Booked at Midnight

Also by E.W. Andersen

───○───

Midnights On the Square Series
The Midnight Book Club
Booked at Midnight

Booked at Midnight

By
E.W. Andersen

Copyright © 2026 by Emily W. Andersen

All rights reserved. No part of this publication may be reproduced, stored or transmitted in any form or by any means, electronic, mechanical, photocopying, recording, scanning, or otherwise without written permission from the publisher. It is illegal to copy this book, post it to a website, or distribute it by any other means without permission. Emily W. Andersen asserts the moral right to be identified as the author of this work.

This novel is entirely a work of fiction. The names, characters and incidents portrayed in it are the work of the author's imagination and, in some cases, the imaginations of authors whose work is in the public domain. Any resemblance to actual persons, living or dead, events or localities is entirely coincidental.

NO AI TRAINING: Without in any way limiting the author's exclusive rights under copyright, no part of this book may be used or reproduced to "train" artificial intelligence (AI) technologies or systems.

Cover design: Lena Yang

ISBN (print): 979-8-9987477-2-4

ISBN (ebook): 979-8-9987477-3-1

For my friends near and far—
with love and thanks for cheering me on

1

It was a cold and drizzly January morning, the perfect excuse to sleep in, but Aurelia had woken up well before her alarm and, surprisingly, felt relatively well rested. Surprisingly, because she'd been up until the wee hours of the morning chatting with fictional characters in the bookshop below her flat. Or maybe not so surprisingly, since limited sleep had become something of a routine by now, just over a year after she'd discovered her shop's secret.

Her shop—it still took some getting used to when it had been her aunt Marigold's for as long as she could remember. In addition to the shop and the flat, Aurelia had also inherited her aunt's tuxedo cat, Fezz. The very cat who was nosing her face to encourage her to get out of bed and make the most of being awake early by feeding him. She obliged him, then got herself ready and went down to the shop to work on her latest book before opening. Settled on the window seat on the mezzanine with a cup of tea, her laptop, and a notebook, Aurelia looked over her notes for a bit, then started pulling them together into an outline. She had just finished typing out an idea for an early chapter in the book when movement from outside caught her eye.

Looking through the large window that ran along the window seat, she spotted someone crossing the square. Her fingers hovered over the keyboard, a smile spreading across her face as she watched a man corralling an overexcited dog toward the shop while trying to hold an umbrella over his head. Aurelia checked the time—it was just past nine, and Oliver was usually at work by now. She frowned for a moment, but her smile returned as she saw his dog, Biscuit, straining against the lead in his rush toward the building. Biscuit had short legs, a long body, and floppy ears, looking something like a blond lab and corgi mix. Despite his size, he was making good progress in pulling Oliver along, so Aurelia collected her things and headed for the spiral staircase at the other end of the mezzanine. From there, she looked back at the window seat where Fezz was still curled up in a ball.

"Good idea. Biscuit is incoming, so you'll be happier right where you are."

Fezz, of course, did not acknowledge this in any way.

At the bottom of the stairs, Aurelia deposited everything on her desk, grabbed the towel she kept in a drawer for wet-dog days like this one, then walked over to unlock the shop door just as Oliver and Biscuit arrived.

She greeted them with a cheerful "Good morning!" only to see Oliver shake out his umbrella and let out some incoherent grumbling as Biscuit yanked him inside. That definitely wasn't his typical greeting.

"*Bad* morning?" she amended.

"Very bad."

Aurelia's eyes ran over him, trying to figure out just how bad. Oliver undid Biscuit's lead and dropped it on the floor along with the umbrella, his usual messenger bag, and another large bag he'd had slung over his shoulder. He looked slightly damp and annoyed, but not as though anything too terrible had happened.

"'Very bad,' is it? What's wrong?"

Aurelia squatted down to pat Biscuit, who she knew wouldn't stop jumping and whining until he'd been properly acknowledged.

"I took Biscuit out early this morning and we ran into my landlord—literally."

"I thought he'd moved out of the country?"

"Well, he's back, and he was very unhappy to see a dog in the building—especially after Biscuit nearly knocked him over."

She looked down at the dog, who was now belly up and happily letting her run the towel over his wet fur. 'Unhappy' and 'Biscuit' were two words that didn't belong in the same sentence.

"Did you explain that his daughter told you it was alright to have him in the flat?"

"I did, and he said she should have known better."

"She's twenty-something, not a child," Aurelia scoffed.

"Exactly. But... the lease very clearly says no dogs. And I didn't have a dog when I moved in."

Aurelia knew that was because Oliver had moved into the flat after a breakup. His ex-girlfriend had taken custody of Biscuit, only to return him to Oliver a few months later, once she'd realized the dog was miserable without him.

"Any room for negotiation?" Aurelia ventured.

"None. And Biscuit tripping him and begging for attention didn't help."

Oliver shot a stern look at Biscuit, who was now sitting at his feet and looking up at him adoringly. Aurelia laughed, only to have Oliver turn that stern look on her. That only made her laugh more since he couldn't keep it up for long before finally breaking into a smile.

"I know he's adorable," Oliver conceded with a sigh. "But he's just got kicked out of the flat."

Aurelia's own smile vanished.

"What? What do you mean?"

"Biscuit isn't welcome back in the building. The landlord let us go inside to get a few of his things"—Oliver pointed to the large bag on the floor—"but that was Biscuit's last time in the flat."

"And what about you?"

"He's letting me out of the lease, but I have to move out by the end of the month so that he can 'un-dog' the flat while he looks for a new tenant."

"The end of the month..." Aurelia trailed off as she realized that was just two weeks away.

"Do you think... Could Biscuit stay here until I find a new place?"

"Of course!" Aurelia said, bending down again to pet the dog's furry head. "Poor Biscuit, banished from home."

"Poor *me*. I've got to find a flat that's dog-friendly, pack up, and move within two weeks."

Aurelia stood and stepped in to give Oliver a kiss.

"We'll figure it out," she promised, her voice low and soothing. "Biscuit can stay here for as long as you need, and I'll help you pack."

Oliver wrapped his arms around her waist, pulling her closer.

"And as for a new flat—"

She broke off, realizing that the words she'd been about to say—*you can move in here*—were weighty. It was an offer she'd been thinking about making, knowing that his lease was up in August, but she hadn't had a chance to ask him yet. Throwing the offer out as a last resort, a 'well, if you must' sort of thing, didn't feel right.

"You'll help me look?" Oliver finished for her.

"Definitely."

It wasn't what she'd planned to say, but it seemed best for now.

After a few more minutes of reassuring Oliver that they'd get it all sorted, he left for work. Aurelia chewed at her lip as she watched him cross the square, waited for him to turn and wave at her, then waved back. He'd been unsettled over the sudden eviction; that was another good reason to give it a day or two before asking him to move in with her. She was fairly confident his answer would be yes, but it felt like something they should discuss when he wasn't late for work and anxious. Maybe tonight, she thought, once he'd settled down a bit—she could ask him then.

Turning to walk back to her desk, Aurelia's eyes caught on the small, round Recommended Reads table at the front of the shop. The very table where stacks of four different books were set out. The very books that had released characters at midnight last night—almost every night for the past month, in fact. And before this group of characters, there had been another batch, and before that—well, there had been the very first group, the one that had opened her eyes to the shop's magical and wonderful secret.

Secret. As in a very big, major reason that inviting Oliver to move in might be... complicated.

"Oh. Right."

Aurelia let out a nervous sigh. Biscuit nudged her leg and she looked down to see him staring up at her, tongue lolling out of his mouth.

"You're a very cute complication. As is your owner."

The dog started happily thwapping his tail against the carpet, oblivious to the chaos he'd created.

2

Twenty minutes later and Aurelia was still pacing back and forth in front of the shop's Recommended Reads table, with Biscuit's head following her movements as though she were the ball at a tennis match.

She *wanted* Oliver to move in. She loved him; he loved her. And moving in together would mean they could spend more time together. There wasn't a doubt in her mind that they were both ready to jog their relationship along to that next step. But figuring out how to have the man she loved permanently in her flat when she liked to sneak out at midnight to meet with fictional characters was going to be a challenge.

So far, she'd been able to manage it while they were living apart, with help from their respective pets. Fezz was used to having dogs in the shop, but whenever they brought Biscuit upstairs to the flat, the cat drew firmer boundaries. Every time Biscuit came within a few feet of him, Fezz would let out a warning hiss or growl. Biscuit would back off... before deciding to try his luck again minutes later with the same result. Over and over. It was hard to get through a conversation or a movie with the two animals constantly testing each other's limits. And with her open-plan flat, the only way to really separate them was to lock one of them in the bedroom or in the shop. A few times, she and Oliver had tried shutting Fezz in the bedroom with them to give him an overnight break from Biscuit's desperate efforts to play with and befriend him, but then Biscuit would scratch at the door, feeling left out. And when they'd tried shutting Biscuit in with them, Fezz yowled outside the door, indignant.

Their solution had been to either have Aurelia stay at Oliver's, or to have Oliver come over in the evenings without Biscuit, then leave before it got too late so that he could get home to walk the dog. But it was hardly a long-term solution; Aurelia missed the characters on nights when she was at his flat and missed waking up next to him on nights when she was alone in hers. Which meant this was the perfect opportunity for a change.

Aurelia's phone rang and she pulled it out of her pocket, answering without checking to see who was calling because she knew it would be her sister.

"Good morning."

"Is it? Then why do you sound so mournful?" Antonia asked.

"I'm going to ask Oliver to move in with me."

It came out as a declaration, as though Aurelia were trying to convince herself that she could do it. Which, of course, she was.

"I'd try for a little more enthusiasm when you ask him," Antonia said with a laugh.

"I *am* excited—I *do* want him to move in."

"Then just pack up his things and move him in already. It's obvious you two are forever. Might as well start now."

Aurelia smiled at her sister's confidence. She felt it, too, when it came to Oliver. But as she paced past the Recommended Reads table again, her smile drooped a little.

"There's still a lot I need to work out before I ask him."

"Like what?" Antonia demanded.

Like how I'm going to sneak out of the flat at midnight most nights to visit fictional characters in the shop.

The words were on the tip of her tongue, but Aurelia managed to hold them in. She hadn't told anyone about the shop's secret—not Oliver, not her best friends, not her father, not even her sister. How could she when the truth was too hard to ask them to believe? She couldn't exactly prove that her fantastical story was true when the characters could only ever appear to the shop's owner—her. She'd never bothered bringing someone into the shop after midnight because the characters had told her about all the times her aunt, great aunt, and great-great aunt had tried it, only to have the characters disappear the second anyone who didn't own the shop stepped inside. She'd snuck down a few times on the rare occasions when Oliver had slept over, and she'd found the characters there waiting for her. That was how she'd learned that someone else could be in the flat after midnight, just not in the shop.

Aurelia didn't like keeping such a big secret from Oliver—from everyone in her life—but she didn't see an alternative. Maybe she should just stop visiting the characters or visit less often... but she loved learning more about them than their books had shown her and, even more than that, she loved hearing their stories about her aunt Marigold, her great aunt Lucy, and her great-great aunt Cristobel. It was a link to her family, to a past she'd never have learned about on her own. It made her feel close to the aunts, the one she'd lost and the ones she'd never met. And she'd started to see herself as a steward for the shop's magic, keeping it going so that when her niece, Julia, was old enough to take over, she'd get to experience it too.

No, abandoning the characters wasn't an option. And not asking Oliver to move in just to keep him from becoming suspicious about her nighttime habits wasn't an option, either.

"Aurelia? Where'd you go?"

"I'm here," Aurelia insisted, shaking her head and bringing her focus back to her sister.

"You said you've got a lot to work out about Oliver moving in. And I asked what you needed to work out."

"Just... just a few things." Her eyes caught on Biscuit, who had made his way up the spiral staircase and was now trotting toward the window seat and Fezz. "Like figuring out the dog and cat situation."

Fezz spotted Biscuit and gave a lazy hiss before moving further back on the window seat, just out of Biscuit's view. Aurelia shook her head at the cat's studied indifference.

"I think exposure therapy is your best option."

"It's our only option," Aurelia agreed, smiling as she watched Biscuit lie down in front of the window seat, head on his paws as he looked longingly up in Fezz's direction. "Oliver got kicked out of his flat this morning."

"*What?* Really?"

"Yes, really. The landlord spotted Biscuit and told Oliver he has two weeks to find somewhere else to live. And in the meantime, Biscuit has been banished."

"Poor Biscuit."

"That's what I said!" Aurelia laughed. "It's sort of the perfect time to ask Oliver to move in, but…" She trailed off, reminding herself again that she couldn't tell her sister the real reason for her hesitation. So instead she said, "I don't want him to think I'm asking just to be nice—just because he has nowhere else to go."

"Well, he doesn't have *nowhere* else to go. He could find another flat somewhere, but what's the point in that? Tell him you'd been thinking of asking him anyway and it makes sense for him to move in now, since he'll be all packed up."

"How romantic."

They both laughed and Aurelia relaxed, letting her shoulders drop as she stopped her pacing. Feeling better, she decided to wind her sister up a bit. "Still… It'll be such a pain. All my stuff moved around, his boxes everywhere, the dog…"

"No! Think about the good things, like waking up to him every morning, saying goodnight to him every night—"

"Finding his dirty dishes in the sink, falling into the loo when he doesn't close the lid…" She had to bite her lip to keep from laughing.

"You're just making things up. I've met Oliver and he seems much better house-trained than that."

"He is," Aurelia agreed, letting out her laugh.

"Now that you've had your fun, I've got to go. Keep me posted on the 'move in with me' proposal."

"I will," Aurelia promised. "Know I love you."

"You too."

As they rang off, a couple walked into the shop and Aurelia switched into shopkeeper mode to greet them. They started to browse and she sat at her desk, eyeing the mezzanine to check on Biscuit. He was looking at the customers with curiosity, but he stayed put, as though determined that today was the day Fezz would finally let him get within sniffing distance.

They could make this work. *She* could make this work. Aurelia pulled a notebook out of a desk drawer and started thinking of ideas for bringing her two favorite worlds together: her life with Oliver and her life with the characters.

3

It had been a busy few days as Aurelia helped Oliver pack and they managed the Biscuit and Fezz acclimation process. She'd come up with a few ideas to get down to the shop at midnight without alarming Oliver, but she'd been too busy to try them out. Just like she'd been too busy to ask him to move in with her.

Maybe not too busy, more like she hadn't found the right time. She didn't want to ask him fresh off his frustration with his landlord's ultimatum, so she hadn't asked him that first night. And the next night, he'd been exhausted after a full day at work and a few hours of packing up his flat. She'd been exhausted too, since she'd been there helping him after closing the shop.

They were back at his flat packing again the following night when Aurelia decided this was it: she was going to ask him right then. She opened her mouth to speak, but Oliver beat her to it with a question of his own.

"How's your book?"

"My book?"

Her eyebrows drew together as her mind switched gears from serious relationship talk to work talk. Oliver had edited her first book, the one she'd written the year before about Count Vronsky from *Anna Karenina*. Well, she'd written it *about* Vronsky but also *with* him, since he was one of the first characters she'd met in the shop. Aurelia had a master's in creative writing and had published a few short stories before she'd inherited the shop, but took a long break after her mother's and aunt's passing. Then, because of his unhappy ending and the fact that she was a writer, she'd volunteered (or been volunteered by the other characters) to write Vronsky a sequel. And it had worked; she'd written him a new ending, one where he wasn't doomed to live the rest of his life under the shadow of tragedy and heartache.

"Right, sorry. I've done a bit more outlining, but I haven't really started writing yet. I'm still trying to figure out who this guy is, whether he's sort of naïve and has been thrown into the art world's underbelly, or whether he's a little more sophisticated and cunning."

Aurelia usually got story ideas from things she'd overheard or read about, but this time it was from something her friend, Kali, had overheard. Kali gave guided tours to children at a handful of London's art museums, and during lunch a few weeks ago she'd told Aurelia about a long-running forgery scheme that had been uncovered—reluctantly—by an auction house that had sold dozens of the fakes without their experts realizing.

"Both could work, really," Oliver said thoughtfully, handing her a roll of packing tape as she started putting together a few more boxes. "You still have him discovering one of the forgeries early on?"

"That's what I'm thinking. It'll start with his first week at the auction house, he's feeling lucky to have landed a job there, when he notices something's not quite right with one of the lots."

"So either he's a guy who's sort of lost and doesn't know what to do, or he's a guy who's trying to figure out whether reporting it—or not—will work to his advantage and how."

"Exactly! I might try writing a first chapter for each character and see which one I like better."

"I'm leaning toward the crafty one."

"I'll take that under advisement, Mr. Editor," Aurelia said in a mock serious tone, nudging him with her hip as she dropped an empty box next to him.

"I'll be ready to read your chapters whenever you're ready to share them, Ms. Writer," he retorted in a mock serious voice of his own.

She stood there smiling at him, lost for a moment in fancying him. They'd started their relationship as colleagues, at a time when Aurelia was grieving and he was getting over a breakup and getting used to being the new owner of a mad dog. (A mad dog who was currently locked up in the shop while Fezz was locked up in the flat—a time out for both of them while Oliver and Aurelia were away.) Their teasing and bickering over edits to her book had morphed into something real and playful, mixing lightness and seriousness in a way that made her feel like this could really be 'forever,' as Antonia had said.

"Do you want to move in with me?"

She wasn't sure if he'd heard her at first, but then Oliver opened his mouth and closed it, and she was certain he was trying to work out what to say.

"It's okay if you don't want to, if you think it's too soon—"

"No—I don't."

She couldn't help but frown at that, and he quickly went on.

"I mean, I don't think it's too soon. And I do want to move in with you. But... Are you sure?"

Now she couldn't help but grin.

"I'm sure."

"I've been wanting to ask if you wanted to, once my lease was up, but I don't want you to feel like you have to offer now, just because I have to move."

"I've been wanting to ask, so it's not just because of Biscuit's inconvenient banishment, I promise."

"Really?" His eyebrows shot up, his tone hopeful.

Aurelia set down the box she'd been assembling, walked over to where he was holding bubble wrap and a dinner plate, and put her arms around him.

"Really. I know the lady who owns the place, and she likes pets."

"Does she?" he asked. He freed up his hands and put his arms around her, swaying them both back and forth as he held in a laugh.

"She does. As a matter of fact, she has a cat. And she runs the bookshop downstairs, so she's a very smart, business-savvy type."

"Mm... Tell me more about this lady. She sounds like someone I'd like to meet."

Aurelia laughed and kissed him, then broke away, her face a little more serious.

"As the lady in question, I should warn you... I have some odd habits."

"I think I've figured out your odd habits by now," he said with a laugh.

Aurelia was about to demand a list of whatever habits he'd found odd but reminded herself to press on with her agenda.

"No, but we haven't really spent many nights at my flat, so you haven't seen them all. Like... you don't know that I like writing late at night. Downstairs."

"In the shop? In the middle of the night?"

"That's right. I'll try to be quiet, but if you hear me—or any other strange noises—at night, you can just go back to sleep."

He let out a soft laugh, waiting for her to tell him it was a joke, but she bit her lip and gave a little shrug.

"Huh. Okay," he said after a moment. "How often am I going to wake up to an empty bed, then?"

"Not that often! And I'll be there when you wake up in the morning. Just... not between, say, midnight and dawn. Sometimes."

He laughed again, then kissed her.

"Alright. If late-night writing is your thing, I'm on board. Any other odd habits?"

"That's it for now," Aurelia said with a sigh of relief.

In her planning over the past few days, preparing him in advance for her late nights in the shop had seemed like the best way forward. It was one half-truth she could tell him, something he apparently found charming instead of odd. Or maybe charmingly odd. Either way, she took it as a win.

"I guess we should keep packing, then. And maybe take some boxes over tonight?"

"Good idea," she agreed. "Might as well start moving you in before you change your mind."

"Oh, I won't be changing my mind. I still want to meet this landlady of yours."

He ducked away from her reach when she tried to swat him, and soon they were back to packing, each of them much happier now that they'd decided on their next big step together.

4

With two of them packing they should have made more progress the night before, but they'd quickly lost their momentum when Oliver had walked past and given her a light kiss, then two, then a much longer one that led to abandoning packing full stop.

Eventually, they'd gone back to Aurelia's flat with a few boxes in hand and started what seemed like their new nighttime routine: Oliver walked Biscuit while Aurelia fed Fezz and then set the alarm on her phone to vibrate a few minutes before midnight so that she could get downstairs to see the characters. She planned to put a new set of books on the Recommended Reads table in the morning—inspired by Oliver's arrival—and wanted a chance to say goodbye to the characters she'd been chatting with over the past few weeks. Goodbyes were always bittersweet since she never knew if she'd meet them again the next time she put their books on the table, or whether a new set would appear. But with so many books and so many characters to meet, Aurelia didn't want to miss the chance to meet others, to hear them share stories about their novels and their memories of meeting the aunts that had run the shop.

Getting downstairs and back up again wasn't at all the challenge Aurelia had been expecting. As Aurelia and Oliver got into bed that night, Biscuit dropped onto the floor next to Oliver's side of the bed, apparently having used up all his energy over the past few days on his excitement over the move. When her alarm went off and she tiptoed out the bedroom door, Biscuit didn't seem to notice. And when she snuck back into the bedroom and climbed into bed at dawn, she heard the dog pick his head up to listen before dropping it back on the carpet. *That was easy enough*, she thought as she drifted to sleep, mentally patting herself on the back for her cleverness.

Oliver was up and off to work just an hour later, which should have given Aurelia a chance to catch up on missed sleep from her night in the shop. But when Fezz and Biscuit—very much awake now—started having a standoff in the living area, she pulled herself out of bed to observe and intervene if necessary. Oliver usually took Biscuit into the office with him, but they'd decided to leave him with her for a few days to get him used to being in the shop and seeing customers come in and out without barking at them or tripping them as they browsed the shelves. After a few more halfhearted hisses from Fezz as he settled on the sofa, Aurelia showered and started her day.

She'd planned to swap out the books on the Recommended Reads table first thing, but the shop was busy that morning. Biscuit did just fine—he perked up every time someone came through the door but mostly stayed on the extra dog bed they'd put next to Aurelia's desk at the back of the shop. Of course, he also perked up every time a customer came over to pet him or tell him what a good boy he was. Soon he started to roll onto his back when someone walked by, in both invitation and expectation of belly rubs.

When things got quiet around lunchtime, Aurelia took her chance to reshelve the books from the Recommended Reads table. Then she went into the back room and carried out the box of books she'd ordered. Before they'd started dating, talking to Oliver about books had been one of the first things to thaw his reserved exterior. And maybe, very possibly, it had made Aurelia feel more at ease too. During one of his early visits to the shop, he'd admitted that he didn't like Charles Dickens' novels, and she'd insisted he'd got it wrong. To prove it, she'd made him read two of her favorites, *David Copperfield* and *Little Dorrit*. Just as she'd predicted, after some initial complaining he'd not only finished but liked them, and already had *Bleak House* on his nightstand as his next read. Marigold had also been a fan; she'd even named Fezz after Mr. Fezziwig, a character from *A Christmas Carol*.

Now, she'd decided to celebrate Oliver's move by filling the table with Dickens novels. She couldn't tell him, of course, but her plan had the extra benefit of giving her a chance to meet the rich, flawed, and endearing characters Dickens had created. *Little Dorrit* and *David Copperfield* were on her list, of course. One was about a young woman, Little Dorrit, who'd been raised in a debtor's prison with her family before they eventually found freedom, and the other traced the life of David, who'd lost his family at a young age and later became a successful writer like Dickens. Then there was *Bleak House*, which focused on a long-running legal battle over an inheritance and the many people whose lives became entangled in it. And last was *Great Expectations*, about a young boy, Pip, whose life was forever changed when he helped an escaped convict flee during a chance encounter.

While Aurelia unpacked copies of each and arranged them on the table, a smile spread across her face as she wondered who would appear from the books that evening. She wanted to meet Little Dorrit, and Peggotty from *David Copperfield*, but there was also a list of characters she'd prefer not to meet. Still, Aurelia had learned there were no guarantees when it came to which characters would show up each time she put a new set of books on the table. The shop's magic seemed to have a mind of its own, so she would just have to wait until that evening to find out who would join her for the next few weeks.

After dropping the empty box in the back room, Aurelia made a cup of tea and carried it to her desk. She heard a noise up on the mezzanine and knew it must be Fezz, jumping onto the window seat for a nap. Biscuit opened one eyelid at the sound, then went right back to sleep. Other than Fezz's movements and the soft ticking of the mantel clock behind her, the shop was quiet for a change, giving Aurelia time to plan for the final stage of Oliver's move, which they'd scheduled for that Sunday. The shop would be closed, allowing them to carry the rest of his things in through the shop and up to her flat without knocking over the customers.

The phone rang and Aurelia scooped it up in one hand while holding her warm mug of tea in the other. She knew it would be Antonia, but as it was the shop phone, she answered, "Hello, On the Square Books."

"Hi, Relia."

"Hi, Tonia. How're things in Paris?"

"That's why I'm calling. The bookshop near me is asking if you'll come over and do an event. They said you could read a little from your book and answer a few questions. What do you think?"

"Did they really ask, or did you suggest it?"

"Either way, the shop owner is inviting you and he wants to set a date. I was thinking sometime next month?"

"Next month?" Aurelia frowned. "Look, I don't know... It's not exactly a runaway bestseller. I don't want to trouble him if it's just going to be a reading for you and the kids."

"No, he thought it was a great idea! He said he'd love to host an event for you."

Aurelia was doubtful. As the owner of a bookshop herself, she was conscious of not wanting to put another bookseller out by having to plan for an author event. She'd never hosted any in the shop herself since the authors of the mostly nineteenth-century books on her shelves had all passed decades ago, but still, it seemed like a lot of work.

"If he really wants me to, and not just because you're pushing him, let's wait a bit since I just saw you all at Christmas. We can make it an excuse for a visit when I'm desperate to see you again."

"Alright," Antonia sighed. "We'll put off the reading for now, but you should know your book is flying off the shelves here."

"*Flying?*" Aurelia asked, more doubtful still. Oliver's publishing company was small; they had limited resources to market her book in the U.K. let alone anywhere else.

"All my friends bought copies. And I've been giving them out as gifts."

"Aw, thank you, Antonia," Aurelia said, touched once again by her sister taking on the unofficial role of Aurelia's hype woman. "I'll have to tell Oliver."

Seemingly on cue, Aurelia looked up at the sound of the bell on the shop door and saw Oliver walking in. Biscuit jumped to his feet—somehow recognizing the sound of Oliver's steps since he hadn't said a word yet—and ran over to greet him.

"Hang on, he's just come into the shop," Aurelia informed Antonia.

"Tell him your 'agent' needs to talk to him," Antonia said, putting on a businesslike tone. "I'll wait."

Aurelia put the phone to her chest and stood to kiss Oliver over the ledge of her desk.

"Hello, you."

"Hello," he said, smiling as though they hadn't seen each other a few hours ago. "I just finished up a meeting nearby and thought I'd stop in."

Biscuit gave a short bark to remind them of his presence, and Antonia gave a shout through the phone, likewise reminding Aurelia of hers.

Oliver bent down to pet Biscuit as he asked, "Antonia?"

"She wants to speak with you. She's pretending to be my agent again."

Aurelia handed Oliver the phone and watched him wander the shop as he spoke to her sister. Seeing Biscuit trail close behind him—nearly under his feet—made her laugh until she heard Oliver telling Antonia, "Absolutely, I agree."

"Now, wait a minute," Aurelia interrupted, stepping out from behind her desk. "I'm highly suspicious when you two agree."

Oliver was silent for a moment, listening to Antonia.

"Tell my sister I can *sense* her conspiring even if I can't hear it," Aurelia added.

Oliver said goodbye and hung up as he walked back toward Aurelia, nearly tripping over the dog.

"Biscuit!" Oliver could never muster up real anger toward him—he was too sweet and clueless to register it anyway. Oliver sighed, waiting for Biscuit to step aside and clear the path to Aurelia. "Antonia says she's lined up a book reading for you in Paris but you need persuading."

"She wants me to go next month, but I'd rather wait a bit. It'll be a pain for the shop owner to set it up, and I'd hate to disappoint them with an audience of family members who already own the book."

"Actually, I think you could pull in more than just Antonia and her crowd. An English-language reading could bring in expats, bookish tourists... It might be fun for you."

"Maybe," Aurelia said, considering. "Is my editor insisting?" She squinted an appraising eye at him.

"No, your editor won't force your hand. Nor will your boyfriend. But we do suggest you think about it."

"Suggestion noted. Business over?"

"Yes, I'm hanging up my publishing hat for the moment."

"Oh good," Aurelia said, putting her arms around his neck and leaning into him for a kiss. "Hello, Boyfriend."

"Hello, Girlfriend. Or should I say Flatmate?"

"Much too impersonal," Aurelia said, shaking her head. "What about… 'Sharer of the Boudoir'?"

Matching her seductive tone, Oliver asked, "How does 'Doer of the Dishes' sound?"

Aurelia gasped and pretended to faint in his arms.

"You know just what to say to make a woman swoon!" Laughing, she kissed him again before bending down to appease a desperate Biscuit, who was jumping and yipping at their feet for attention.

Aurelia petted him, then remembered the Recommended Reads table.

"Oh! Did you spot this month's selections?" she asked. "I just swapped them out this morning."

Oliver walked over and smiled as he caught onto the theme.

"Trying for more converts?"

"Well, since I managed to get you on board, I figured I might as well work on the rest of London. How're you getting on with *Bleak House*? Do we need to negotiate a few reading breaks while I help you pack tonight?"

"I almost forgot," Oliver said, his face falling. "My mum called and insisted we go and see Jack's play tonight. It's the last night of the run, otherwise I'd try to put it off again."

"Jack—your *brother*, Jack?"

"That's the one," Oliver said flatly.

Somehow, Oliver had met Antonia—who lived in another country—but Aurelia had yet to meet Oliver's younger brother,

Jack, who lived in the same city. Jack was a set designer, a *junior assistant* set designer as Oliver liked to clarify, at University College London. He and Oliver weren't particularly close for reasons Aurelia hadn't yet figured out, which meant Oliver wasn't in any rush to introduce them. Given Aurelia's preternaturally close relationship with her sister, she hadn't yet wrapped her mind around the fact that someone would want to avoid spending time with their sibling.

"So that's tonight, then?" she asked.

She wanted to meet Jack, finally, but realized that without the chance for a nap that day, she'd most likely miss meeting her Dickens characters for the first time that night.

Oliver cocked his head to one side, trying to read her face.

"You don't want to go? We don't have to. I can just tell Mum that—"

"No! No, let's do it. I was going to do a few things around the shop later, but it's no problem. I want to meet Jack. And if your mother is insisting we go, that's an end to it."

Now, Oliver's mother she'd met. His mother, like Oliver, had a slightly cool exterior, but Aurelia was certain she'd seen signs of thawing by the end of their most recent encounter. She wasn't about to cross the woman, though, especially when it came to a plan involving her sons.

"What's the play?" she asked.

"Oh, I've no idea," he said indifferently.

Aurelia gave him a look of disapproval, but he just smiled back at her.

"Let's hope it's something short," he said, teasingly planting a wet kiss squarely on her nose. "I'll pick you up at seven?"

"Excellent," she said, scrunching up her nose as she rubbed at his kiss.

Aurelia walked him to the door and stood as he strolled through the square, waiting until he'd turned to wave at her. She waved and smiled after him for a moment, running a finger over her nose where he'd kissed her.

Turning back into the shop, her brows pulled together as she spotted the table with its display of Dickens novels. With the play and then a likely stop at Oliver's place on the way home to pick up a few more of his things, they might not get home before midnight. And if she wasn't in the building by then, the characters wouldn't appear and she'd miss them.

It would be fine, she told herself. She could wait until tomorrow night to meet the characters. She knew her habits and routines would shift with Oliver's more permanent place in her life, and she was only too willing to make it work.

5

Walking across UCL's campus to the theater, Aurelia's spirits lifted as memories of her undergraduate years on that very campus came flooding back to her. Meanwhile, she noticed a distinct dip in Oliver's spirits. His mood deflated still further when they got to the steps of the theater only to see posters for the play: *King Lear*.

"Oh, come on," Oliver groaned. "This is going to be ages."

"It looks like it might have a modern twist," Aurelia said, pointing to the photographs of actors in suits and ties. "Maybe it'll be a bit faster-paced," she added hopefully.

As they took their seats, Oliver flipped through the program peevishly before repeatedly slapping it against his thigh. Aurelia took it from him and hunted down Jack's name.

"There he is—he's famous."

"Yes, a famous junior assistant set designer for a university theater program."

A woman sitting in the next row turned and gave Oliver a scolding look.

"A very well-known and respected university theater program," Aurelia said loudly, smiling at the woman before turning back to Oliver. "What's wrong with being a junior assistant set designer?" she continued more quietly. "He has to start somewhere, doesn't he?"

"He started here five years ago and hasn't budged since."

"Maybe he's happy where he is," Aurelia reasoned.

"That's just it—he'd be happy being a junior assistant forever," Oliver finished in a whisper as the lights went down and a hush fell over the crowd.

Hours later and the play finally ended. Oliver tried dragging Aurelia away, but she insisted they wait to say hello to his brother.

"I'm sure your mum wanted you to actually see *Jack*, not just his play," Aurelia said, pushing him toward the lobby.

"She did say something about meeting him out front," Oliver admitted.

Aurelia poked his side. "Honestly—you're impossible!"

The crowd had thinned considerably by the time Jack appeared. Aurelia, never having seen him before, was still looking around expectantly when someone approached them and gave Oliver a few friendly pats on the shoulder.

"You're here! Thanks, big brother."

"Well, Mum sort of insisted," Oliver began before Aurelia nudged him. "No, I mean—it was interesting. I've never seen Shakespeare set in the 1980s."

"Right?" Jack asked eagerly. "It was a fun challenge."

Aurelia was smiling, trying to contain a laugh as she looked from one brother to the other. There was Oliver, so reserved and stiff until you broke through to him, and there was Jack, a bundle of energy and positivity. She couldn't help thinking of Biscuit, trailing after Oliver with adoration and joy at every moment. Any nervousness she'd felt at meeting another member of Oliver's family had completely vanished.

"Who's this, then?" Jack asked, looking to Aurelia and smiling. "Is this her, at last?"

"I'm sorry," Oliver said suddenly, straightening up. "Yes, this is Aurelia."

She felt Oliver's hand at her waist and got the sense that he was reassuring himself, rather than her. She put one hand on his and reached out the other to shake Jack's hand.

"At last is right!" Aurelia said with a grin. "I'm sorry it's taken us so long to meet. But what a lovely way to be introduced—the play was wonderful."

"Did you really think so?" Jack asked, looking like he truly wanted to know. "We've had some mixed reviews. Most people like their Shakespeare nice and traditional."

"No, I loved it! I felt transported back to the eighties. But this was the last performance—are you sad to see it ending?"

"Oh, a little. It's alright, though. We strike the set tomorrow and get started on the next one. It's *The Caucasian Chalk Circle*, by Brecht."

Oliver groaned, just loud enough for Aurelia to hear, though she didn't think Jack had picked up on it.

"We'll look forward to seeing it," she said, trying to cover for Oliver's apparent annoyance. "Can you join us for a drink?"

"I can't tonight, I'm afraid," Jack said, looking disappointed to turn them down. "We've got a cast party since it's our last show, and I really can't miss it."

"We'll make a plan soon then, once Oliver's moved in and settled."

"You're moving?" Jack asked, turning back to Oliver. "Mum didn't mention it."

"It was sort of sudden," Oliver said with a shrug.

"But you'll still be in London, won't you?"

"Yes, I own a bookshop in town and the flat's just above it. Here," Aurelia added, rummaging through her bag and pulling out a bookmark. "This is the address."

She looked to Oliver, whose expression had finally cleared into something closer to his usual smile. She knew he was remembering their very first date, when she'd handed him one of her bookmarks. He'd been completely flummoxed by it until he learned that it wasn't just any bookmark, but one for her own shop. And the fact that he'd held on to it for months afterward had helped cement in her mind that Oliver, too, was worth hanging onto. The sweet memory had Aurelia leaning into him.

"I think I've walked past this place," Jack said as he flipped the bookmark over.

"Mum can give you the address if you lose that."

"I won't lose it," Jack insisted. To Aurelia he added, "Always the big brother."

A group had entered the lobby from the theater and was heading toward the exit, calling out for Jack to join them.

"We'll let you go. It was good to finally meet you, Jack! See you again soon."

"Good to meet you, Aurelia. Thanks for coming!" Jack gave them both a very contented smile before running to catch up with his friends and colleagues.

Aurelia and Oliver watched them leave in a loud, exuberant crush, and then followed them out into the cold night.

6

"There's no way I'm sitting through a Brecht play," Oliver complained as they pushed past the boxes in his flat in an attempt to find a duffel bag of clothes he'd packed the day before and wanted to bring home. "I've never seen *Caucasian*-whatever-it's-called, but judging from his other plays, I'm not interested."

"Oh, come on. It'll be one night—not even! A few hours. Anyway, it's months away. And also, I think it's Brechtian—'a Brechtian play,' not 'a Brecht play.'"

Oliver looked unconvinced of every one of her points.

"You want me to go to Paris to entertain Antonia with a book reading, so you can't complain about sitting in a dark room for a few hours here in London."

"Sure I can," he insisted.

"Your brother's adorable. How have I not met him until now?"

"Studied avoidance."

Aurelia made a face and pushed him into a stack of boxes, finally breaking through his crabbiness and eliciting a laugh.

"We're just not that close. He's seven years younger and you see how he is."

"Sweet? Friendly? Eager?"

"Exactly."

"I'm sorry," Aurelia laughed. "How are those bad qualities?"

"Because they go hand in hand with him being flighty and immature."

"Well, he's younger than us by quite a few years. You've got to give him a bit of a break."

"Yes, Jack's always getting a break," Oliver said under his breath.

Aurelia was ready to tease him for acting like a child when she realized his tone wasn't as whiny as she'd first thought but instead sounded a little hurt. Oliver could be reserved sometimes, but dodging her questions wasn't like him. Seeing Jack and talking about him had hit a nerve that was apparently quite tender. She was about to ask him about it when he seemed to sense the shift in atmosphere he'd created and pulled her to him.

"Thank you for suffering through *King Lear*." He kissed her and added, "And thank you for agreeing to pack up a few more boxes while you're here."

Aurelia scrunched up her face in a question mark.

"When did I agree to that?" she asked, trying and failing to suppress a smile.

"It was implied," Oliver answered with a grin. "You... coming here... late at night... unchaperoned."

She rolled her eyes at him as he moved off to keep looking for his bag. Her smile faded slightly as she thought back over the night. Oliver clearly didn't want to discuss his irritation over his brother right now, so she decided to give him some time and space before bringing it up again. Still, questions about what had happened between them—an argument when they were younger? Some grudge he'd held on to?—ran through her mind as they gathered up a few more things before heading home.

7

It was Sunday, and Oliver was finally moved in. Well, they were still unpacking boxes and trying to sort through the debris, but he'd turned in the key to his old flat and was officially living with Aurelia.

As she carried a few now-empty boxes down into the shop to leave out for recycling, Aurelia began worrying her bottom lip, thinking about what might happen that night. She still hadn't met Dickens' characters. First it was Jack's play, then it was two nights in a row of being much too tired to stay awake and meet them after helping Oliver to finish packing and cleaning his flat. Which meant they'd appeared and were likely wondering why no one had been there to greet them. She wondered if she could chance going downstairs later without waking Oliver. She'd managed it just a few nights ago, and Oliver and Biscuit hadn't even noticed. But she had several hours left to decide, so she focused on the task at hand and went back upstairs to keep at it.

The first hour of unpacking had been mild chaos, with Biscuit jumping and barking at their heels as they moved from room to room and tried to organize the boxes without falling over what suddenly seemed like far too much stuff. Eventually, they cleared a path of boxes in the living room, Biscuit passed out on the carpet, and they started unpacking Oliver's books onto Aurelia's already-full bookshelves.

Now that he'd be sharing the space, she'd been ready for Oliver to critique her outsized collection of books, her penchant for knick-knacks, her worn and favorite armchair. But clearly those were just her own criticisms since he hadn't said a word. He didn't seem daunted by the boxes or the uncertainty of where his things would fit and whether they would suit hers. Instead, he was happy, smiling, and had seemingly unflagging energy for shifting boxes and unloading them.

Pausing a moment as she tried to stuff his copy of *David Copperfield* next to hers on a shelf, Aurelia looked over at him, a smile growing as she did.

"Hey, you," she said.

Oliver turned, eyebrows raised as he balanced a small stack of books against his chest. Aurelia climbed over a box, nearly put her foot into another, and kissed him.

"Thank you for moving here." She kissed him again. "And thank you for not complaining about all my things."

Oliver shifted his stack of books to one side and put his free arm around her.

"I like your things," he said, kissing her back. "And I figured I'd give it a week before I start with my list of demands."

Aurelia laughed, then carefully helped him maneuver his stack of books onto a nearby shelf to free up his arms before wrapping her own around him. As he eased the books onto the shelf, he pointed to a mismatched set of notebooks.

"What are these?"

Aurelia had been kissing her favorite spot, just under his jaw, and looked at the shelf distractedly.

"My notebooks—for writing."

"Is this where Count Vronsky got his new start?"

She pursed her lips in a secret smile as she thought of the hours she'd spent working on the book with Count Vronsky, the excitement of not only writing but finishing and then publishing her first novel, and the fact that she'd found herself a boyfriend who could get sidetracked from a romantic moment by the possibility of discussing fiction.

"It is indeed," she said, resting her head against his chest.

"We'll have to make room for all the notebooks for all the books you'll write next."

"Let's focus on the one, for now," Aurelia said with a huff of a laugh. Then, looking up at him, she asked, "Are you really ready to go through the editing process with me again?"

He tightened his arms around her. "If I remember, last time *you* were the one who was unsure about going through the editing process with *me*."

"Revisionist history," she scoffed, shaking her head. He leaned down to kiss her, and soon all thoughts of fiction were replaced by the reality of standing there, together, in *their* apartment.

Stumbling over boxes, they made their way to the bedroom at the back of the flat. Unpacking could wait.

8

Waking with a start, it took Aurelia a moment to process her surroundings. It was dark, and there were boxes and piles of clothes strewn around the room, but eventually her eyes adjusted and she realized she was in her flat. Their flat. Oliver was fast asleep next to her, his breathing a step away from a snore.

A muffled sound of tapping was coming through from the living room, which she thought must be what had woken her. She looked to the clock on her bedside table, saw that it was just before one in the morning, and a realization struck her: there was plenty of time to go downstairs and meet the characters before dawn. She slowly sat up, careful not to jostle the bed as the tapping continued. Aurelia turned to look at Oliver; he seemed to be deeply asleep, unfazed by the noise. What *was* it? She gingerly stood up and picked her way around the boxes in the bedroom, making it to the door with only a few muffled yelps as she banged a shin against one box and struck a toe against another. Looking back, she saw that he was still asleep. So far, so good.

Aurelia pulled the bedroom door shut behind her as she stepped into the hallway. It was a little brighter out there as they hadn't closed the curtains over the front windows, allowing light from the streetlamps to pour across the open space. She spotted a blond shape standing at the top of the stairs and recognized Biscuit, his tail beating a steady tattoo as it knocked against a nearby box. As she stepped closer, she could see that all his attention was focused on the door to the shop at the foot of the stairs. And now she could hear them: light voices filtering up from downstairs. She caught her breath and smiled.

Biscuit suddenly took notice of her and gave a small yip of excitement. Aurelia dropped into a squat and then nearly toppled over as the dog hopped up and around her. Clearly he'd recovered from his exhaustion over the move with a few overlong naps.

"Alright, I'm here," she whispered. "You've caught on, hey?"

Biscuit seemed to have forgotten the voices downstairs and was pleased to have found Aurelia. She rose and was about to step onto the first tread to go downstairs when she saw her bare foot, then her bare leg. She was wearing one of Oliver's old sweatshirts and not much else; it wasn't an ideal outfit for greeting a group of nineteenth-century characters. Part of her advanced planning for Oliver's move-in had included setting out clothes in the bathroom so that she could change out of her pajamas before going downstairs each night. But she'd forgotten earlier—she'd been distracted—and now she'd have to go back into the bedroom, find something to wear, and get back out again without waking Oliver.

Uncertain of her next move, she stood still for a moment, Biscuit breathing heavily at her feet, the characters chatting below. Right, missing tonight was not an option, but neither was showing up to meet them in her underwear. Aurelia caught her breath at her brilliance when she remembered the laundry hamper in the bathroom. She scuttled in there, scooted Biscuit inside, closed the door, and turned on the light. Lifting the lid on the hamper, she peeled through days of wrinkled clothes—*must do laundry tomorrow*, she told herself—trying to find something vaguely presentable. She found a wrinkled black top and a dark pair of jeans with a jam smear on the thigh from her breakfast two days ago. They were the best of several bad options, so they'd have to do. Tossing them on, she swept her eyes over her reflection, then stopped to tidy her hair as it had worked itself into a nest of tangles. She smiled a moment, thinking of how those tangles had gotten there.

That thought and the risk of waking Oliver before she could get downstairs had her heart rate picking up speed. She turned the light out and opened the door, giving her eyes a moment to adjust back to the darkness. Biscuit scrambled out the door and ran to the top of the stairs, with Aurelia behind him.

She started down the stairs but stopped short when the dog began following her. She turned to look at him and saw his tongue hanging out of his mouth as he stared happily back at her.

"Stay, Biscuit," Aurelia whispered. She took another few steps and heard him once again padding behind her.

"Biscuit, stay!" she whispered more urgently.

Maintaining eye contact, she took one slow step down and he did the same.

"Damn."

She got to the bottom of the stairs with Biscuit landing beside her as she slipped on a pair of flats. Attempting to open the door just enough to get herself out while keeping the dog in, she started sliding a foot, then a leg through the opening.

Once it was wide enough to squeeze her body through, however, Biscuit himself squeezed right past her and out into the shop.

"Damn," Aurelia whispered again.

She watched as Biscuit made a beeline for the window seat and plopped down below it, eyeing Fezz, who had decided against coming into the flat for the night.

Suddenly, Aurelia was aware of a hush that had fallen over the shop. As always on nights when characters were visiting, the shop was filled with a beautiful, diffuse light that looked and felt like the glow of a dozen candelabra. She walked over to the railing along the mezzanine, feeling a mix of apprehension and excitement as she looked down at the curious faces turned upward. Her heart leapt at the sight. She didn't think she'd ever get used to it and she didn't mind that at all.

"Good evening!" she called down to them as she moved quickly to the spiral staircase and spun down the steps. "I'm so sorry I couldn't join you before tonight. I hope everyone's alright?"

There was a collective murmur of agreement and greetings.

Stepping onto the shop floor, she looked around and smiled at the group.

"Hi! Welcome to On the Square Books. This is my shop and I'm so happy to have you here."

Aurelia took in the crowd that began gathering around her. So many of Dickens' characters had lived vividly in her imagination for so many years, but she still struggled to place each one with their respective novel. A middle-aged man walked over to her. His hair was greying at the temples, and he wore a well-tailored dark grey waistcoat and a white shirt with a few ink splotches around his cuffs. *Someone in business*, Aurelia guessed, but that hardly narrowed down the list of possible characters. On his arm was a plump woman, her salt-and-pepper hair pulled back into a loose, wild bun and the buttons on her dress straining as she tried to contain her apparent good humor.

"Marigold?" the man asked doubtfully.

"No, my name is Aurelia. Marigold was my aunt—she owned the shop before me. I'm sorry to tell you… She passed away."

The news had gotten easier to share with each new group of characters, though Aurelia still felt bad delivering it when so many of them had been fond of Marigold.

"That is sad news indeed. I am sorry for your loss, Miss… Aurelia?"

"Yes. Thank you, Mr.…?"

"Pardon, madam. I'm Mr. Copperfield. David Copperfield." He inclined his head toward her.

Aurelia's eyes widened and she was sure she'd blacked out for a moment. She was standing in front of *the* David Copperfield! Dickens had said *David Copperfield* was the closest he'd come to writing a memoir. Meeting David, then, was like meeting Charles Dickens himself—one of the greatest writers in history. And the ink on his sleeves wasn't because he was in business, but because David was a writer, just like Dickens.

"Miss Aurelia?" David asked, leaning in as if to confirm she was still present despite her vacant stare.

She shook her head, trying to shake loose her nerves at meeting a literary hero.

"Yes! I'm sorry. I'm so very happy to meet you," she said, ducking her head as she felt a blush creep up her cheeks.

"May I introduce Peggotty," David continued, patting the hand of the woman whose arm was linked in his. "That is, Mrs.—"

"I'm your Peggotty, Davy, I may as well be hers!" she said happily. "Pleased to meet you, Miss Aurelia."

Peggotty! Aurelia's smile grew as she took in David and his old nurse, a woman who had cared for him as a son after his mother passed away.

"You can just call me Aurelia," she said, looking around to include everyone.

As she spoke, an older man stepped forward, also arm in arm with a woman. She was much younger than him, perhaps in her early thirties. Both were dressed simply but elegantly, reflecting a comfortable wealth, though their warm smiles showed they weren't stuffy or snobbish. Aurelia had a guess that they might be John Jarndyce and Esther from *Bleak House*. Esther was a central figure in the novel and narrated half of it, while John Jarndyce was her guardian. In Aurelia's mind, he was 'John Jarndyce'—not just 'John'—partly because Dickens often referred to him by his full name, and partly because some people's first and last names just stuck in her brain as a complete unit.

"Mr. John Jarndyce?" she hazarded.

He stopped and looked at her in wonder. "You know my unfortunate name, do you?"

Right, Aurelia remembered with a wince. His family, and name, was connected to a long legal battle that he'd found upsetting. She'd have to try and get used to calling him John, if he'd let her.

"Never mind my guardian, Aurelia. If you know of him then I hope you also know that his good disposition reflects better upon him than his name."

"That's certainly his reputation."

Aurelia smiled; from the woman's age and quiet confidence, Aurelia now felt certain she knew who the woman was.

"And you must be Esther?"

As one of *Bleak House*'s narrators, Esther had described her face as deeply changed after an illness that Aurelia thought must have been smallpox, but in person Esther was lovely. There was, perhaps, a trace of scarring, but it looked like nothing more than a few mild acne scars.

"I am. And I am very pleased to make your acquaintance. When I last visited the shop it looked quite different, but perhaps that was many years ago now? I believe it was owned by a Miss Lucy then."

"Lucy was my great aunt, so yes, that would have been many years ago. Welcome back!"

They smiled at each other as two men, one large and well-built, perhaps in his sixties, and the other younger and trimmer, approached.

"I met Miss Lucy myself on more than one occasion," said the older man, his baritone voice resonating with kindness. "Joe Gargery, miss, pleased to meet you," he said, raising a hand to his head as if to remove a hat that wasn't there.

Ah, Aurelia thought, Joe was from *Great Expectations* and had been a devoted father figure to his young brother-in-law, the central character, Pip. Could the younger man with him be—

"And this old chap here," Joe added, clapping a rough hand on the younger man's shoulder, "is Pip."

"Philip, miss, but I'll answer to Pip." His accent was smoother and more polished than Joe's, but his smile was just as genuine.

"Happy to meet you both," Aurelia said, nodding to them in greeting.

Pip and Joe started asking her about the shop, telling her when they'd visited and which of her aunts they'd met. Aurelia wanted to hear every detail and was spilling over with excitement at finally meeting this new batch of characters. *This is going to work!* she told herself. She'd managed to get out of the flat easily enough—Oliver was sleeping and Biscuit was oblivious. She might just be able to keep up with her evening visits to the shop.

9

Just as Joe started telling Aurelia another story about her great aunt Lucy, Esther stepped forward and raised a hand to catch her attention.

"I am sorry to interrupt your conversation, Aurelia, but there is a young woman here who is quite tearful. Something seems to have upset her, and I've tried comforting her to no avail. Perhaps you could try?"

"There's another charac—*person* here?"

It was hard not to think of the shop's visitors as characters, but it always felt strange to Aurelia to refer to them that way when they were standing right in front of her. She looked around, trying to get a glimpse of the woman. As Esther led her toward the armchair at the front of the shop, Aurelia realized it must be someone from

Little Dorrit, but which character? As they got closer she saw that the woman was young, no older than eighteen or nineteen. She was slouched over in the chair, crying into a handkerchief. Seeing how genuinely sad she was, Aurelia's heart went out to her.

"Hello," she said gently, lowering herself into a squat at the girl's side.

The girl paused her tears to look up from her handkerchief, then began crying again. Aurelia and Esther made eye contact over her head, both looking worried.

"Aurelia, this is Harriet."

Harriet? At first, Aurelia couldn't think which character that could be, until she remembered Tattycoram. Her real name was Harriet, but she'd been given the thoughtless nickname by the Meagles family, who had taken her from an orphanage to be a maid to their daughter.

"Harriet and I made each other's acquaintance a few nights ago, on our first evening in the shop together," Esther explained to Aurelia. She then settled herself on the arm of the chair and placed a comforting hand on Harriet's shoulder as she said, "Please, do tell us what has saddened you. Perhaps we can give you some comfort?"

Harriet leaned into Esther, still crying into her handkerchief.

Aurelia took a turn and said, "If these past few nights have been your first time here in the shop, I'm sure it's been a lot to get used to. Is there anything I can do to help? Do you have any questions for me?"

"It's—it's not my first time—here," Harriet said between sobs.

"Well, I should say welcome back then, shouldn't I?" Aurelia offered with a smile. "Which of my aunts did you meet the last time you were here?"

Harriet's face crumpled as she turned back into Esther's side, and Aurelia and Esther exchanged another look.

When characters appeared in the shop, it was always from the end of their novels, and Aurelia's mind raced to remember what happened at the end of *Little Dorrit* that might have upset Harriet. But then Harriet began to collect herself, looking as though she was preparing to speak.

"The last time... the last time I was here..." She paused to steady herself. "It was with Marigold. It was always with Marigold."

"Oh..." Aurelia trailed off, thinking she understood—all too well. "Were you and Marigold friends?"

Harriet drew the handkerchief up to her face again and nodded.

"I'm so very sorry, Harriet."

Tears welled in Aurelia's eyes to see how moved Harriet was by Marigold's loss. Her own grief had knocked Aurelia's life out of orbit. First her mother had died, then her aunt not long afterward. Other characters she'd met had been saddened by news of Marigold's death, but Harriet was the first to look so... devastated by it.

"Did you know she was ill? Did she get a chance to tell you?"

"Mm-hmm. She set out her favorite books, near the end," Harriet said with a sniffle. "She said she was doing very poorly and wanted us to meet you before she passed, to help explain how the shop worked."

"Then you must have been here with Sergeant Cuff! Do you remember seeing me?"

"Just barely," Harriet said with a tentative laugh.

"That's right." Aurelia exhaled a laugh at the memory. "I was a little scared when I saw all of you down here."

"A little," Harriet agreed. "When we saw you, we realized... that we might never see Marigold again, but I still held out hope. She'd had a plan, Aurelia. She wanted to show you, to introduce you to us. Us especially."

Aurelia remembered Sergeant Cuff telling her that Marigold had left his book out on purpose; she hadn't realized that *all* the books on the table had been part of a plan. And it was only luck that Aurelia had left Cuff's book there since she'd been planning to swap out all the books that day. Aurelia wanted to ask which other characters Marigold had wanted her to meet but decided to hold her questions for now and concentrate on Harriet.

"Unfortunately, her plan didn't work. Things went very quickly for her, at the end. She'd been up and about, still running the shop while getting treatment." Aurelia paused to swallow down threatening tears. "Then suddenly she was so weak she could barely speak to us let alone get up from her hospital bed. We thought she had more time, but..."

"I wish I'd had a chance to make Marigold's acquaintance," Esther said quietly, likely recognizing that Harriet and Aurelia needed a moment to pull themselves together.

After taking that moment Aurelia asked, "You said she wanted me to meet you?"

Harriet nodded, a small smile spreading across her tear-stained face.

"She thought you and I... that we might be able to help one another. She said she loved us both very much and thought we might need each other, after she'd passed."

Aurelia had known Marigold well enough to suspect she'd wanted Aurelia to comfort Harriet. She was younger, like a little sister Aurelia had never had but always wanted. Perhaps she'd even been something like a daughter to Marigold, part of her secret family here in the shop. Tears sprang up in her eyes again as Aurelia thought of the ways Marigold had been looking out for both of them, even in her last days.

"How very perceptive," Esther observed, wrapping an arm around Harriet. "What a very good friend she was."

"I'd love to hear more about Marigold while you're visiting," Aurelia said. "Maybe I can tell you a bit about her life outside the shop, and you can tell me a bit about her life here with you?"

With a broad smile, Harriet wiped away the last of her tears.

"I'd like that. I'd like that very much."

10

Harriet stood, and Aurelia pulled herself up as gracefully as she could from her crouching position. John Jarndyce approached their small circle, handing Harriet a dry handkerchief while leaning in to speak with her.

"No more tears, now. Yes?" His voice was so very gentle, as though he were speaking to a frightened child. "Let's find our joy in being here, together. What do you say?"

He held his arm out to her and she took it with a shy smile as he led her over to join the rest of the characters.

"You have brought together a delightful group of visitors, Aurelia, and I look forward to getting to know each of them, and you," David said with a nod first at Aurelia and then at Harriet, a subtle show of kindness after her tears. When Harriet gave him a nod in return, he continued. "My understanding is that, amongst us, I have visited the shop most frequently and have met several of its previous owners—Marigold, as I mentioned, Lucy, and Cristobel."

"Goodness, then you've met all of us. My great-great aunt Cristobel opened the shop and passed it down through the family. I've only ever met one other character—person—who'd met all of us."

"I consider it something of an honor, then," he said, his voice booming as he laughed and inclined his head again.

His loud voice and laugh reminded Aurelia that Oliver was asleep upstairs, so she'd need to keep the group's volume to a dull roar. The other night, when she'd said goodbye to the last group of characters, she hadn't had to worry about making noise; they'd all been socializing together for a few weeks, so it was a more subdued evening. Tonight, with a new batch of people eager to get to know her and one another, not making noise was proving more of a challenge.

"Won't you tell us about yourself, Aurelia?" David asked, his voice seeming to double in volume now that she'd reminded herself of the need to keep quiet.

"Me?" she asked. She'd been making a mental list of questions to ask him—what books he'd written and what story he was writing now—and had to switch gears to try and think of what he might want to know about her.

"Um, sure," she said as softly as she could. "But first—please, make yourselves comfortable. The shop is entirely open to you. You should wander, walk up to the mezzanine, sit, whatever you like."

Joe, who was standing in front of her desk with Pip, moved to lean against it, while Peggotty settled herself into the armchair that Harriet had vacated. The others remained standing, scattered around the shop floor in front of Aurelia.

"You were asking about me, David?" Aurelia confirmed, and he nodded encouragingly. "Well, I run the shop now and I live upstairs," Aurelia added, pointing to the door on the mezzanine that led to the flat, and lowering her voice again as she thought of Oliver sleeping there. "And I'm a writer."

"As am I!" David declared, not without pride. "I do enjoy speaking with fellow writers. I look forward to talking shop, as it were."

David Copperfield wanted to talk with *her* about being an author! Aurelia tried to keep her face neutral but was sure it had 'fangirl' written all over it.

"I'd like that," she said in the understatement of the century.

"I have often become lost in the world I am creating, as I'm sure you have," David said, shaking his head in wonder. "I can only imagine what you must have thought when you discovered that the words on the pages of your shop's wares came to life!"

"It took me a while to believe I wasn't just having some very vivid dreams," she agreed with a laugh. "But once I learned that everyone had met my aunts, and then seeing them here night after night..." She paused, remembering to speak quietly. "Well, eventually I figured out that I wasn't dreaming at all."

"I'm sorry, Aurelia, I didn't hear that last bit," Peggotty called from the armchair, straining forward to listen.

Aurelia panicked at Peggotty's raised voice and looked nervously toward the door to the flat. Rather than raise her voice, she stepped closer to Peggotty.

"I said I've loved getting to know the visitors in the shop."

"Ah," Peggotty said, nodding.

"Have you had many guests since you discovered your first visitors last year?" Esther asked.

"Hmm… I've had a little over twenty, I'd say," Aurelia said softly. "I should mention, there may be nights when I can't join you, but I hope it won't happen too often."

"Are you unwell?" Esther asked with concern. "You seem to be losing your voice. Are we keeping you too late?"

"Oh, no! Not at all."

She opened her mouth to explain Oliver, then realized: she couldn't tell these nineteenth-century characters that she was living out of wedlock with her boyfriend. But she also wouldn't be able to erase him from their conversations or keep up the pretense of living alone without slipping up at some point.

"My… husband is asleep upstairs and I don't want to disturb him."

The lie slipped out of her mouth so quickly that it surprised her. He'd moved in less than ten hours ago and already she'd promoted him to her husband. She shook her head, pressing on.

"He doesn't know about this," Aurelia added, pointing around the shop.

"Your aunt Lucy had a time of it trying to keep her husband in the dark," David said knowingly.

"Did she?" Aurelia asked, instantly distracted from her fib. Lucy hadn't been married; Aurelia knew that for a fact. Had Lucy told the same lie to cover up her boyfriends? Aurelia smiled at the thought, wishing Lucy—or any of the aunts, for that matter—had shared some of their tricks for keeping the shop's secret.

"She did, indeed. Fortunately, her husband snored loud enough to drown us all out and was none the wiser."

Aurelia raised a silent prayer that Oliver, too, would develop an ability to snore through her nightly visits.

"I had not realized you were married, Aurelia," Pip said. "Is it no longer in fashion to wear a wedding ring?"

Aurelia looked down at her hand, surprised for a moment that a ring hadn't materialized to corroborate her story.

"No, I must have forgotten to put it on today," she said, laughing falsely at her imagined forgetfulness and hoping her latest lie wouldn't give her away.

Just then, Biscuit let out a happy bark from the mezzanine. Everyone looked up, surprised at the seemingly sudden appearance of a dog. He was looking down at them with his head between the railings as his tail wagged his entire back end.

Aurelia looked at him, confused. Somehow, Biscuit had only just registered the characters and now kept up a steady, cheerful barking in their direction.

"Biscuit! Come!" Aurelia whispered loudly.

But he continued barking and wagging his tail, completely ignoring her.

"I'm so sorry," Aurelia said, turning to the characters. "I don't know what's got into him." Then, back to Biscuit, she added, "Will you stop?"

He wouldn't, so Aurelia quickly climbed the spiral staircase, determined to quiet the dog before he woke Oliver. Squatting down beside Biscuit, she leaned against the mezzanine railing to apologize again to the characters below when suddenly they all dissolved into swirling clouds of white printed with words and were rapidly drawn back into their books on the small table.

Aurelia's breath caught in her throat, and she stood gaping at where they had just stood. She knew it couldn't possibly be dawn, but her eyes moved to the window to confirm it was definitely still dark outside—much too early for the characters to leave.

"Aurelia?" Oliver's sleepy voice called to her from the door to the flat.

Her head spun so quickly that she pulled a muscle in her neck. Wincing, she rubbed at it as she saw Oliver standing in the doorway. The shop was cast into darkness now that the characters had disappeared, and he was silhouetted by light from the stairwell.

Aurelia tried but couldn't read Oliver's expression—it was too dark and he was too far away. With a slow release of air, she stood and started walking toward him. She needed to come up with an explanation for why their first official night living together in the flat was ending with a bang. Or a bark.

11

It was a quarter to ten in the morning and Aurelia was still nibbling on her toast while sitting at the flat's small dining table, looking out on the square and thinking over last night's events.

Oliver had been half-asleep when she'd found him at the shop door, and what with Biscuit's excitement at seeing him and Oliver's confusion at being woken, she'd managed to chivvy him back to bed without much of a story. Since he'd found her in the dark and without her notebook or laptop, she couldn't pretend she'd been writing, as she'd planned. Instead, she told him that she'd heard a noise and come down to investigate, and that Biscuit had followed her, seen Fezz, and set off barking. It wasn't necessarily a lie... It was just the beginning and end of a story, minus the middle.

Fortunately, the sound of nearly a dozen voices hadn't woken Oliver, just Biscuit's barking. That was some relief, anyway.

Poor Oliver, she thought as she finished her tea, *waking to find me out of bed and Biscuit barking.* She blushed a little to think of how she'd told the characters they were married. Not even a week into living together and she'd already pushed them into a pretend marriage. Though being married to Oliver wasn't an idea that scared her. Just as moving in together had felt like a natural next step they were both ready to take, Aurelia thought that—later, at some point—saying 'I do' might feel just as natural. But, of course, one step at a time. And trying to figure out how to visit the characters without waking Oliver every night was a step that needed to come first.

When the characters disappeared the moment Oliver walked through the door between the flat and the shop, Aurelia saw first-hand that Sergeant Cuff and the other characters were right; he'd never be able to come into the shop after midnight to meet them. As much as she'd believed everyone and suspected it must be true, it was still disappointing to have confirmation that she couldn't share it with him, that it was a secret she'd have to continue to keep from the people she loved most.

With Oliver at work and Aurelia facing what was likely to be a quiet Monday, she decided she might as well start her day. Soon she was in the shop, had opened the wooden blinds, and was just sitting at her desk when the bell on the door set to ringing. Biscuit, who had settled himself on the floor near her desk, jumped to his feet, ready to investigate. Looking up, Aurelia smiled as she recognized the man who had just come in.

"Mark!"

She was surprised to see him. He used to stop by every Monday but had been coming by less often now that he, Aurelia, and Oliver had been spending time together outside the shop. For years, Mark had been in love with Aurelia's aunt Marigold, though it had been an unrequited love. After her aunt died over a year ago, he'd started a routine of weekly visits, which gave him and Aurelia time to commiserate in their shared grief.

And now Oliver had helped them transform that mournful companionship into a functioning friendship, with dinner dates, walks, and the occasional event. She wasn't sure exactly how Oliver had done it, but it seemed to have something to do with breaking them both out of the shop. Why hadn't Aurelia ever asked Mark to dinner or coffee before? She simply had no answer. He had always come to the shop, and she had believed he wanted to be there, nearest to the place that Marigold had called home for so many years. Yet one day, Oliver had been there during one of Mark's visits and spontaneously invited him to join them for dinner that evening. She'd waited for Mark to make an excuse, assuming he wouldn't be interested, but was surprised to hear him eagerly accept.

That one night had set off a regular cycle of outings and gatherings. Which was why she hadn't expected to see Mark today since they'd invited him to dinner the following week with the hope that it would motivate them to unpack all of Oliver's boxes in time for his visit.

"Can I get you some tea?"

"No, thanks. I was just a few streets away and couldn't resist stopping in for a minute. How are you?"

"I'm good! Oliver's settling in, though we can't find the floor for the boxes at the moment," Aurelia said, laughing. "You said you were nearby?"

"Yes, I'm meeting... a friend. For coffee. We hadn't seen each other in years, but we bumped into each other a few months ago." Mark bent down to pet Biscuit, who was sitting at his feet waiting to greet him.

"That's nice you reconnected. Were you friends at university, then?"

"No, we were in primary school together, if you can believe it. My family moved when we were in third form and we lost touch until now."

"All these years later! I'm glad you found him again."

Mark opened his mouth to speak but then hesitated before saying, "Yes, it's been good catching up." He looked at the clock at the back of the shop, then confirmed the time against his watch. "I'd best be off. Don't want to be late."

"Have fun, then. See you next week."

Mark waved as he headed out the door. Aurelia watched him walk away and was happy when she spotted him smiling to himself. He'd been looking better these past few months. His smile was more genuine, his face less careworn. She felt guilty for not having realized before that he might have needed a push to get through his grief, not just mutual sympathy. As it happened, she'd needed a push as well. Oliver had provided a push for Mark, while Aurelia's push had come in the form of Count Vronsky, who had needed a new ending. Which set her back to thinking about the characters and their brief visit to the shop the night before.

Looking down at Biscuit, who had settled on the floor by her desk, she decided she'd need to make a better plan for getting him used to the shop's evening visitors. Waking Oliver every night with a barking Biscuit wasn't fair, and it certainly wouldn't give her much time with the characters.

12

Aurelia managed to sneak out of the flat once again that night, though Biscuit had once again insisted on joining her. This time she remembered to set aside some clothes to change into, grabbed her notebook and a pen as props, and was able to get to the shop a few minutes before midnight. Fezz was already settled on the window seat, but before Biscuit could skitter away toward the cat, she scooped him up and carried him down the stairs. She hoped that, despite the unique way the characters appeared, if she could get him to meet them all at the start of the evening, they might be able to avoid surprising him at an inconvenient moment.

As the mists started to rise up from the books on the table, Aurelia squatted next to Biscuit and held him firm. She spoke reassuringly as his tail wagged and he let out a few whines of excitement, but he kept his barking in check even as he watched the figures appearing all around him.

Once Biscuit seemed to understand that the characters weren't out to get him or Aurelia, she released him and stood, smiling at her guests. "Hello! Welcome back!"

"Good evening, Aurelia!" John Jarndyce stepped forward and dipped his head. "We had quite a sudden departure last night. I hope all is well?"

The other characters gathered closer, nodding and murmuring the same concern.

"Yes! I'm so sorry. The dog woke Oliver, my… husband. He came down to see what was going on and, well—poof! I hope everyone's alright?"

"No harm done, dear," said Peggotty, smiling.

"None at all. We're made of strong stuff, aren't we, old chap," Joe declared, pounding Pip on the shoulder with his large hand. Pip was tossed forward a bit but laughed as he gave Joe a gentle pat on the shoulder in return.

Fortunately, none of the characters seemed to be afraid of dogs, and instead smiled as Biscuit wandered between them, sniffing at their skirts and trousers, trying to figure out who these new visitors were. His wagging tail set some of their clothes into wisps of mist with a scattering of printed words shifting across them, which he had fun chasing until the mists materialized back into the characters' forms.

Joe leaned down, reaching out a hand as if to pet the dog, but Biscuit's curious nose turned Joe's hand into a momentary mist before it resolved into a human hand again. Joe gave a hearty laugh and stood.

"I thought maybe I'd be able to give him a scratch behind the ears."

"We can't touch the shop owners or their animals, I'm afraid," came a quiet voice from the back of the crowd.

Aurelia looked around and saw that it was Harriet, who appeared timid and alone even though she was surrounded by others. At the sound of Harriet's voice, Biscuit had walked over to her, and she bent as if to pet him. Just like Joe's, her hand swept through Biscuit's head before shifting back into shape. He seemed unperturbed by it and sat down at Harriet's feet.

"Ah, I see," Joe said. "Lucy didn't have any pets when I visited her. I've never yet been able to touch anything other than a chair or a table in this shop."

Others chimed in to agree.

"Fezz?" Harriet asked uncertainly, just loud enough for Aurelia to hear her over the conversations that were starting up around them.

"He's still here," Aurelia promised. "He's up on the window seat if you'd like to go and see him?"

Harriet smiled and nodded.

"I'll join you," Esther said, stepping forward.

"What about you, Peggotty? Are the stairs too much for you?" David asked kindly, walking toward the armchair she had just dropped into.

"It's not getting up them, Davy, it's the coming down them again," Peggotty laughed. "I'm comfortable enough here for now."

Aurelia watched as Esther followed Harriet up the spiral staircase. They circled the mezzanine once, then settled near Fezz on the wide window seat. Movement nearby caught Aurelia's eye, and she saw that David had taken a small notebook and pencil out of his pocket and was jotting something down. She moved closer to him as Peggotty and the others started chatting, wondering what he might be writing before gathering the courage to ask him.

"Are you working on a new story?"

David made a dramatic flourish with his pencil before tucking the notebook away again, smiling as he nodded.

"I am writing a book set in Paris during the Revolution, and ideas and lines seem to strike me at the oddest of moments," he explained. "There is one line I keep working over from the first chapter—'greatest of times, most horrible of times'—something to that effect."

Aurelia smiled to hear that David really was just like Dickens. He was describing the story and first line (though not quite there yet) of *A Tale of Two Cities*.

"I'm sure the right phrasing will come to me if I let it," he added. "And you? What story are you writing at present?"

"Oh—" Aurelia broke off, once again trying to be cool (even though she knew that was a status she'd never managed to achieve) in the face of David's talent. "Um, I'm just starting a new book, actually. The main character works at a struggling auction house and discovers—his first week there—that not only is one of the upcoming lots a forgery, but several lots of art sold over the past few years have been forgeries, too."

David stared off into the distance and began rubbing at the beard on his chin, as though envisioning the story as Aurelia laid it out.

"At first I thought perhaps he'd be a naïve type," she continued. "Someone who is unsure what to do next and then sort of stumbles through telling everyone as they work out what the auction house should do."

David made a face, clearly rejecting that idea, so Aurelia rushed forward.

"But then I realized it would be more interesting if he was a little more conniving. I think he's going to play the auction house and the forger against each other—threatening to expose them or keep the secret, depending on what he can get from each."

"Much more intriguing," David agreed. "And is the auction house in on the scheme? Did they hire the forger?"

"I don't know yet," Aurelia said with a smile, loving that David was tapping into the ideas and questions she'd been working through herself. "I'm thinking they aren't, but that they still wouldn't want the secret to get out—about how they'd somehow missed detecting the fakes—without being able to control how and when. Especially when they're up against major art auction houses and their business has been in the red. And maybe the main character knows that and is waiting to tell them, wanting to see what he can get from the forger first."

"Money for his silence?"

"Or maybe a cut of the profits if he promises to keep putting up the forger's works for auction."

"Ah," David said appreciatively. "Many different ways to build in drama and excitement—the only trouble will be choosing."

"I think so too," she said happily, feeling like she'd just gotten Dickens' stamp of approval.

Aurelia was about to walk over to grab her own notebook so that she could flip through it and tell David some of her other ideas for the book, when she spotted Biscuit climbing up the spiral staircase. She watched as he made his way over to Harriet and Esther, worrying that he'd spot Fezz and start his barking again.

"I'm sorry, David—I see Biscuit is on a wander and think I'd better keep an eye on him. Do you mind if I run upstairs for a moment?"

"Not at all," he said kindly. "I will keep having a think over your story and will be ready to share some ideas the next time we speak."

Aurelia barely managed to hold in her squeak of excitement before thanking him and heading up the stairs.

"I'm sorry to interrupt," she said as she joined Esther and Harriet, "but I think Biscuit might need some supervision to keep him from barking you back into your books."

They laughed and made room for her on the window seat, and as she sat down, Biscuit dropped to the floor and rested his head on one of her feet. Fezz, who'd been sleeping on a far corner of the seat, stood up lazily, stretched, and moved to curl up next to her. Harriet reached out a hand as though offering it for Fezz to sniff. He looked up at her and gave a slow blink, like he recognized a friend, and Harriet smiled back at him.

"We have a dog at home, but I've always wanted a cat," Esther said thoughtfully as she watched them.

"If I remember, Esther, you have a family now?" Aurelia asked.

Esther's face broke into a smile. "I do. I have two daughters. And then there's my Ada—I was her companion for a time, before she reached her majority," Esther explained to Harriet. "Ada has a son and I think of him as one of mine, as well."

"Do you mind being away from them? Would you rather not come to the shop?" Aurelia hated to think that her simple decision to put *Bleak House* on the Recommended Reads table might make Esther worry over leaving her family behind.

"I am quite happy to visit," Esther said, reaching a reassuring hand out as if to touch Aurelia's arm. "They never seem to miss me when I arrive home again, and I enjoy the chance to make new friends."

Aurelia smiled, relieved. "And you, Harriet, at the end of your story I think you're back with the Meagles family again?"

Harriet looked upset for a moment before she seemed to master her emotions. The sight made Aurelia regret using the word 'again,' which must have alerted Harriet to the fact that Aurelia knew the ins and outs of her story. She'd run away from the Meagleses, hurt and angered by their insistence on treating her as a maid instead of as a daughter, but she went back to live with them by the end of her novel.

"Yes, that's right. I've returned to the family." Harriet paused and added, "To serve them."

"I had a wonderful maid who came to work with us when she was quite young, after her parents died," Esther said kindly. "I miss her very much now that she is married, though I see her often when I am in town."

"I am sure she enjoys your visits," Harriet said, attempting a smile.

"It is a pity we cannot meet one another's families."

"Yes," Aurelia agreed, "I'd have liked to meet all of them." With a gasp, Aurelia realized she still hadn't met the other character from *Little Dorrit*. "Harriet! Who else is with you?"

"I'm sorry?"

"Who else is here with you? From your book?"

"No one. Everyone from other books always arrives in pairs, but I'm always here alone."

Aurelia's expression fell in shock. She leapt up from the window seat and looked down to the shop floor to confirm there were only five characters below. But in her hurry to check, she'd nudged Biscuit awake and set Fezz leaping onto the floor. Biscuit immediately began barking and Aurelia paused her counting to shush him.

"Biscuit, quiet!" He continued barking at a steady pace, seeming to simply enjoy the sound since his tail was wagging and he didn't look at all put out. Aurelia looked over at Esther and Harriet.

"I'm so sorry about this. It's my fault for waking him."

"Not at all," Esther said, letting out a laugh that suddenly erupted into vapor along with the rest of her.

"Esther!" Aurelia cried out, forgetting to whisper.

Harriet was disappearing too, as was everyone else. Aurelia tracked the mists as they were pulled back into their books before closing her eyes for a moment. As she opened them she turned to the flat door, knowing Oliver would be there, as he was, tousle-haired and confused at being woken up yet again to find her in the darkened shop with a barking Biscuit.

13

The next morning found Aurelia experiencing déjà vu as she sat at the table in the flat, but this time her breakfast was practically untouched. Pushing her toast around her plate, she was trying to process a dozen thoughts at once, which meant she hadn't managed to get to any sort of resolution with any of them. Adding to the confusion inside her head was the detritus of Oliver's half-unpacked boxes surrounding her, though Fezz seemed undisturbed by it as he sat on the table looking serenely out the window, while Biscuit lay on the floor below, belly up and legs in the air.

Fortunately, last night Oliver had allowed her to shuffle him back to bed again without much complaint. He hadn't even noticed that she didn't have her notebook with her or that she was in the dark again. She'd wanted to laugh at the absurdity of a barking dog setting off a chain reaction two nights running. And she might very well have laughed if it wasn't for the thoughts she was working through about Harriet.

Harriet had come to the shop alone, the only character from her book. The last time that had happened was with the first set of characters Aurelia had met. Then, the solo character was Count Vronsky from *Anna Karenina*, who, she'd learned, had appeared alone because he was unhappy with his book's ending. This had set Aurelia off on the project to fix it by giving him a happier ending than the one Tolstoy had. And then Oliver, as her editor, had helped her turn Vronsky's manuscript into a published book. When Aurelia had put it on the shop's Recommended Reads table, two characters appeared to let her know that Vronsky was doing well in his new story.

Vronsky had wanted to believe that a happier life was possible. Was that why Harriet had arrived alone from her novel? If Sergeant Cuff from *The Moonstone* were here again, she was sure he'd know what to do. Though knowing him, he'd likely make her figure it out on her own anyway. She couldn't decide what to do next. If she asked Harriet outright, that would probably seem rude. *Are you unhappy?* was a very direct question for someone she'd only just met. And how exactly did Harriet's story end, anyway?

It was nearing time to open the shop, so Aurelia stood and carried her plate and mug into the kitchen. Walking back into the living room, she searched the bookshelves and found her copy of *Little Dorrit* tucked behind a few of Oliver's books. Once downstairs, Aurelia sat at her desk and began flipping through to the end of *Little Dorrit*, looking for Harriet's last appearance. Not too long ago, she'd done the same thing with her copy of *Anna Karenina*, trying to remember exactly what Vronsky's ending had hinted about his future. Aurelia paused at a section that described Harriet's return to her adopted family, her apology for leaving them, her promise to return and fulfill her role as a maid to their daughter, and their admonition that she should remember her 'duty' to them. Aurelia paged forward but couldn't find any other mention of Harriet.

Little wonder Harriet had appeared in the shop alone, then. No warm return to the family she'd left, no apology for treating her as a servant instead of a family member, no promise of a future beyond fulfilling her duties as a maid. Aurelia leaned back in her chair, her eyes unfocused as she thought.

Harriet had been an orphan at the Foundling Hospital, a London orphanage that, if Aurelia remembered right, had been a real-life institution for children who'd been born out of wedlock. Esther, too, had been born out of wedlock, but she'd avoided an orphanage and eventually was hired as a companion—a rung above a maid on the social ladder—and married into a middle-class life. Esther's birth mother had been middle class and later moved into high society while Harriet's parents were unknown—maybe that was the difference? Aurelia sighed to think that the old stereotype about the English being obsessed with social class had been confirmed through Esther and Harriet's diverging paths.

If Harriet's unhappy with her ending though, what then? Aurelia wondered. Should she offer to write Harriet a sequel, just as she'd done for Count Vronsky? Was that her future, to run the shop and write sequels for unhappy characters? That possibility made her sit up in her chair. There were loads of unhappy characters in every book in the shop and Aurelia was bound to run into more of them. As much as she'd come to embrace running a magical bookshop and fitting in writing during her spare time, giving up the possibility of ever writing her own ideas—her own characters, even—felt like being required to permanently ignore her imagination. Sure, she had come up with unique ways to make Vronsky's story interesting, but she'd had a prescribed main character (Vronsky, of course), plot (get him to a happy ending), and purpose (give Vronsky hope).

It felt selfish not to help every character that might need her. As for Harriet, she would keep arriving in the shop unhappy from the ending of her story for as long as Aurelia kept her book on the table. And now Harriet was even more unhappy by the news of Marigold's death. Aurelia felt for Harriet and naturally wanted to comfort and help her. But did that necessarily mean writing her a new ending? Aurelia liked the story she'd been working on, the one about the art forgeries that Oliver was looking forward to editing and that David Copperfield himself had thought was full of possibilities for drama and intrigue. Granted, she hadn't written much of it yet, but her mind was in that world, in the same way David's mind was focused on the world of his new story. Her thoughts were working through who her main character was and what he'd do, and she wanted to see where the story might take him.

Maybe all this worry was for nothing, Aurelia decided. She would find a way to ask Harriet if she was unhappy with her ending before making any rash decisions about offering to help and abandoning her book.

Even with that decision made, though, Aurelia couldn't help worrying over what Harriet's answer might be.

14

Aurelia had been so deep in thought over Harriet's solitary appearance that when the shop door opened, it took her a moment to snap herself back to the present. She looked up to greet the customer coming in and nearly jumped out of her seat when she realized it was Oliver's brother Jack.

"Hello—good morning!" Aurelia's surprise at seeing him was quickly overtaken by Biscuit's barking. The dog raced to the door and began hopping up and down at Jack's feet.

"Biscuit!" Jack crouched down and let the dog lick his face as he petted him.

"I see you two know each other, then," Aurelia laughed.

"Oh, yeah. We go way back. Oliver brings him round to family dinners sometimes."

"Well, while Biscuit's busy greeting you, can I get you some tea?"

Jack stood and looked around.

"Oh, I don't want to trouble you—"

"It's no trouble," Aurelia insisted, heading for the back room. "I'll put the kettle on."

"I knew I'd walked past this place before," Jack called after her. "It's a beautiful old shop. I've wanted to come inside but was always on my way somewhere else."

"I'll give you a tour, though you can see most of it from here," Aurelia said as she stepped back onto the shop floor.

"That'd be great," Jack said, walking over to join her. "Is Oliver home by chance?"

"No, he's always off to work early, I'm afraid."

"Of course," Jack said, shaking his head. "I don't know why I thought he'd be home at this hour. I forget not everyone's on my make-your-own schedule."

"It's good to set your own hours, isn't it?" she asked conspiratorially. "Here, let me get our tea."

Mugs in hand, Aurelia led Jack around the first floor, pointing out her favorite spots in the shop and explaining about the long line of aunts that had preceded her. Up the spiral staircase, she pointed out the window seat and the view across the square, as well as the artwork and benches. Jack seemed to take in every detail, as though he were filing them away for future use in one of his set designs.

"Do you want to see the flat? It's a mess right now since Oliver's still unpacking, but you're welcome to come up," she offered, pointing to the door.

Jack hesitated, looking uncertain.

"That's alright," he said. "I'll see it another time, once the dust has settled."

Aurelia was about to ask if he was sure when the phone rang. Jack followed her down the stairs to the shop floor, stooping to pet Biscuit again as she answered it.

"Hello, On the Square Books."

"It's just me," Antonia replied from the other end of the line. "Did Oliver talk to you?"

"Well, yes, he did. We talk every day."

"Don't be smart. Did he talk to you about coming to Paris for the reading?"

"We talked about it and, just like I told you the other day, I'm going to think about it."

Jack signaled toward the door and moved as if to leave.

"No, it's alright!" Aurelia said, waving him back. "It's just my sister."

"*Just*," Antonia said tetchily.

"Yes, *just*. Jack is here—Oliver's brother."

Aurelia watched as Jack looked around the shop again, his eyes scanning up and down the shelves.

"Really? I thought they didn't get along?" Antonia asked.

Aurelia's eyes widened slightly. Though she knew Jack couldn't have heard, she was still embarrassed.

"He stopped by to say hi and see the place." It didn't exactly answer Antonia's question but seemed like the safest answer for both of her listeners. "I'll call you back in a bit, okay?"

They rang off and Aurelia came out from behind her desk to join Jack near the Recommended Reads table.

"I'm sorry—I didn't mean for you to cut your call short."

"It's fine. We talk almost every day, so there's not much to catch up on. Though we'll probably still find a way to chat for an hour about nothing when I do call her back," Aurelia laughed. "That's the joy of having a sister."

Jack's smile faltered for a moment. Aurelia was about to ask if he was alright before she realized it was probably hard for him to hear about how close she and Antonia were when he and Oliver were... not as close.

"I was just thinking," Jack said, seeming eager to change the subject. "This would be a great place for a lecture or a book talk. Have you ever done that sort of thing here?"

"Lectures? No. Not that I remember, anyway."

"We're surrounded by universities. I bet you could ask any literature professor you like to come and give a talk about one of these old books. They'd probably jump at the chance."

It seemed like such an obvious draw for her customers that Aurelia was ashamed not to have thought of it before. She'd always focused on the fact that the books' authors were gone, but that didn't mean no one was around to talk about them and their works.

"You know, that could be interesting... Invite different professors—maybe even Ph.D. students?—to give talks on a book or an author. I could order extra copies of whatever they were discussing..." Aurelia trailed off as she thought of the possibilities. "That's a great idea!"

Jack puffed his chest out and then laughed at his pretended pride.

"Well, I'm sorry to have missed my brother, but glad to have inspired you." He began heading for the door. "Thanks for the tea and company."

"I'll tell Oliver you stopped by. We're hoping to have all his things unpacked and sorted by next week. You'll have to come over for dinner."

"Really?"

At the sound of hope in his voice, Aurelia realized she should have talked to Oliver before extending that invitation. It had just been so natural to invite him. He was Oliver's family, after all. But Oliver had seemed out of sorts after the last time they'd seen Jack, and he had a right to decide whether and when he wanted to socialize with his brother—even if Aurelia couldn't understand why he wouldn't want to. Still, now that she'd put the offer out there, she couldn't very well take it back.

"We'd love to have you," she insisted, and tried to sound as though she meant it.

15

Aurelia had to face her impulse to invite Jack to dinner when Oliver arrived home from work and immediately asked how her day had been.

"It was good. There were some lulls in the shop, so I got some writing done."

"Excellent."

Oliver started searching the cabinets for the makings of their dinner, and Aurelia got up from the sofa to help.

"I also had a visit from Jack."

"Jack. My Jack?" Oliver froze with his hands full of spices, a box of pasta, and a large pot.

"Your Jack," Aurelia confirmed, taking the spices and pasta from him. "He came by to say hello but didn't realize you'd left for work already."

"Most people call before stopping by," Oliver mumbled as he filled the pot with water.

"Most people don't live above a shop that's open to the public," Aurelia reminded him.

"Mm."

"The thing is, as he was leaving, I might have mentioned something about him coming round for dinner."

Oliver froze again, this time raising an eyebrow at her.

"Might have?"

"Definitely did," she admitted with a wince. "I'm sorry. I wasn't thinking. It just came out, and I know I should have asked you first. He looked so disappointed to have missed you. And he was excited about coming back for a visit when you're here."

"It's alright. I know how he is. That look he does, it's like…"

"Like a lost puppy," Aurelia said with a chuckle.

"Exactly."

She walked over to where he was leaning against the counter and stood in front of him.

"If you really don't want to, we can put it off. This is your home now—you have a say in who we invite over."

"No, it's fine." Oliver sighed as he brushed a reassuring hand across her cheek. "If you hadn't invited him, then I'm sure my mum would have started hinting about it. I'll call him tomorrow to set it up. What do you think… Should we have him over the night after Mark?"

"Sure, why not? We'll be a well-oiled hosting machine by then."

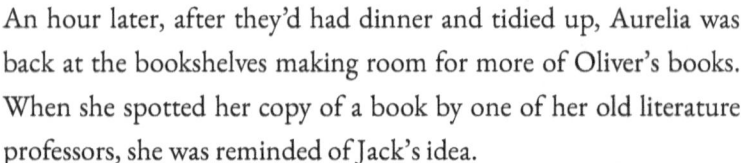

An hour later, after they'd had dinner and tidied up, Aurelia was back at the bookshelves making room for more of Oliver's books. When she spotted her copy of a book by one of her old literature professors, she was reminded of Jack's idea.

"Oh—I forgot to tell you," she began, turning to Oliver.

He made a vague noise from across the room, where he was unpacking a box of old photo albums.

"Jack asked if we ever had people come into the shop to give lectures on books or authors. I don't remember Aunt Marigold ever doing anything like that, but it was an interesting idea."

Oliver straightened and Aurelia could see he was thinking it over.

"It is, actually," he admitted reluctantly.

"I'd never thought of it before. I guess I'm used to bookshops having live authors read from their books, which has never been an option here," Aurelia said with a soft laugh.

"You have a good number of regulars that would pop by for something like that."

"I do, yeah."

"And if you put the word out, you might get some new faces in as well."

"I'm just sort of stuck on how to arrange it. I mean, the shop is pretty small, so we couldn't fit too many people. And I don't think I could afford to pay anyone very much to come and give a talk."

Aurelia had never put on an event like this; the fuss and trouble of it had been keeping her from committing to doing a reading at Antonia's local bookshop.

"You could charge a fee for people to attend—maybe five quid, something modest to cover the cost of wine and renting out some chairs."

"Chairs! And wine... Of course, I hadn't thought through all the particulars."

"It wouldn't take much work. I think the whole thing could be easy enough to pull together."

"Not too much work then?"

"Not at all," Oliver said with a smile. "And sales of whatever book is being discussed, plus a small fee—that could definitely cover your costs."

"So you think I should try it?" Aurelia asked.

"Might as well. See how the first one goes," he suggested. Oliver looked thoughtful for a moment before asking, "Was this really Jack's idea?"

"It really was," Aurelia said hopefully.

But Oliver's only response was to make a noncommittal sound before going back to unpacking.

16

Standing near the Recommended Reads table just before midnight, Aurelia was congratulating herself on getting down to the shop in time.

After unpacking for a while, Oliver had announced that he was tired and they turned in early. As she lay in bed trying to fall asleep, Aurelia's thoughts bounced between plans for Jack's lecture idea and ways to get Harriet talking about how she felt about the end of her story. Not long after she'd fallen asleep, Aurelia was up and changing back into the clothes she'd purposefully left hanging on the back of the bathroom door. And with the alarm on her phone set to vibrate, she'd been able to wake just before midnight without bothering Oliver.

Biscuit was another matter. He'd insisted on coming with her into the shop and Fezz had followed, unwilling to be left behind. Having lost the battle, she sighed, hoping the dog could contain his excitement over anything that might happen that night. Fezz, of course, was well used to the characters appearing and disappearing by now and viewed the whole thing with an air of disinterest—an emotion Aurelia was certain Biscuit had never experienced.

The clock at the back of the shop began striking midnight, and Aurelia watched as mists slowly formed over the stacks of books on the table. They grew in height, white with twisting words traveling over and around each other as they eventually flowed over the edge of the table and onto the floor, rising up to form the shape of each character. Biscuit managed to keep his enthusiasm in check, though as soon as the characters were fully embodied, he began walking amongst them, sniffing and wagging his tail as he greeted each one.

"Welcome back—and I'm sorry!" Aurelia said.

"Quite alright," Esther said, laughing. Others were smiling at the dog as Esther continued, "This time we knew what to expect."

"I wish I could promise that would be the last time Biscuit's barking wakes Oliver. They've only just moved in, and the dog is still getting used to everything, including my cat, Fezz." As she spoke, she pointed up at the mezzanine, where Fezz sat assessing them from between the railings.

"I did not realize you were newly married, Aurelia. Best wishes are in order!" John Jarndyce said as he began clapping.

Aurelia looked around in confusion as the others joined in. Then it dawned on her: she'd already told them Oliver was her husband, but now she'd let slip that he'd only just moved in with her. Of course a roomful of nineteenth-century characters would assume that meant they'd only just gotten married. Her cheeks reddened a little at their kind response to her tall tales. Now she really was a blushing bride.

"Thank you. It's all... very new," she managed to say.

"That explains why you've forgotten your ring again," Pip said, pointing to her hand.

"Uh, yes—it does," Aurelia said, touching her left hand and feeling the absence of a ring that had never been there. "I'm sure I'll get into the routine of it eventually."

Must find a ring to wear at night, Aurelia told herself.

The characters wanted to know more about Oliver, like how he and Aurelia had met, how long they'd been engaged, and whether he worked in the shop with her. Esther asked if anyone had helped Aurelia with her trousseau, which required an explanation about the fact that, in the present day, women generally didn't sew the linens and things they'd need for a new household. Aurelia tried to imagine having to sew bedsheets and tablecloths before moving in with Oliver and decided they were both lucky that was no longer a tradition. Eventually, everyone split off into groups, sharing stories about weddings they'd been to or been in, and the trials and tribulations of life as a newlywed.

Aurelia soon began chatting with David and Peggotty. She'd been eagerly swapping ideas with David about each other's books, with Peggotty smiling and adding in a few ideas of her own, when she noticed Harriet perusing the bookshelves by herself. Earlier in the day she'd hoped to find a way to speak with Harriet and Esther, or Harriet, Esther, and Peggotty, thinking that some combination of the ladies—all kind and open-hearted—might make Harriet feel more comfortable sharing her story. And as much as she'd like to keep talking about writing with David, Aurelia knew this was a good opening for that conversation.

"Peggotty, I see Harriet's on her own. Should we go and have a chat with her?"

"You ladies go and enjoy yourselves," David said. "I'll see if Mr. Jarndyce will tell me more about that case of his. It does seem like a brilliant story—lost wills... wards and guardians... I own I am quite envious of Esther for getting first crack at it."

David's disappointment reminded Aurelia that, like David, Esther had 'written' her own story, with Dickens having each of them narrate their lives in the pages of their books.

"Well," David continued on a sigh, "perhaps Esther will indulge me with a few more details."

He strolled across the shop toward John Jarndyce and Esther, leaving Aurelia and Peggotty to walk over to Harriet.

"Peggotty and I wondered if you'd like to join us for a chat?" Aurelia asked once Harriet had spotted them. "What do you say, Peggotty, should we see if we can get you up the stairs this evening?"

"Certainly, if your Oliver will oblige me by helping me to disappear back down again," she laughed.

"That I can't promise. We'll have to leave it up to the dog," Aurelia said wryly.

"I'll help you up and down," Harriet declared. "It's a shame if you don't get a chance to see the rest of the shop." She'd been slightly shy around the others that evening but seemed to come alive at the injustice that someone might be left behind.

"Alright, then," Peggotty said, clearly surprised by Harriet's sudden enthusiasm.

Aurelia led them upstairs, looking back now and then to check on their progress, but Peggotty did just fine. Once she'd cleared the landing, she looked around the mezzanine, seeming quite pleased with herself. After they'd walked the mezzanine loop, they made themselves comfortable on the window seat. Aurelia let their conversation wander for as long as she could before she jumped in to start her line of questioning.

"Remind me, Peggotty—you live with David and his aunt, Betsey, at the end of your book, don't you?"

"That I do, Aurelia. She terrified me to bits when I first knew her, but I warmed to her. I decided that anyone who loves my Davy as much as I do is alright by me."

"And you like living together?"

"I do indeed. We see plenty of Davy and his young 'uns. It's lovely having your family close."

"And, Harriet..." Aurelia trailed off, still not sure how to navigate this conversation. "You reminded me the other night that you live with the Meagleses at the end of your story."

Harriet nodded, her eyes downcast.

"And... are you happy there?"

Harriet shrugged, then paused before shaking her head, still avoiding eye contact.

"It always bothered Marigold," she said quietly. "That I had to go back to them."

Aurelia drew in a breath.

"You and Aunt Marigold talked about your ending?"

"We did—often. She always wished it were different, that Mr. Dickens had put me in a nice home with a nice family, somewhere

I'd feel wanted and—" She broke off, looking embarrassed to have shared so much.

"Dear girl." Peggotty tutted, taking Harriet's hand in hers.

Aurelia's heart sank a little. Marigold had wanted to help Harriet but couldn't; Aurelia knew how to help her and could.

"Did you and Aunt Marigold ever talk about what you'd like to do in your future?" Aurelia asked.

"We talked about me finding friends and being happy, but mostly ways to make life with the Meagleses better since I'm stuck with them. She gave me suggestions for how to tolerate living together. How to look for a bright side every day. Even days when I didn't think there was one."

Aurelia's heart sank a little more. Making the best of things was all Marigold could offer Harriet, while Aurelia—after her experiment with Count Vronsky—could offer much more than that.

"She used to leave my book out nearly all the time, just to give me an 'escape' as she used to call it."

Harriet gave a soft smile at the memory, and Aurelia's heart nearly sank to the floor. She remembered that Marigold had always called reading her 'favorite escape.' Marigold had loved recommending books to her customers and helping them find their next great adventure. But since she couldn't give Harriet that kind of escape—not when Harriet couldn't touch any of the shop's books—she'd given Harriet the only way of fleeing her life she could offer. But visiting the shop, just like reading, was only a temporary freedom—a few hours at a time. A sequel would certainly give Harriet a more permanent freedom from her unhappy life in *Little Dorrit*. And from what Harriet had shared and what Aurelia knew about her aunt, Marigold would have jumped at the chance to make that change in Harriet's life.

Still, Aurelia hesitated to take it on. To be fair, writing a sequel wasn't an easy thing. It would be work, hard work, and Aurelia was just picking up steam on her own book. They'd need to work long hours together, she'd need to research Harriet's options based on the time and setting of the novel, and she'd need to explain to Oliver why she'd suddenly decided to switch projects. But no matter how she tried to rationalize it to herself, Aurelia kept coming back to the same set of facts: Marigold had cared for Harriet; Marigold had wanted a better life for her; Marigold hadn't known how to help Harriet; and Aurelia knew exactly what to do.

"What about your life before the Meagleses?" Aurelia asked after a moment. "Do you remember anything that happened before you arrived at the Foundling Hospital?"

"Oh... Well, my very first memories are of being pushed and tumbled about with other children in a house out in the countryside."

"It sounds like you had a large family, then?" Peggotty asked.

"No, they weren't my family. An older couple looked after us, but they weren't my parents, nor were the children my brothers and sisters. We weren't treated poorly, but there were so many of us crowded together. I wasn't all that sad when they came to take some of us to the Hospital."

"Who took you away?" Aurelia asked, imagining a grim scene.

But Harriet's expression was neutral when she responded. "A few men and women who worked for the Hospital. I was four—or maybe five—when they came. The couple explained things to us quite plainly and we had seen other children come and go. We always knew, then, that we would be taken away when we were old enough. The day we left it was me, Margaret, and Stephen."

"Those were your friends?" Peggotty asked.

"I never liked Stephen very much," Harriet said with a frown. "He was always pushing me when we played together. But Margaret was like a sister to me," Harriet added, smiling at the memory. "She was a little younger, but we cried so when they tried to separate us. They decided it wasn't worth the bother to keep her there without me, or to send me away without her."

"What was it like, at the Hospital?"

Aurelia felt a little guilty to be pestering Harriet with questions but she needed to know, needed to understand the ins and outs of Harriet's life if she was going to offer to help her. *If*.

"It was very strict, very regimented. Every minute accounted for, with lessons, chores, meals, and prayers."

"And that was your life, until the Meagleses?"

Harriet nodded. "Most of us stayed there until we were around fifteen. Margaret left a year or so after me. We write to each other, but it's been hard not to see her for all these years. She works in service for a family in Dorset, and I never get a day free from the Meagleses."

"So, you don't know anything about your parents or your family? Didn't anyone from the Hospital ever tell you about them?"

"No, never."

Aurelia thought about little Harriet alone in an orphanage, then scooped up to live and work with the Meagleses. If anyone deserved a happier ending to a sad and tragic life, surely it was her? But Aurelia had many other questions to answer for herself before making such a big commitment. And worse than offering Harriet some hope would be to decide she wasn't able to help after all.

Peggotty began telling Harriet about some of her memories of David's childhood, making Harriet laugh and relieving some of the tension from their unhappy conversation. Aurelia nodded along, but the thin sound of Harriet's laughter caught at her ears, making her feel as though the answer was right in front of her, inevitable as the dawn that drew nearer as they talked through the night.

17

Aurelia woke the next morning to an attempted kiss from Oliver, who had squatted down at her bedside to say good morning before he left for work. At first, she pushed him away to save him from her hazardous morning breath. But after he offered her a few sips of his tea to equal the playing field, she gave in to an enjoyable morning snog.

She thought she just might get used to having a live-in boyfriend, after all.

A few hours later, Aurelia was sitting at her desk in the bookshop with her notebook and her copy of *Little Dorrit* in hand. In between greeting and helping customers, she'd started to collect her thoughts about Harriet. What kind of new ending would Harriet want? Would it be something that would appeal to readers?

To Oliver's publishing house, or any others? Would it be something that Aurelia would feel confident about writing? Where would she even start?

Writing with Vronsky had been so comfortable; they'd bonded over their respective grief first, then became friends before sitting down to plot out the rest of his life story. But Aurelia felt as though she hardly knew Harriet. She knew facts about her life, knew that she was unhappy, knew that she'd loved Marigold and that Marigold had set her book out many times over the years. Still, who *was* Harriet? Aurelia had no idea what she liked to do for fun; what made her laugh; what her favorite kind of treat was, or her favorite book.

Tolstoy had given so many details about Vronsky—his likes and dislikes, his strengths and his character flaws—that Aurelia had felt as though she'd known him just from reading his book. But Harriet was a side character. Dickens hadn't spent nearly as much time developing who she was and what she wanted out of life. Aurelia could ask her, obviously, but as much as Harriet had shared details about her life's circumstances, Aurelia wasn't certain she'd be open and willing to share the aspects of herself that would make for a good story. With a sigh, Aurelia acknowledged that her doubts didn't mean she shouldn't give it a try.

It was a surprise when the clock behind her chimed noon. It felt like only minutes had passed since she'd sat down to think. Aurelia and her friend, Kali, had planned to meet for lunch at a café that was a few minutes' walk from the shop, so Aurelia ran upstairs to get a jacket before closing up, nodding to Fezz and then waving at Biscuit—who stared longingly at her from the shop door—before setting out.

She got there before Kali, so she found a table and took out her notebook to keep writing down questions about Harriet while she waited.

"Nose in a book as usual, I see," a deep female voice boomed.

Aurelia looked up to see Kali standing next to the table, her long black hair pulled into her usual tight bun, with one hand on her hip as she pretended to scold Aurelia.

"Well, if someone could keep time..." Aurelia teased her right back, and she stood to hug her.

"It's not my fault," Kali insisted, sliding into her seat and shimmying out of her coat as Aurelia dropped her pen and notebook into her bag. "I have a tour scheduled at the National Gallery next week and they've been giving me trouble."

"What kind of trouble?" Aurelia sat up, immediately on the defensive for her friend.

Her indignation had to go on pause for a moment as a waiter came over to take their order, but Aurelia raised an eyebrow as soon as they were alone again, urging Kali to fill her in.

"They allow private tours that aren't affiliated with the museum, but they say mine are 'overcommitted'—which just means that even when I try to limit the number, mums show up with their kids anyway or spot my tour as I'm going through the galleries and join in."

"Scroungers!" Aurelia exclaimed. "I'm going to start showing up and charging everyone who tries to jump in."

"No, it's alright," Kali laughed. "It's actually good advertising—sort of a try before you buy thing. I've started carrying around postcards with a link so they can sign up for other tours. But in the meantime, museum staff at the National Gallery aren't very happy with the crowds I seem to attract."

Aurelia shook her head, smiling in spite of her annoyance on Kali's behalf.

"Do you remember when you told me about this idea and you called it 'mad,' as if no one would want you leading them around and telling their kids about art? And look at you now—people are *gate-crashing* your tours!"

"It's a good problem, I know," Kali said resignedly. "But I'm not sure how much longer I'll be able to run tours there. I've got plenty of other museums on my list, but that one's my favorite. I love going through the galleries there and kids really seem to like it."

"Kali!" Aurelia said with a start as realization struck her. "I have a new customer who works at the National Gallery! She just moved to London, so she's only been at the museum for a few months. I've chatted with her a bit—she's obsessed with the Brontës—and I'm sure she'd be happy to talk to you. Her name is Sarah something... I think it's McClellan."

Kali's jaw dropped before she confirmed, "You know Sarah McClellan? *The* Sarah McClellan?"

"You've heard of her?"

"Aurelia!" This time it was Kali's turn to burst out her friend's name, and she added a laugh. "Sarah is the new head of the museum!"

"Is she?" Aurelia felt proud even though the woman's title had nothing to do with her. "She's very nice. And she's coming in next week to pick up a special order. It might not be in time for your next tour, but I'll ask if she can talk to you and help work something out."

"That would be fantastic—thank you! I'm sure dealing with outside tours is far below her paygrade, but at least she might be able to put me in touch with the right person. I don't seem to be getting anywhere on my own."

"I'll let you know as soon as she comes in," Aurelia promised.

Their food arrived and they caught up about Kali's son Ben and husband Tom, and Oliver's big move.

"How's the book coming?" Kali asked in between bites. "You were scribbling away when I came in."

The question caught Aurelia off guard since she knew Kali was thinking of the art book she'd been working on—the one that had grown out of a story Kali had shared a few months back.

"Um… I've been making progress. I have an outline and I started working on the early chapters."

"Oh—I told you I was going to talk to my friend in art conservation, and I did. He said he actually knows a forger. Well, a former forger. He was caught a while back, and now he consults about tricks of the trade. I asked my friend if he'd connect you and he said no problem."

"A forger!" Aurelia had started doing some research, reading accounts of forgers and how they worked—their tricks of the trade, as Kali had said—but speaking to one would give her a whole new kind of insight. "I have a million questions already. This could be a huge help!"

"Excellent. Look at us, networking and working our connections," Kali said with a shoulder shimmy. "I'll give your contact info to my friend."

Aurelia's mind worked quickly as she thought through how to approach this new source and what he might be willing to share with her. She pulled out her notebook to write a few of those thoughts down before she could forget them, but as she flipped through the pages to find a blank spot, she caught sight of one repeated word: 'Harriet.'

"Those are your notes for the book?" Kali asked, nodding toward Aurelia's notebook.

"These? No. Actually... I've been working on an idea for something different. Something I might work on first."

"Whatever it is, it can't be more interesting than an art scandal," Kali deadpanned.

"You're probably right," Aurelia admitted. "I'm sort of on the fence about it, to be honest."

"What about Oliver—which story does your editor like?"

"I haven't told him about the new one yet," Aurelia said, making a face at yet another admission. "It's so new and I'm not sure about it. And we haven't had time to talk about my writing—we've both been busy."

"Busy with the move, or busy with other things..." Kali trailed off suggestively.

Aurelia rolled her eyes at first but then smiled and felt it grow into a sappy, impossible-to-control grin as she thought about that morning's kiss goodbye and where it had led.

"That is an X-rated smile, Aurelia Lyndham!" Kali said, pretending to scold her.

"It is, indeed," Aurelia laughed, twitching her eyebrows mischievously.

They finished their lunch with much laughter and whispered teasing. Aurelia walked back to the shop smiling and looking forward to meeting Oliver out for dinner that evening. Those thoughts were a good distraction, for a few minutes at least, from her internal debate over what to do about Harriet.

18

In spite of the boxes and piles of Oliver's things that still littered the flat, Aurelia and Oliver had made a dinner reservation rather than stay home and unpack. Although she preferred early nights—mostly because they made it easier for her to catch up on the sleep she missed when visiting with the characters—she'd agreed to meet Oliver at the restaurant at eight that night. It was crowded and service was slow, but they nonetheless enjoyed being away from the lingering disorder of their flat for an evening.

During dinner, there were a few moments when Aurelia thought she might tell Oliver about Harriet and the new novel she was likely-probably-but-maybe-not going to write, but something kept holding her back. She'd been honest with Kali when she'd said that the only reason she hadn't told him about the idea sooner was that she'd only just started thinking about it. But now, hours later, there was something more.

It had occurred to her that sharing the idea with Oliver carried extra significance because he likely wouldn't be able to listen without mentally editing it. They hadn't been dating when they'd started working together on her first book; that had only happened once the book was done—even though she could admit that she'd been pining over him for most of that time. Now that they were not only dating but living together, it seemed like she might need to create some sort of divide between their dating and working relationships.

But as they walked home from dinner and Oliver asked about her progress on her new book, she realized that she couldn't create a dividing line without running it past Oliver. And that they shouldn't create one until they'd figured out whether that was even necessary.

"Actually, I have an idea I've started working through. An idea for another book," she told him.

"The art one, right? You've already been working on that," he said, sounding confused.

"No, a different book. I might put the art one aside for a bit."

"Really? You were keen on that—I was looking forward to reading it."

"Yeah, it's just that something else is sort of on my mind, and I think I might need to shift gears for a while. I could work on this new thing, and then go back to the art thing."

I really hope I can go back to the art thing, she added to herself, *and not another sequel and another and another.*

"Alright, then. What's this new idea?"

She heard his tone shift into editor mode: eager, curious, and ready to dissect her idea.

"Do you remember Harriet, from *Little Dorrit*?"

He quirked an eyebrow.

"Tattycoram," Aurelia added.

"Oh, right. Yes."

"I'm thinking of writing about her. She grew up at the Foundling Hospital—an orphanage—and had such a hard life. I thought I'd try writing her a happier next chapter."

"So... it would be a sequel? Like Vronsky's?"

"That's the idea, yeah."

"And why Tattycoram?"

Aurelia looked away, then realized she could be honest in one respect, at least.

"Aunt Marigold really loved her. I mean... She loved her as a character. I only just found—" She broke off. She was making all sorts of mistakes. "I just found out because... I found something of hers, some... notes—about books she liked. She loved *Little Dorrit*. And she really connected with Harriet."

Oliver nodded slowly, then observed, "That would be two sequels for characters from nineteenth-century novels on your C.V."

"Mm-hmm."

"Hmm." He kept nodding, his eyes on the pavement.

Aurelia waited as long as she could before blurting, "What? You hate it?"

They'd gotten to the shop door and Oliver took out his keys to let them in. It took a minute for them to greet Biscuit and start up the spiral staircase before he responded.

"I don't hate it. It's just a bit niche. The first one was different, unique. Now, with two... I wonder if you're locking yourself into a sort of genre?" In response to her blank stare, he continued. "Or *is* that your genre? Is that what you want to write?"

Aurelia sighed. Oliver had opened the door to the flat and was waiting for her to go through, but she looked out across the shop and leaned against the doorway.

"I don't know. I'm not really sold on the idea, to be honest. I'd like to keep working on my art book, to figure out who that character is, how deep the conspiracy could go, but... I feel like I *have* to write Harriet's story. Like I'm being pulled to write it."

"Because of Marigold?" he asked softly.

"That and..." *That and if you could see how sad Harriet looks...* "Mostly that."

"I never got to meet your aunt, but I don't think she'd have pushed you to write something you didn't want to write. A novel is a big undertaking, a lot of time and energy. It's hard to keep at it if you don't love the story or the characters you're writing about."

"I know."

She did know; she'd had those very same thoughts herself.

"I'm not saying you shouldn't write it," he said, taking her hand as he led her up the stairs. "But I think it could have an impact on your career that you should think over before you chase the idea too far down the road."

Aurelia squeezed his hand as Biscuit raced past them to find Fezz.

───○───

It wasn't until they'd gotten into bed and she'd had a good look at the clock on her nightstand that Aurelia realized how late it had gotten—a quarter to eleven. She feigned exhaustion and tried to speed along their nighttime routines, but they didn't make it to bed until half past eleven.

Aurelia lay there, hoping thirty minutes would be enough time for Oliver to fall into a deep sleep. At five minutes to midnight, she slowly swung her legs out of bed and sat up. She paused, listening for the cadence of Oliver's breathing. Shaking her head after a minute, she laughed to herself at the oddity of trying to assess her boyfriend's state of slumber so that she could sneak out for a wild night with a bunch of literary figures. She touched her feet to the floor and took a few tentative steps toward the bedroom door. Hearing Oliver shift in bed behind her, she froze.

"You alright?" he called out.

"Yeah, I'm fine!" Aurelia whispered loudly. "Just going to the loo."

She walked to the bedroom door and closed it behind her, exhaling in relief. She went into the bathroom and collected the clothes she'd left hanging from a hook on the back of the door. As she started to pull off the top she'd worn to bed, she heard the bedroom door open.

Once again, she froze. Oliver's footsteps passed the bathroom door and moved to the kitchen. *What was he doing?* She pulled her top back on as she heard the kitchen sink running and guessed he was getting a glass of water. Aurelia strained her ears, waiting to hear him walk back to the bedroom, but she couldn't hear anything. After another minute, she opened the bathroom door to investigate.

Oliver was squatting on the floor in the hallway, ruffling Biscuit's fur.

"Everything okay?" he asked.

"Yeah, I'm fine."

"Thought you needed the loo?"

"I did."

"Oh. I didn't hear the flush."

"Didn't hear the...?" Aurelia said slowly. Then she put the pieces together. She'd told him she needed the loo and now had been caught in her own simple, silly fib. "No. I thought I had to go, but... as it turns out, I didn't."

"Right." Oliver smiled indulgently at her. "Back to bed?" He nodded toward the bedroom and started walking over there, giving her no choice but to follow him.

Lying in bed next to Oliver once again, Aurelia tried to fight off sleep as she listened for his breathing, but it was a losing battle. At one point in the night, she woke to the sound of laughter coming from the shop below, but sleep quickly pulled her back under again.

19

Aurelia took advantage of the opportunity to sleep in that Sunday morning, happy to have a chance to catch up on the rest she'd been missing due to her nights in the shop. When she was at last willing to leave the warmth of her bed, she found Oliver out in the living room, unpacking the last of his boxes.

"Don't let me disturb you," she teased, tiptoeing theatrically toward the coffee pot. "Wouldn't want to distract you."

"Very funny," he said in his best 'we are not amused' tone. "Distraction isn't an option anymore—we've got Mark in for dinner on Tuesday, then Jack on Wednesday. We can't very well ask them to sit on one of my boxes or on a stack of our books."

Aurelia carried her mug of coffee into the living room and sat on the sofa next to Fezz, who uncurled himself to greet her.

"Where's Biscuit?"

"He crashed out over here," Oliver said, pointing to a gap between boxes. "I unpacked his stash of toys and he went hyper for a bit."

"How did I not hear that?" Aurelia laughed, taking a sip of her coffee.

Oliver resumed his unpacking and asked, "Don't suppose I can tempt you to help me?"

"Oh, I don't know. Watching you unpack those boxes and organize your things... This might be better than television." Aurelia leaned back against the sofa. "Actually, can you take your shirt off? Then I can pretend I'm watching one of those American reality shows."

"I'm not here to make friends," Oliver said, his voice a feigned snarl.

Aurelia drew in a giant, dramatic gasp of surprise as her eyes widened. "I thought you'd try to pretend you've never seen a reality show, but now we have it! You watch them every week, don't you?"

Oliver laughed as he picked up one of Biscuit's squeaking toys and tossed it at her, but Aurelia managed to dodge it while keeping her coffee from splashing.

"You're a very cranky contestant!" She laughed, getting up from the sofa. "Right, I can help you for one hour, then I'm meeting David for a walk." She picked up a handful of his books from where he'd unpacked them on the coffee table and added, "Though I feel I should warn you that your insistence on keeping your shirt on will be a big impediment to advancing to the final round."

———◯———

Very little of the next hour was actually spent sorting out where to put his things, but neither Aurelia nor Oliver minded very much. She eventually showered and raced out the door to meet David. And though she was five minutes late by the time she got to his flat, she was spared a scolding since he was running ten minutes late himself.

They'd planned to walk up one side of the Thames and then back along the other, so they picked up coffee and started off toward the river.

"Let's hear it. How's your new flatmate?" David asked, grinning.

He and his partner, James, had set Aurelia and Oliver up last year and David was still gloating over their successful matchmaking.

"He's very shaggy. Has trouble getting onto the sofa by himself. Gets over excited about visitors."

David nudged her hard.

"Oh, not the dog, then? In that case, Oliver is good."

"Good, but not great?"

"He's great. Wonderful. Fantastic—any and all of the above." Aurelia paused. "Are you waiting for another 'thank you'?"

"I mean, only if you think it's well deserved. Which, from 'great, wonderful, and fantastic,' I take it—"

"Thank you again for setting me up on the worst blind date of my life."

David cleared his throat.

"I wasn't finished: the worst blind date of my life, which ultimately led to dating bliss."

"That's better."

"Very near bliss, anyway."

"Wait a second—did you just downgrade?"

"No. Not really." Aurelia hesitated, serious now. "Everything's been good, really good. I just have this writing thing that's weighing on me."

"Shouldn't Oliver help you sort it out? Isn't that what editors do?"

"He tried. I'm just not sure I can follow his advice."

"You two are usually annoyingly in sync. I think the only thing I've ever heard you two argue about is books."

"This *is* about a book. A potential book. But it's not really an argument." Aurelia sipped her coffee. "It's just that I've been thinking about writing something new and he doesn't like the idea."

"Why not? What's it about?"

"Well, Oliver would probably describe it as another sequel to an old book," she said with a laugh.

"Then I wouldn't let him write a blurb for the book cover."

That set them both laughing.

"What's the old book this time?" David asked after a minute.

"It's *Little Dorrit*. I was going to write about Harriet, an orphan who was adopted from the old Foundling Hospital to be a servant."

"Adopted into service? That sounds dismal."

"I know. She thought she was going to be adopted as a daughter. Her adoptive family went to visit the Hospital, felt bad for the children who had no parents to love them, but then took her home, only to make her their maid. It's very sad."

"It sounds like she told you all that herself," David said with a laugh.

"I... Does it?"

Aurelia knew it did. Of course it did, since she'd been talking to Harriet just last night.

"That must mean you've read the book too many times."

"Right. I have. I definitely have read it a lot."

Do I sound like I'm covering something up? I think I sound normal, Aurelia thought, trying not to look suspicious.

"So, the Foundling Hospital... There's a museum about that place. I think it's near the British Museum," David went on.

"Oh, I think you're right."

Aurelia let out a little sigh of relief, grateful that her friend had let her strange comment go without further discussion.

"You should go and visit, do some research for your story."

"That's a good idea. I'll have to get over there and take a look around."

The wheels in Aurelia's brain started turning as she considered what she might learn at the museum. Maybe details that would give some missing color to Harriet's story.

"So, writing about characters from old novels—is that your thing, then? Your, what... your theme?"

Aurelia's face fell at the echo of her conversation with Oliver. She'd already been worried about being creatively boxed in by writing sequels for every unhappy character ever written; now she'd be worrying that everyone would question the same thing—why she only ever wrote about other people's characters.

That's if *I decide to write it*, she reminded herself. *I might not, after all.*

"What's wrong?" David cocked his head in concern.

"It's just... When I got the idea, I didn't consider that people might think it's strange for me to write two books in a row that are sequels to someone else's books."

David shrugged his shoulders. "If that's what inspires you, you have to go for it. Don't think of it as strange, just… unique."

"Mmm, if you say so."

"And what does Oliver say? He doesn't like it?"

"Not really. And he's made some good points, but I'm not sure I can take his advice on this one." Aurelia let out a long sigh. "Still, I hate the idea of writing something he wouldn't like. It's hard enough trying to write a book without also feeling like your editor isn't on board. I wouldn't want him to have to slog through edits if he isn't excited about it."

"I wonder…" David began and then looked at Aurelia. "You fell in love working on your first book, but maybe it was sort of a lightning strikes only once type of thing?"

"Meaning?"

"Meaning, maybe you should be happy you found each other and were able to put out one book together. But now that you're dating *and* living together, maybe that's enough 'together time.'"

"I had that thought the other night—that working on another book might be too much now that we're together. Like maybe we need to have some dividing line between work and home."

"Look, it might be great and you both get through it and everything's wonderful. Or it could be too hard to live with the person who's criticizing your work during the day." He paused, a grin spreading across his face at his own quick thinking. "And then wanting to get down to business at night."

"Oh, honestly!" Aurelia nudged him this time, both of them laughing until Aurelia broke off with a sigh. "There is a tricky dynamic there. But I'm just not sure I can do anything about it. It would be like breaking up with half of him. And I don't know how he would feel if I said I wanted to work with someone else."

"Well, you don't have to decide right now. But there might come a time when you've got to decide which half of him you want to keep around." David steered Aurelia toward the embankment wall. They looked out over the river before he continued, "I suggest you keep the boyfriend half, Aurelia. I feel like I've got you back since you've been with Oliver."

"I wasn't much fun for a while there," she said softly.

"Well, you know, you lost your mum and your aunt, so I gave you a pass on being fun."

He leaned into her and she rested her head on his shoulder.

"It felt like everything was upside down, like at any moment someone could come and shake it all up again." Aurelia paused. "I think writing gave me a sense of order in the chaos. Or maybe... Maybe it made me realize I could order the chaos myself. And that's what Oliver does too, isn't it, with his editing? Maybe that's part of what clicked for us at first. Anyway," she said, pushing back from the wall and smiling broadly as she put aside her introspection, "we're well clicked now."

"And it's all..." David offered, waiting for Aurelia to finish his sentence as he waved his hand with a flourish.

"It's all thanks to you, yes," she said, rolling her eyes. "Debt acknowledged yet again."

They continued teasing and nudging each other for the rest of their walk, covering topics from the hideous tiles James had chosen for their bathroom remodel (which David needed to criticize in private since James loved them), to swapping second-hand stories about old friends from school.

After they said goodbye, Aurelia walked home, dragging her feet a bit as she thought about the book she'd been so eager to write, and the one that was pulling her away.

20

Over the next two nights, Aurelia tried to draw Harriet out and learn more about her with minimal success, and over the next two days, she continued helping Oliver to incorporate the rest of his belongings with hers. As planned, their invitation to Mark helped get them over the finish line just in time for his arrival on Tuesday.

As she and Oliver set to work making dinner that evening, Aurelia realized that she wasn't sure whether Mark had ever been in the flat. Despite his years' long love for her aunt Marigold and their long friendship, Aurelia wondered if her aunt's decision not to pursue a romance with him would have kept his frequent visits limited to the shop.

But when he followed her up the stairs and into the flat, he said, "It looks just the same, doesn't it?"

He and Oliver shook hands and greeted each other, which gave Aurelia a few seconds to wipe the curious look from her face.

"A few changes, but mostly the same," she agreed. "Did you visit Aunt Marigold here often?"

"Not often, no. But she'd have me up for tea sometimes." His voice grew a little quieter. "Especially near the end."

After a shared smile of commiseration, she put her arm through his and led him into the living room. "We're so glad you're here. Not least because we can show off the fact that we've unpacked and arranged all Oliver's things."

"Fortunately, with everything put away, it'll be too much work to kick me out," Oliver said, coming into the living room with glasses and the bottle of wine that Mark had brought.

"Yes, that'll be the only reason I keep him around, now," Aurelia teased.

They chatted over wine for a bit, then sat around the small table to eat. Mark was telling them about a new exhibit he'd seen at Tate Modern when he let slip the word 'we.'

"'We'?" asked Aurelia. "Is that your new friend? Or, your new old friend, I suppose."

Aurelia saw Mark exchange a glance with Oliver. She gave Oliver a questioning look, but he didn't respond.

"That's right, my 'new old friend,'" Mark said. "We've been spending a lot of time together lately. It's been lovely."

"That's wonderful. Oh!" Aurelia said, struck by a thought. "We should have invited him too. I'd love to meet him."

Mark paused. "Actually, *he* is a *she*. Rebecca."

"Rebecca? The old friend? The new old—she's a woman?"

"Yes. And for that matter... she's become more of a girlfriend than a friend." He paused. "I didn't know how to tell you. I wasn't sure if you'd be upset?"

"Upset? I'm... No, I just didn't..."

She trailed off, looking first to Oliver, who seemed as though Mark's news wasn't a surprise, then Mark, who seemed worried about how she was taking it. But she couldn't quite process what she thought or felt. Mark, who had been friends with and had loved her aunt for years, had finally moved on.

Maybe I am a little upset, she thought.

"I'd like you to meet her. Maybe I can bring her by the shop sometime?"

Aurelia pulled herself together and said, "Of course, bring her by sometime."

"It's great that you're spending time with her," Oliver said, his tone reassuring and steady. "I'm glad you've found someone."

"Yes, Mark," Aurelia said, recovering a little more and taking Oliver's cue. "I'm very happy for you." She nodded at him and smiled, feeling guilty for her reaction but still not quite over the shock.

Oliver changed the subject then, telling them about a book he was editing for one of his longtime authors. After a few minutes, they all shifted back into lighter chat that carried them through to the end of the evening.

Aurelia said goodbye to Mark, and Oliver walked him down through the shop. She turned back to the kitchen and started gathering up plates and glasses to wash. But her self-command was starting to wane as she finally had a chance to digest Mark's news unobserved.

Minutes later, she was standing at the sink and gave a small jump when she felt Oliver's arms coming around her. The water had been running while she'd been holding a sponge and dish in midair, thinking instead of washing. He turned off the water and she set everything down before wiping her hands on a tea towel.

Oliver turned her around and she looked up at him, tears brimming in her eyes.

"I know it's silly—"

"No, you're alright."

"You knew?"

"He told me a few weeks ago. We didn't know how to tell you. When you asked about 'him,' though, I think Mark was right not to lie."

"No, I'm glad he told me," Aurelia said, shaking her head and trying to move past the sadness she felt creeping over her.

"Why don't I finish the dishes, hey? Do you want to sit for a bit? Watch a show, read something?"

Aurelia looked around the flat, her eyes seeming to catch on every piece of furniture or object that had been her aunt's.

"I'll walk Biscuit. It'll give me a chance to clear my head." She attempted a smile, which became a little more heartfelt when she saw Biscuit trotting into the room, clearly having heard her mention a walk. He gazed up at them and stretched his legs exaggeratedly, as though he hadn't moved in hours.

Aurelia walked to the bottom of the stairs, Biscuit beside her, and put on her coat and shoes. Biscuit's lead now had its own hook, and she lifted it off as she opened the flat door. The dog pushed out in front of her, but Aurelia stood still for a moment, closing the door behind her as she looked across the shop, the lights dim. Her shop;

Aunt Marigold's shop. How many times had she seen Mark here, first to visit Marigold and later to mourn her?

She could hear Biscuit below, pawing at the door. Aurelia sighed and pulled herself down the stairs, then outside to walk him around the square.

Once they were back, Biscuit waited impatiently for Aurelia to undo his lead, then he raced up the spiral staircase. She spotted the clock at the back of the shop as she moved to follow him—it was ten thirty. She started to sigh again then stopped herself, feeling frustrated at her own confusing emotions.

After opening the door to let Biscuit up to the flat, she turned out the shop lights. She was about to follow when she hesitated, finding she wasn't ready to set aside her feelings just yet. As she walked a few slow laps around the mezzanine, her mind was a mix of memories of Aunt Marigold, Mark, and thoughts and feelings that wouldn't seem to come into focus. Eventually, she sat on the window seat, looking out across the now-darkened shop.

The door to the flat opened, spreading light from the stairwell across the mezzanine floor. Oliver walked toward her, then stood at her side and ran his hand over her hair.

"I'm in a bit of a mood," she said softly. "I thought I'd try to leave it down here."

"Your moods are welcome upstairs, you know."

Aurelia was quiet for a moment. They were both still, Oliver with his hand cupping her neck as Aurelia leaned against him.

"It feels like I just lost a little bit more of Aunt Marigold." Her voice was strained and her throat hurt as she tried to keep her tears in check. "I'm happy for Mark. I know he's been lonely," she added quickly.

"I know you are. So does he."

"I don't know why it hit me so hard. Maybe just the surprise of it, but... I think it's also knowing that he's moved on. It feels final in a way, like the last person who loved her as much as I did has let her go."

"No one's let her go—not you, not Mark. She's here, Aurelia. In this shop, all around you. And Mark is still here too. You can't get rid of him that easily."

Aurelia nodded. Maybe that was part of it. In a way, Mark was family now. He'd been there for her when her mother died, and they'd been there for each other when Marigold died. He was a constant, reliable presence in the shop and in her life.

"Do you think I upset him?" Aurelia pulled back to look up at Oliver.

"Not at all. He told me he'd be by next Monday for his usual visit."

"Good. I'll be ready to ask him all about her by then."

"Come up to bed?"

Aurelia thought for a moment. Midnight wasn't too far off now, but she wanted a night off from engaging with other people. She could sneak back up just before midnight and make her apologies to the characters the following evening.

"I just want to sit here for a bit. I'm okay," she added, seeing the concern on his face. "I am."

"Alright, then." He squeezed her shoulder and started to move away when Aurelia reached for his hand. Oliver wasn't 'other people.'

"Will you stay?"

He paused, then walked back to her. "Of course."

Oliver sat sideways, with his back against the wall and one leg stretched out along the window seat. Aurelia moved close and leaned against him, her arms wrapping around his middle. As he slid his arms around her, they relaxed into each other.

Aurelia's thoughts started turning again, but this time they were crystal clear.

One way not to let her aunt go was to do what Marigold always wished she could do—help Harriet. How could Aurelia visit with Harriet and then take her book off the table in a few weeks, fully aware of the sadness Harriet would be facing for the rest of her life and how that sadness had affected Marigold?

Aurelia would write Harriet's story. She'd stop being selfish and just do it. It would mean something to Harriet, it would honor Aunt Marigold, and she could work on her own book afterward. She could do it. It would be fine. And Oliver would help—he'd understand.

They sat together—both of them eventually drifting in and out of sleep—until the shop's clock struck midnight. Oliver's presence kept the characters in their books, and the clock ticked on, the only sound in the quiet shop.

Aurelia registered this and knew it was time to get up. No more stalling. She stood and stretched, her muscles tight from sitting for so long. She turned and reached out a hand to help Oliver to his feet, then they walked across the mezzanine and up to bed.

21

Aurelia awoke the next morning to Fezz's paws stepping across and in between her ribs. She flinched and pulled him close to her, turning to her side with him tucked into her chest. He started purring and she was nearly lulled back to sleep before eventually opening her eyes and committing to being awake.

Spotting a note leaning against the lamp on her bedside table, Aurelia reached out a finger to trace the outline of the words written there: 'Love you.' She smiled, feeling lighter than she had the night before. It was surprising sometimes to think she was well past a certain stage of grief, only to have it trip her up when a moment or memory brought back the glaring absence of her loved ones. But the initial shock of Mark's news had worn off and now she felt only happiness for him. He had pined for Marigold long enough; it was finally time for him to be with someone who could love him back.

Shifting Fezz, Aurelia got out of bed and began her day. She made tea, had breakfast, showered and got dressed, then went downstairs to open the shop. But when she sat at her desk and pulled out her notebook to start writing ideas for Harriet's new story, nothing came to her. She was back to the same problem, which was that she didn't know enough about Harriet to guess what she might like to do with her life. Instead of writing down ideas, then, Aurelia made a list of to-dos: ask Harriet if she was even interested in a sequel; ask Harriet what she'd like to do with her future; tell Oliver she'd decided to write Harriet's story; and visit the Foundling Museum over the weekend to learn more about what Harriet's life had been like. It was a start, at least.

As much as Aurelia had taken some convincing to consider the project, she knew she needed to be enthusiastic about taking it on. She wanted to do right by Harriet, and if she was going to do the thing, she ought to do it well.

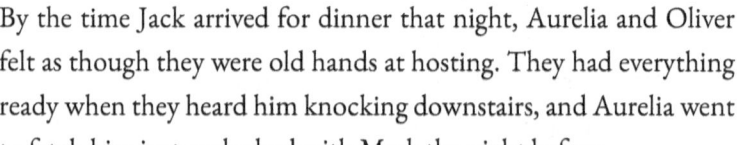

By the time Jack arrived for dinner that night, Aurelia and Oliver felt as though they were old hands at hosting. They had everything ready when they heard him knocking downstairs, and Aurelia went to fetch him just as she had with Mark the night before.

"It's so funny to think your front door is the shop door," Jack was saying as he came up the stairs. "Funny, but very cool! How old do you reckon this building is?"

"Well, it's been around since at least 1920, when my great-great aunt opened the shop. I'm not sure how long it was here before that."

"I love a building with history!" Jack gushed.

Spotting Oliver in the kitchen, he walked over and the two exchanged awkward shoulder pats before Jack handed him a bottle of wine.

"This is great, Oliver. What a place!"

"It's pretty great, yeah," Oliver said, his flat tone failing to match Jack's exuberance.

Oliver had been so warm and welcoming with Mark the night before. His coolness now made Aurelia wonder why Oliver hadn't taken her up on her offer to find a way out of her accidental dinner invitation. She raised her eyebrows at Oliver from behind Jack's back, silently begging him to try and make the night go a little smoother, and Oliver tried again.

"Thanks for the wine, and for coming by."

Just as they had the night before, they settled on the sofa with wine before moving to the little table for dinner. As they ate, Aurelia filled Jack in on her plans for the lecture series.

"I called one of my old professors at UCL and he seemed excited. He thought it could be a great outlet for Ph.D. students to test out their dissertations. I think that might be the bulk of the lectures, but he said he'd be happy to do an inaugural lecture, sort of kick the whole thing off for me."

"That's brilliant!" Jack enthused. "I'm glad it's going to work out."

"All down to you. Thank you! I'm going to be on campus next week to meet with him and figure out the details. Maybe we can meet for a coffee while I'm there?"

"Definitely—I'm in."

As he spoke, Jack tapped his index finger on the rim of his wine glass. Aurelia's eyes moved from Jack to Oliver, who was tapping his own index finger on the rim of his glass. She smiled. She'd seen Oliver tapping away dozens of times and had never thought much of it. Seeing the brothers tapping simultaneously made her wonder which one had picked up the habit from the other though she guessed that Jack, as the little brother, had borrowed it from his older brother.

Spotting Aurelia's gaze, Oliver looked to Jack and, seeing him tapping, stopped. Aurelia frowned.

"My sister was giving me grief yesterday, saying I should be concentrating on setting up my own readings instead of other people's," she said, trying to get them on common ground.

"You have time to do both," Oliver said diplomatically.

"That's what I told her. If the lecture thing works out, I don't think it'll be too much trouble to keep them up once I get the first one under my belt."

"A bit of wine, a few chairs. It shouldn't be much trouble at all," Jack agreed.

"That's what Oliver said!" Aurelia laughed. "Wine and chairs, nothing to it."

Jack smiled, then seemed to grow serious as he turned to Oliver.

"Aurelia and her sister were chatting when I was in the shop last week. It made me miss Lottie, hearing them."

Oliver stiffened. Aurelia could see something was wrong from the set of his jaw, but she didn't understand what was happening.

"Sorry," Jack said, clearly aware he'd hit a nerve. "It just made me wish... I wish we had the chance to know her like that. Having her just call for a chat."

Aurelia waited, but no one stepped in to explain. At last, she asked, "Lottie?"

Jack nodded. Silence reigned again until Jack spoke up.

"Lottie—Charlotte—was our sister. Oliver, haven't you—?"

"No, I haven't."

Aurelia looked from one to the other. Oliver had never mentioned a sister before and questions filled her head. But she kept quiet, having the distinct impression that she needed to let them play this out between themselves.

"Why would you even—" Oliver began, staring down Jack and shaking his head. He turned to Aurelia. "She died when we were young. I was eleven and Jack was just a baby."

Aurelia's hand shot out to hold Oliver's.

"I wasn't a *baby*. I was nearly five," Jack said, stung.

"Lottie was only seven when she died," Oliver continued, ignoring Jack. "She was born with a heart condition and there wasn't really anything they could do for it, at least not back then."

"I'm so sorry," Aurelia said, her voice coming out in a near whisper as she wrapped both hands around Oliver's. "She was so young. Goodness, all of you were. It's just too sad."

"It was a long time ago," Oliver said, squeezing her hand. "It was hard—really hard—but... It was a long time ago," he said again, his voice stony as he looked at his brother.

Jack seemed cowed by Oliver's stare.

"I'm sorry, I just... Well, I was thinking of her. The other day, it just reminded me..." He trailed off and left the rest unsaid.

Aurelia looked between them and felt the weight of the silence that began stretching out.

"I understand," she said. "I've lost people I love too, and sometimes it's surprising when something, or someone, reminds you of them. It can catch you off guard—the memories."

Jack nodded appreciatively.

"I just had one of those nights last night," Aurelia went on, trying to lighten her tone as she could see Oliver was still in his head, upset. "My aunt owned this shop and she lived in this flat before she died."

Jack opened his mouth as if to offer his condolences but Aurelia waved her hand.

"It's alright. One of her old friends came round for dinner, Mark. We'll have to introduce you to him, actually. He's becoming something like family, isn't he?"

She knew she was chattering on but didn't know how else to keep the night from devolving. When Aurelia looked to Oliver, he finally came back to life with a nod.

"I think you'd like him," Aurelia continued. "Maybe we should bring him to your next play. Speaking of, how's the new set coming along—have you started it?"

Sensing the lifeline she'd just tossed him, Jack started describing his latest efforts on the upcoming show.

Aurelia held in a sigh of relief at having gotten them past that terrible moment.

It didn't take them long to get through dinner. Oliver had little to say for the rest of the night, and Aurelia felt further relieved when Jack announced that he was going to head home. She walked him out and then gave herself exactly one minute to gather her thoughts before heading back upstairs.

22

Oliver was carrying dishes in from the table when she returned. She stood at the top of the stairs and watched him for a moment, having no idea what state he might be in after Jack's visit. She waited for him to put the dishes on the counter and turn toward her before she spoke.

"Are you okay?"

"I'm fine," he said with a weary smile.

She walked over and put her arms around him.

"I'm sorry. I can tell that's not how you wanted that story to come out."

"No, it wasn't," he said with a sigh.

She pulled back to look at him, his face in her palms.

"I want to hear it, all of it, but if you're not ready or you want to do it another time…"

"No, I want to tell you. Let's do it now—tonight." He took her hands in his and kissed each one.

"Should we sit? Walk around a bit? Whatever you want."

"Let's walk. We can take Biscuit."

They pulled on jackets and scarves, put the lead on Biscuit, and headed out into the cool January night. After walking in silence for a few minutes, Aurelia linked her arm in his and Oliver began.

"I'm sorry it came out like that. I should have told you sooner, I know. But there's never really a great opening for 'Hey, I used to have a little sister,'" he said, attempting a chuckle.

"Okay… But I feel terrible. All those times I was sad about my mum or Aunt Marigold, and you never said you'd been through something like that, too."

"Hearing you put it that way… It must seem awful that I didn't say anything sooner," Oliver said with a groan. "It just—it was so fresh for you, so recent. Lottie died almost twenty-five years ago now. I mean, it was awful and horrible, and I do still think about her, but it just didn't occur to me to say 'Oh, me too.'"

Aurelia nodded as she tried to process it all. Part of her felt hurt that he hadn't told her before now. But… she wasn't in a position to complain about keeping secrets, especially when this one—like her own—wasn't intended to hurt anyone.

"You were eleven?" she asked.

"I was. Lottie'd had a few surgeries in the first year or two after she was born, and she was a little weak after that, but she was normal—like anyone else's little sister. She was just four years younger than me, so we were closer than I was with Jack. She'd drive me completely mental, messing up things in my room, insisting on playing with me when I had friends round. But we'd also spend hours together, playing a game or reading to each other. I taught her how to read."

Aurelia's eyes pricked with tears at the sound of pride in his voice. Lottie may have died almost twenty-five years ago, but his memories of her were clearly still with him. She squeezed his arm.

"I knew she was getting worse, that year. She wasn't running around as much, had more visits with doctors. My parents didn't tell us, but Mum was crying all the time—I started to figure out that she wasn't going to get better. The last few weeks, they arranged for her to be home. It was such an odd time. Moments that felt almost normal and then moments when I could hear Mum and Dad either crying or arguing. I remember reading to her because she couldn't read on her own anymore. I didn't know it then, but I think that was because of whatever medication they had her on, for the end."

His voice wavered slightly and Aurelia wondered—had he said these words before? Was this the first time he was telling someone about what it had been like? After seeing his reaction when Jack brought it up earlier, she understood his grief was a wound that might not have healed properly. One that, because he was a child when he'd gotten it, had left a different kind of scar to hers.

"She died in June. That day... It was so strange to feel the heaviness of everything that was happening inside the house and then to step outside and have the sun beating down and birds flying about. I felt this urge to run away, to go and hide somewhere. As if things could go back to normal if I wasn't there to see that she was really gone."

They'd come to a small park and Aurelia led Oliver to a bench to sit. Biscuit dropped down at Oliver's feet, and he reached down to stroke his ears.

"And Jack was five when she died?"

"A few months shy, yeah. He spent most of his time with a sitter or with family friends during those last weeks. I don't know why he said... I mean, he was so young, he didn't really understand what was going on. I doubt he remembers her at all. I don't know why he'd even bring her up like that."

"It sounded like he might remember her," Aurelia said gently.

"He couldn't possibly. I'm sure he just thinks he remembers her from things my parents have said. I know he remembers them arguing, before the divorce, but that was over a year later and he was a little older, then."

"The divorce—that was right after?"

He nodded, stretching an arm across the back of the bench.

"It was textbook, really. I don't know that they were all that happy to begin with, so it just made things harder, with Lottie being sick. They both loved her and were gutted about it, but they just couldn't get past it together."

"I'm so sorry, Oliver. I can't imagine how hard that must have been for you. First Lottie, then your parents..."

"Yeah, it was a rough couple of years," he said, attempting a light tone, as though trying to reassure her that he was alright now.

"What Jack said tonight, about wishing you'd had the chance to grow up with her and chat with her—I wish you'd had that too."

"Me too."

They were quiet for a few minutes, sitting on the bench and thinking their separate thoughts. Eventually, Oliver stood and reached for her hand. They walked home, with Biscuit happily leading the way. As they entered the shop and Aurelia turned to lock the door behind them, Oliver began laughing softly.

"What?" she asked. "What's funny?"

"I'm just thinking how our first two nights of hosting people in the flat left both of us with major revelations."

"It does suggest a pattern," Aurelia said with a smile.

"That's it, then. We can never invite anyone over for dinner ever again."

"Definitely not," she agreed, and they climbed the stairs to bed.

23

Aurelia missed another night with the characters, but she didn't regret it at all. There was so much to think about after talking with Oliver that she wasn't ready to put it all aside and casually chat with everyone. And it didn't feel right to sneak out on Oliver after everything he'd shared with her.

He'd seemed better once they'd gotten back from their walk. Aurelia half expected him to break down and cry or to want to be alone, but she had to keep reminding herself that he'd had over two decades to process his loss. Having only just learned of it, for Aurelia it felt more immediate, like it had just happened.

As they got ready for bed, she asked if he had any photos of Lottie, and he promised to dig them out and share them with her.

———○———

She woke with Oliver the next morning, wanting to see him before he left for work. He was fine, just as he'd been the night before—just as he always was, in fact. He kissed her goodbye and, as soon as she'd heard the door to the shop close behind him, she rang her sister.

"I know it's early, but I couldn't wait."

"It's nearly half past nine. It's not all that early," Antonia said, ignoring the fact that Aurelia hadn't said 'hello.'

"Oh, right—well, it's only half eight here. But never mind the time, I have to tell you something. Oliver had a sister."

As she said it, Aurelia realized how much she'd needed to process the information with Antonia.

"*Had?* No! What happened?"

"She died when they were young. She was just seven years old."

"Oh no. How terrible... His poor family."

"I know. He keeps saying it was a long time ago, but I can't stop thinking about it now that he's told me."

"You're not mad he didn't tell you sooner, I hope?" Antonia asked, a note of reproach in her voice.

"No! I mean, I wish he had, but I can't be mad at him for it."

"Good. He probably wasn't sure how to mention it. It's not exactly something you can just throw into a conversation."

"That's exactly what he said. I get it, I do. It's just that it's this new piece of him that's only now fallen into place—a big piece. I'm still trying to wrap my head around it."

Aurelia was distracted for a moment, thinking about the big piece of her own life, her nights in the shop, that Oliver would never learn about, let alone get a chance to wrap his head around. The very same big piece she was keeping from Antonia, her father, and friends.

"Sorry, what?" she asked, realizing Antonia had spoken.

"I asked if it was him, Jack, and his sister, then?"

"That's right. Jack's the youngest, and their sister, Lottie, was in the middle. Jack was here for dinner last night, and when he mentioned it, Oliver got very upset."

"Did he? Well, he probably wanted to tell you himself."

"That was part of it, but he said something later, that he thinks Jack doesn't remember Lottie, so he shouldn't be talking about her. Or he shouldn't be sad about her? Something like that."

"That's a bit harsh, isn't it? She was Jack's sister, too."

"I'm thinking maybe that's why he and Jack don't get along very well. Oliver went through this awful time and Jack was too young to really understand it all."

"Maybe. Is that your professional opinion then, Doctor?"

"It is. You know I've got an advanced degree in armchair psychoanalysis."

"Well, me too," Antonia said, switching into her bossy big-sister tone. "And I think it's probably very complicated. I'm sure there are lots of bits and pieces to their relationship that you're not going to be able to work out. So."

"So?"

"So don't start trying to interfere."

Aurelia was about to insist that she wasn't going to do anything of the sort, until she remembered how she'd wrangled Oliver into having Jack over for dinner in the first place.

"I'll try... But Jack is so sweet. He and Oliver could be such good friends if Oliver would just let Jack in. I can tell Jack wants to—"

"Leave it, Aurelia," Antonia intoned. "Oliver must have his reasons. He's a grown-up and he can reach out to Jack if he wants to."

"But, but, but... I know," Aurelia finished with a dejected sigh. After a moment, she added, "I'm going to be thinking about it all day."

"I know you are."

Aurelia could hear the smile in her sister's voice and picture the accompanying smirk on her face.

"I want to do something nice for him. Any ideas?"

"Yes: it would be really nice of you not to get in the middle of him and Jack," Antonia laughed.

"That would be nice, but I'm thinking of something more tangible, more achievable in the immediate future," Aurelia said, feigning an acid tone.

"I mean, don't be too weird about it. Don't buy him flowers or something. It happened a long time ago."

"I want to do *something*, though. He was so upset last night. Maybe I'll just do something subtle, like make him dinner tonight."

"There you go. Make him his favorite meal and don't say anything like 'This is because you might be sad about your sister.'"

"Right, thank you," Aurelia grumbled. "I'm not completely socially inept."

"No, only partially," Antonia laughed.

24

Aurelia ran out at lunchtime to gather up the ingredients for Oliver's favorite meal, boeuf bourguignon. She was grateful for a cold day as it wouldn't have gone over quite as well had she been trying to cheer him up in, say, July. As it was, she was happy to have a complicated recipe to keep her busy, and she closed the shop a little early to give her time to throw it all together.

Fortunately, she kept having to wait for things to boil or simmer, which gave her time to think through her two primary preoccupations: Oliver's news and how to begin work on Harriet's story.

"What's all this?"

Aurelia hadn't heard Oliver come in. She'd moved to the living room to jot down notes about Harriet as their dinner sat ready and warming on the stove.

"You're home!" she exclaimed, jumping up from the sofa. "I made dinner."

Oliver had to placate Biscuit before he could get past the top step, but once that was accomplished, he went over to the stove to see what was on offer.

"Boeuf bourguignon? Really?"

He turned to her and took the glass of red wine she was pushing toward him.

"Yes, with fresh bread and a meringue from that bakery near the Tube."

"Wow—thank you!" Oliver seemed astonished by his good fortune. "I figured after entertaining all week, we were due for takeaway for the next few nights."

"I just wanted to—" She stopped herself, remembering her conversation with Antonia and her own insistence, now completely disproven, that she could be smooth. "To... eat... boeuf bourguignon. Had a real craving for it."

"Did you?" Oliver said, narrowing his eyes at her.

"I did."

She walked over and gave him a kiss. As she stepped away, he pulled her back to him.

"This is very thoughtful," he said, looking meaningfully into her eyes. "Thank you."

Her plan for subtlety had failed, but she was glad to see he didn't mind.

"You're very welcome. And tomorrow night we're definitely ordering in for dinner."

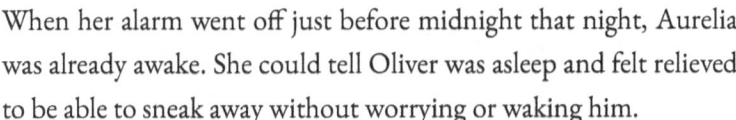

When her alarm went off just before midnight that night, Aurelia was already awake. She could tell Oliver was asleep and felt relieved to be able to sneak away without worrying or waking him.

After changing in the bathroom, she was just about to walk downstairs when she caught sight of her hand as she touched the newel post. She'd forgotten to find a ring, and Pip's eagle eye was sure to spot her oversight—again. Aurelia didn't usually wear rings, but she thought she must have something that could work as a makeshift wedding band. But... all her jewelry was in the bedroom.

Casting a disparaging eye at the heavens, she tiptoed back down the hall. Somehow, she managed to get into the bedroom and grab her jewelry box without Oliver so much as changing the rhythm of his breathing. From the doorway, she looked back at him and smiled. He looked so handsome, even dead asleep with an arm thrown over his head, that she was tempted to climb back into bed to stare at him for a bit. Deciding that would probably cross the line from sweet to creepy, she held in a laugh at herself before closing the door to let him sleep.

In the bathroom, she foraged through her jewelry box and found a gold band inlaid with three moonstones. Aurelia stared at it a moment, trying to place it, then remembered it had been her mother's. She'd given it to Aurelia somewhat casually a few years before she died—*I never wear this anymore. Do you want it?*—and

Aurelia had worn it for a couple of days before forgetting to put it on again.

Aurelia felt a momentary rush of emotion at the memory and the discovery of this object that was connected to her mother. Slipping it on her ring finger, her mouth twitched into a smile to see that it was a perfect fit.

She went downstairs, with Biscuit trailing behind her, and as she opened the door into the shop, the lights were just coming on while clouds of words began falling over the table's edge. By the time she'd gotten down the spiral staircase, everyone was gathered before her, solid and smiling their greetings.

After saying hello and apologizing for missing them the night before, Aurelia managed to get Harriet, as well as Esther and Peggotty—the two characters Harriet seemed most comfortable with—upstairs and settled on the window seat.

"Harriet, I've been asking you about your novel, and about how it ends for you. And I'm sorry if I seemed nosy, but there's a reason I've been asking. I've been wondering... If you had the choice, would you want to stay with the Meagleses or try something new?"

There was a long pause.

"It's no use thinking of what can never be," Harriet said, as if trying to convince herself. "Better to accept what I've got than wish for something new or different."

Aurelia thought for a moment. "Peggotty, your brother and niece went to Australia to make a better life for themselves, didn't they?"

"They did. It was hard work indeed, but better than staying put."

"And David made changes in his life, too, didn't he? He worked hard to change careers."

"Indeed, he worked very hard at that, and so much the better for him. He's ever so happy now."

"Making changes in one's life can bring about happier circumstances, it's true," Esther said slowly.

She gave Aurelia a curious look, as though willing to go along with her but wanting in on the plan. Aurelia nodded, knowing it was time to get to her point.

"Harriet, what if you could do anything you wanted? Go anywhere, be anything?"

"But... I can't do anything I want, Aurelia. I suppose I might try to find a position with another family, but they could be worse than the Meagleses."

"No, I mean something bigger than a new job. Last year there was a charac—a man who visited the shop from his novel. He was the only one from his book to come here, just like you, and he was very unhappy at the end of his story. We worked together and I wrote him a new story, a sequel, where he was able to create a happier future for himself." Aurelia paused. "I could write a new ending to your story, if you'd like."

Harriet's dark eyes moved quickly over Aurelia's face, almost as if she were trying to read the truth of Aurelia's words there.

"That man... what happened in his old story?"

"Well, at the end of his book, the woman he loved died and he was on his way to fight in a war."

Harriet pulled a face. "That's how his story ended?"

"Yes, it was very sad. *He* was very sad. But it made him feel better to know we'd created a future for him that would be full of good experiences and happier times."

"And his new story, what happened there?"

"He traveled and did the things he enjoyed doing, like riding horses and painting. He also mended his broken heart and eventually fell in love and got married. I set his new book out on the table downstairs, and met his wife and best friend, and got to hear all about how well he was doing in his new story."

"You accomplished all that?" asked Esther, sounding impressed.

Aurelia nodded enthusiastically.

"Oh, Harriet! You must let her try it!" Peggotty burst out, which sent one of the buttons on the front of her dress popping off and rolling on the floor. She waved her hand at it dismissively and continued, "You might like riding horses—or painting."

Aurelia held in a laugh and said, "Well, we could write anything you want. If you don't like horses, you could have a dog, a cat—whatever you like."

"What an opportunity, Harriet!" Esther said encouragingly.

"I couldn't afford to do those things," Harriet said, still hesitant but curious now.

"That's the beauty of fiction," Aurelia insisted. "I can write anything! You can become an heiress or discover that your favorite brooch is worth a fortune."

"Just like that?" Harriet asked.

"Just like that." Aurelia paused, then added, "I think Marigold would have liked to see you moving forward into a better ending. Don't you think?"

Harriet gave a cautious smile, then asked, "And you can write... *anything*?"

"Anything at all. The only limit, really, is your imagination."

Harriet's mouth opened and closed. She smiled then, and it was the first truly happy smile Aurelia had seen on her face.

"Why don't you start thinking of ideas? I've already started working on a few. And Peggotty and Esther, you'll help too?"

"Certainly we will," Esther promised.

"And don't forget Davy. He's a writer too. He's sure to come up with ideas for you," Peggotty added.

When the other characters heard about the new project, they wanted to know more about Count Vronsky and his story. Aurelia showed them a copy of his book—their book—and explained how they'd come up with ideas together during his nights in the shop, and how characters from his new book had confirmed he was happy in his new story. She also told them that the other characters in the shop had shared suggestions for Vronsky's story and asked them to do the same for Harriet.

There was a familiar hum of excitement as the characters talked about what it all might mean for Harriet. Aurelia had to admit (to herself, since she didn't want to dampen everyone's spirits) it was a little bittersweet to be writing with a new partner. Though there was some comfort in knowing that having a new writing partner meant that what they'd done for Vronsky had worked—and could work for Harriet, too. That idea, and the characters' obvious enthusiasm, helped Aurelia to push away the bitter and focus on the sweet.

During a break in the questions Aurelia had been fielding, David shuffled over and caught her eye.

"And what of your auction house and forger?" he asked in an undertone.

"Oh... I'll have to work on that later. After Harriet's story."

"I suppose writing both concurrently would be a bit of a challenge, what with your responsibilities here, running the shop?"

"Yes, I seem to be a one-book-at-a-time writer," she agreed with a sigh.

"Still, it's a shame. I've had to set aside projects of my own at various times, typically due to circumstances not of my own choosing. I know it can be difficult to shift one's focus to something new."

Aurelia bit her bottom lip to hold in a response, afraid that whatever she might say would seem unkind.

"Well, if Harriet's story is next on your agenda, I shall be happy to assist in any way you like," he offered with a smile.

"Thank you, David," she said, smiling back.

"And when her story is complete, I shall be equally happy to return to discussing your stimulating forgery idea."

Later, just before dawn, Aurelia took Harriet aside.

"I've been thinking—the Foundling Hospital where you grew up is a museum now, so I can go and learn a bit more about how it was run during your time there."

"A museum!" Harriet let out a laugh and then covered her mouth. "Truly?"

"Really and truly," Aurelia said with a smile. "I can go and see what I can learn about it. I thought... Well, I know you don't know who your parents were, but I could find out whether children were ever reunited with their family. It might help us to decide whether that might be an option for you, in your new story."

Harriet's brows drew together.

"I don't know... reunited?"

"Why don't I find out, and in the meantime, you can think about whether it's something you'd like me to write?"

Harriet smiled and nodded, and they joined the others to say their goodbyes.

Seeing Harriet's excitement over the project, and her hope, brought home for Aurelia how much Harriet needed this second chance. Aurelia wished she could touch Harriet—take her hand or hug her. She would just have to pick up a pen, instead.

25

After work the next evening, Aurelia and Oliver were on the sofa, sipping wine and enjoying a tidy, box-free flat. Aurelia sat with her legs draped over Oliver's lap, watching Biscuit and Fezz settle on the carpet just a few feet from one another.

"Look at that! Progress!" she exclaimed, nudging Oliver with an elbow.

"Do we think they're warming up to each other, or is Fezz just resigned to life with Biscuit?"

Aurelia wrinkled her nose as she considered this. "Unclear," she concluded. "But let's mark it a victory for Biscuit anyway."

"His next challenge is your dad's dogs."

"Oh, they're no match for Biscuit," Aurelia said airily.

"That's two weeks from now?"

"Yep. Dad says he's looking forward to it. He always says he doesn't want a fuss for his birthday, but I think he's pleased we're going up this year."

"Good. Biscuit can work on your dad's dogs, and I can work on your dad."

Aurelia laughed. "There's nothing to work on with Dad. He already likes you. The real test will be whether you outrank Antonia's Max."

"What are my odds?"

"Well, you're local," Aurelia said, pretending to size up the competition. "He can see you more often than Max. And you have a dog." Aurelia sat back and looked Oliver up and down approvingly. "I think you're looking like a front runner."

"That's some relief, then."

She leaned forward, put her wine glass on the coffee table, and then took his face in her hands. "I love you, so that's another point in your favor."

They shared a long, slow kiss that carried the promise of something more. Aurelia found herself grinning and opened her eyes to see Oliver grinning back at her. He kissed her again and she fell back against the cushions, pulling him down with her.

Later, they were brushing their teeth in the bathroom when Aurelia remembered something.

"I meant to ask you about tomorrow."

Oliver frowned at her in the mirror. "What?" he asked through a mouthful of toothpaste.

She held up a finger while she spat out her toothpaste and then asked again, this time without a toothbrush in her mouth. "I forgot to ask—I wanted to go to the Foundling Museum tomorrow. Any chance you can mind the shop while I dash over there?"

He nodded and finished brushing. "Sure. What's on at the Museum?"

Aurelia startled at the realization that she hadn't told Oliver she'd decided to write Harriet's story. After Mark's visit she dove right in, wanting to give Oliver a chance to process Jack's visit before telling him about the change.

"Sorry, I—I forgot to tell you. It's been so busy this week... I've officially decided to switch over to writing Harriet's story."

Oliver's brows furrowed as he said, "I thought you were going to think about it?"

"I did. I just—it's like I said, I feel like I have to write this right now. I can go back to my art book afterward, once I get through this."

"'Get through' it? It doesn't sound like you want to write this book."

"I do," Aurelia said, trying to sound enthusiastic. Then, remembering Harriet's tears and eagerness, she said more firmly, "I do."

"Is this... because of Marigold? Because of Mark's visit?"

"That's a big part of it," she admitted.

"What's the other part?"

The other part is that if you saw how much this could help Harriet, you'd understand.

Aurelia held her tongue. She wanted to share this with Oliver—explain what was behind her decision, help him see how she needed to help Harriet, how it was her responsibility as a shop owner who could write, who knew that a sequel would actually make a difference in Harriet's life. That Harriet wasn't just a character, but someone who was real enough to Aurelia and her aunt Marigold, someone who had thoughts and feelings, someone whose past had hurt her and whose future didn't look much brighter.

But she couldn't.

"That's really the only part," she lied. "I just want to have that connection to Marigold, to feel like I'm doing something she'd like for a character and a book she loved."

Oliver sighed—not an exasperated or angry sigh, but a sympathetic one.

"I see," he said quietly. "I understand that, I do. But are you sure?"

"I'm sure. I wanted to go to the Foundling Museum tomorrow since Dickens wrote that Harriet had grown up there, when it was still an orphanage. I thought I'd do some background research to help me get started."

"Okay. Yeah, I'm happy to watch the shop for you."

He pulled her in for a hug and she buried her face in his shoulder, feeling awful for accepting his sympathy when she wasn't telling him the whole truth.

26

Aurelia left Oliver sitting at her desk the next morning with Biscuit at his side. His sympathetic smiles over breakfast gave her a sinking feeling in her stomach that made it hard to eat her toast.

It was a nice enough January day for London, so Aurelia decided to walk to the Museum. She looked at the displays for a while before she met an elderly docent who eagerly answered her questions.

It seemed that Harriet would have been left there when she was under a year old, possibly as young as a few weeks. There was a lottery system to accept children, so her mother must have been lucky, though it was strange to say. Aurelia had overcome thoughts of Harriet's mother being a fiction. Harriet was real enough to her, and though she'd materialized from Dickens' imagination fully formed as a young adult, Dickens had also imagined her growing up here, abandoned by a mother.

Once a child was admitted, their mother's name was recorded and she was given a certificate specific to her and her child. That way, she could return and reclaim her child or simply find out how they were doing. Sadly, it was a system that was rarely used since, as the docent explained, few mothers ever returned. There were likely many reasons for this but one was that in the nineteenth century, every child admitted to the Hospital was illegitimate, marking them as outcasts in a society that didn't welcome them. If a mother hadn't been able to keep her child at birth, it was just as unlikely that she'd be able to bring them back into her life years later.

Just as Harriet remembered, children were sent to the country until they were about four or five years old, then they came back to the Hospital and were given a basic education that, for girls, also included training in needlework and housework. And just like with Harriet, it was unusual for a child to be adopted as a new member of a family. Instead, most girls were hired into domestic service, while most boys entered the military.

Saddest of all were the tokens: small items that mothers had left with their children as little remembrances. But these were never actually given to the children, just kept as part of the Hospital's records. There was a whole display of them—elaborate pieces of embroidery; coins with messages, dates, or names scratched into them; even simple buttons. Aurelia wondered if the mothers had known their children would never see the tokens, or if they just wanted to do something, no matter how small, to mark that someone had cared for and thought of their child.

A few hours later, as she walked back to the shop, Aurelia thought about Dickens again. He'd written that the Meagleses wanted to adopt a child after a visit to the Hospital and to give him or her the love they'd missed when growing up without a parent. But somehow, despite that intention, he'd allowed them to treat Harriet like a servant. It seemed as though Dickens had pulled their heartstrings toward adoption, but not hard enough to overcome Harriet's illegitimacy.

There were a million options for Harriet's future, but Aurelia hoped Harriet would agree to stick to realistic ones—no space travel, no unicorns, no sudden ability to fly or be invisible. Aurelia wasn't sure if readers would be on board for a book with a Dickens character that departed so drastically from Dickens' world. Though, at the memory of Kali's resigned look when Aurelia had given her a copy of *Bleak House* a few months ago... maybe they would be? But, no—that wasn't the sort of story Aurelia wanted to write, and she'd have to cross fingers that Harriet agreed.

In terms of Harriet's realistic options, Aurelia was still struggling. Vronsky had been a wealthy man, so arranging for him to travel through Europe and settle in Paris was fairly straightforward and believable. And not only did he have the financial means to choose any future he liked, but he also had gender on his side. As a male in late nineteenth-century Europe, he could travel alone and wander the streets at any hour of the day without a second thought. But even if Aurelia were to invent a rich relative for Harriet, there would be limits to what Harriet could do, and gender wasn't the only limiting factor.

For one thing, in early nineteenth-century England social class wasn't something a person could overcome with money alone.

Harriet had been working as a maid, so it would be stretching reality—even if it was fiction—to have her suddenly rubbing elbows with London's elite as if she were born to it. Dickens wrote about that exact scenario in *Little Dorrit*, and the characters' acceptance into society wasn't at all smooth. Aurelia could write anything, of course—she could rework history so that London society would accept Harriet as one of their own—but Aurelia chafed at the idea of writing something that was so improbable in reality and in the world Dickens had created.

Returning to the shop, Aurelia thanked Oliver with a kiss for his labors. To make up for taking over his morning, she insisted he go off and enjoy his Saturday. He left to meet up with a few friends for a pint, promising to be home for dinner. Having the shop to herself gave Aurelia time to think over everything she'd learned that morning and to consider how she could put it to use in Harriet's new story.

27

That night, after chatting with the characters for a bit, Aurelia and Harriet started for the spiral staircase to discuss her visit to the Museum. When Esther met them at the foot of the staircase and asked to join them, Harriet readily agreed. She appeared to have developed a friendship with Esther, though at times Harriet seemed almost in awe of her. Aurelia understood the feeling. Esther carried herself with a confidence that came across as reassuring, but it could easily have been intimidating if Esther were a different sort of person.

Once upstairs, Aurelia filled Harriet in on everything she'd learned about the Foundling Hospital. Harriet asked a few questions but mostly wondered what it all might mean for her sequel.

"Like I said, there was a certificate that the Hospital gave to each mother so that she could come back and claim her child. Do you want us to write that your mother used her certificate to find you?"

Harriet was quiet for a moment, then said, "But after all this time? I'm nearly twenty years old. Why would she come to claim me now?"

"Well... Maybe she always wondered what happened to you, but she'd been too afraid to find out in case something bad had happened? Or maybe she moved away and this was the first time she could get to London to check on you?"

"Perhaps," Harriet said doubtfully. "And then what? Would I go and live with her?"

"If you wanted to, sure."

"I don't know that I should like that. I have been thinking... Well, I have thought about it many times in my life."

Harriet paused and Esther took her hand, smiling encouragingly.

"It comes to this: I can't think of what my mother might say that would make those years without her any easier to bear. If she had come to some misfortune and had wanted to claim me but couldn't—that's misfortune on both of us and there is nothing we can do to take it back or change it. And if she had always been able to return but chose not to, I don't think I should like to know that, either."

Harriet looked to Esther.

"I have told Harriet a bit of my own story," Esther said, looking from Harriet to Aurelia. "As you have read my book, you must be familiar with it yourself."

"Yes, I remember," Aurelia said.

Esther's mother had revealed herself to Esther only to insist they could never have a relationship or tell anyone about their connection.

"I have no doubt that, with your pen in hand, you could smooth the way for Harriet and her mother. But even so, it may raise more questions than answers for Harriet. Perhaps it might be easier to form new friendships rather than try to revisit a relationship and circumstances that likely caused both of them pain and sadness?"

Harriet nodded. "I know myself all too well. Whatever story we devise, it's hard to think of forgiving her entirely. I have a fear that part of me would always question her story, and whether she could really love me as a daughter after so many years." Harriet had been speaking quickly and caught her breath. "Knowing that we had made her return, instead of having her return on her own, would make it even worse."

Aurelia couldn't help thinking that someone had written the story that had made Harriet's mother leave her in the first place, but she kept that thought to herself.

Instead, she said, "I understand. This is meant to be *your* story, so we'll do whatever you like. No reunion, then."

"No reunion," Harriet repeated, nodding in agreement.

"In that case," Aurelia said, "there might be another way to use the Hospital to help get your story started."

"Oh? Shall we join the others downstairs and you can tell them your idea as well? Now this first part is settled, I'm happy to let them hear the rest."

"Sure," Aurelia agreed.

They stood and began walking toward the staircase.

"David will be pleased," Esther said with a distinct twinkle in her eye. "He does enjoy conjuring the most intriguing ideas for new stories."

Aurelia thought her idea was positively Dickensian, so the true test would be whether it appealed to Dickens' writer character.

Once they'd gathered everyone around, she began.

"I learned that wealthy Londoners used to visit the Foundling Hospital to see how it was being run and what skills the children were learning. I thought maybe we could invent a visitor who saw Harriet as a child during a tour and asked about her. Then, over the years, the visitor had wondered how she was doing and how they could help her. So, they wrote a codicil to their will—"

"Ah!" David's face lit up as he understood what she was suggesting. Secret wills and mysterious heirs regularly featured in Dickens novels.

"Yes, the codicil could provide a legacy for Harriet," Aurelia continued. "That would give her the means to leave the Meagleses and live independently."

"An anonymous benefactor?" Pip asked uncertainly.

"I was thinking maybe an elderly widow with a large estate and no one to leave it to when she dies? Then there wouldn't be any heirs to fight over Harriet's share and she'd have the money free and clear."

"That's alright then, old chap," Joe said, smiling at Pip. "A nice old widow—very thoughtful like. Can't do better than that, Harriet!"

"Very good, Aurelia," David said encouragingly. "Though there's something to be said for angry heirs as a plot device."

"True," she conceded, "but maybe we should avoid setting a bunch of angry relatives on Harriet?"

"Indeed," said John Jarndyce. "We'll have no wrangling over wills for Harriet. Better, certainly, to spare her all that."

There was general agreement on that point, though David looked slightly disappointed. Excitement in the shop mounted as everyone realized Aurelia had found the first step forward in Harriet's story.

"What's next then, Aurelia," Harriet asked during a break in the chatter, "now that we know how my new story will begin?"

"Why don't I work out a few more ideas tomorrow and then, tomorrow night, we'll start writing."

28

Soon after the characters appeared the following night, Aurelia and Harriet were sitting at her desk. Aurelia had taken the extra chair from the back room so that she and Harriet could work together, just like she and Vronsky had done. The other characters were curious but watched from a distance—even David, who Aurelia would have been happy to have join them—giving the two women space to start their project together. Aurelia had pulled out a few loose sheets of paper and was holding her pen poised, ready to write.

"I thought we'd start with setting the scene. Maybe it's been a few months since the end of *Little Dorrit*, and you've been living with the Meagleses again. You think you've settled there and that your future is going to be with them." Aurelia paused. "Good so far?"

"Yes," Harriet said, sounding uncertain.

"You're sure? Anything you don't like, we can change. It could start the day after you go back with them if you don't want to be there for long."

"No, a few months is fine."

"I just thought it would give you a chance to sort of catch your breath after all those months with Miss Wade."

"That sounds sensible."

"But is that what you want?"

"I think so," Harriet said.

Aurelia looked at her, trying not to show the slight annoyance she felt.

"It really can be anything you like."

"I'm just not certain where to start. But what you said sounds right."

"Okay, then. We'll start there."

Aurelia began writing. She'd been thinking about these first few paragraphs, so the sentences flowed easily. She described Harriet's life back at the Meagleses' tidy little cottage, one day running into the next as she tried to settle back into life in a house that would never be her home. After a little while, Aurelia set the pages out for Harriet to read.

When Harriet was finished, Aurelia asked, "Good?"

"Yes," Harriet said, this time a little more decisively.

"Next, I think a letter will arrive in the post—maybe everyone is surprised because it looks very official. You open it, and it's from the widow's solicitor, telling you about the will and asking to meet with you to discuss it. Does that sound okay?"

Harriet nodded, hesitantly at first and then more deliberately when Aurelia raised an eyebrow as if to ask, 'Are you sure?'

Aurelia began writing again, describing the shock that was delivered to the household along with the letter as everyone wondered who had included Harriet in their will and why. When she finished describing the scene, Aurelia again showed Harriet what she'd written, waiting patiently for a response. Harriet read the pages and then looked up and nodded her approval.

"Excellent. So then the solicitor comes to the house," Aurelia began, diving right back into the story. "I think Mr. Meagles would join you when you sit down to talk to the solicitor, since he's basically your guardian. The solicitor explains how the widow saw you, got your name from the Hospital, and later wrote her codicil."

Aurelia didn't wait for Harriet to approve this time but began writing as she spoke. When she was done, she showed Harriet the pages.

Once Harriet looked up to signal that she'd finished reading, Aurelia immediately began writing again, absorbed in the ideas that were passing from pen to paper. She soon got lost in the world she was creating, losing track of the shop, the young woman sitting next to her, the clock ticking behind her, and the other characters who were socializing around the room. After a while, she came to a natural pause in the story and became aware of the silence surrounding her. She looked up and was startled to see that the characters were eyeing her with curiosity. Harriet was leaning forward on the desk, her head resting on her arm and her breathing soft and slow in sleep.

"Oh," Aurelia said quietly, blinking in surprise.

"You were on a good jog," David said, smiling.

"I was—I'm sorry," Aurelia said, rising stiffly from her chair and stepping away from her desk, all while eyeing Harriet to make sure she didn't wake her.

"No need to apologize. We're in fine company and had good conversation to occupy us," John Jarndyce said warmly.

"Were you able to make a strong start on your story?" Esther asked.

"Yes. Well, Harriet's story, yes." Aurelia looked back at Harriet. "I think I've tired her out, though. I can get a little carried away when I'm writing."

"We'll let her rest. Come and tell us what you've written, then," Peggotty said from her seat in the armchair.

Shaking off the last of her daze, Aurelia joined the others. She grew animated as she described the scenes she'd just written, relieved that writing with and for Harriet seemed like it would be easier than she'd thought. Harriet slept on, and eventually Aurelia tucked the first pages of the story away before joining Esther upstairs for a chat in the last hour before dawn.

29

Mark's tradition of Monday-morning visits had fallen by the wayside over the past few months, but the next morning he came into the shop right after Aurelia had unlocked the door and turned back to her desk.

"Good morning," he said as he pushed open the door.

His progress was halted by a giddy greeting from Biscuit, who leapt around Mark's feet and insisted on being petted.

"Mark! Welcome," Aurelia said warmly. "Were you just passing by?"

"Not exactly," he admitted. "I thought one of my old visits might be in order."

Aurelia blushed slightly, remembering her reaction to the news about his new girlfriend and feeling bad at the thought that she'd made him worry.

"You're welcome here any time, Mark. You and Rebecca—you and anyone you like."

She gave him a long look, hoping he understood she meant what she'd said.

"Thank you, Aurelia."

They stared at each other for a moment before she rushed over to hug him.

"I'm so happy for you. So, so happy."

"I know," he said, hugging her back. "I know."

"Tea?" she asked as they stepped apart. "Please say yes—I'm ready for a cup."

"Then yes, please."

She bustled into the back room and turned on the kettle. As she waited for it to boil, she closed her eyes and took in a deep breath. Then, reaching into the far corner of a cabinet, she pulled out a box of tea that she'd left untouched after discovering it a while ago: an old box of Marigold's secret stash with a note warning Aurelia not to use it. She took out two bags, then tucked the box away again. With a wistful smile, she continued getting their tea ready, certain that Marigold would have approved.

After carrying their tea into the shop, Aurelia and Mark chatted about her upcoming weekend away in Yorkshire, and then set a date for his visit with Rebecca. Aurelia told him about her plan to host a lecture in the coming weeks, and Mark made her promise to let him know once she'd set a date and time, telling her she could count on him and Rebecca to be there.

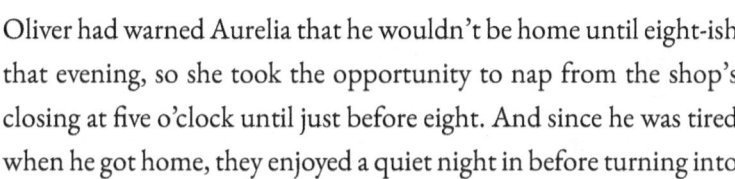

Oliver had warned Aurelia that he wouldn't be home until eight-ish that evening, so she took the opportunity to nap from the shop's closing at five o'clock until just before eight. And since he was tired when he got home, they enjoyed a quiet night in before turning into bed at a reasonable hour.

Given her recent nap, Aurelia struggled to fall asleep, but when her alarm started in at a quarter to midnight, she struggled just as much to open her eyes again. She performed her now-usual ritual of slowly maneuvering out of bed and through the bedroom door before closing it behind her. Then a quick change in the bathroom, where she fished the gold ring out of a drawer, before heading downstairs (with Biscuit in tow, of course) to meet the characters. Aurelia was surprised to see Fezz waiting at the door to the shop, seemingly unperturbed by Biscuit's presence. She rubbed his cheek as she opened the door, letting Biscuit race out, followed by a sedate Fezz.

Minutes later, Aurelia and Harriet were sitting at her desk, discussing what Aurelia had written thus far—how Harriet had gotten her letter and met with the solicitor to discuss the inheritance. They'd also consulted with David and John Jarndyce, who had helped them decide on a sum of money that would allow Harriet to live very comfortably.

Now Harriet just needed to decide what she wanted to do with her newfound wealth.

"Did you and Marigold ever talk about what you might do in the future?" Aurelia asked.

"Only that she wished Dickens had done better by me, or that I hoped I might see my friend Margaret more often."

"But... no big dreams? Thoughts of places you'd want to visit or things you'd like to see?"

Harriet shrugged, saying, "It never seemed worth the time to wish for what could never happen."

Aurelia let out an involuntary and quiet "Oh." To think that Harriet hadn't even let herself dream of a better life—no wonder Marigold had taken her under her wing. Aurelia looked around helplessly. The idea of needing to teach someone to imagine, to hope, to dream... It was so tragically sad and desperate that the heaviness of it felt almost paralyzing. While Aurelia had grown up imagining and writing stories, Harriet had learned to accept her life the way it was, grey and colorless as a rainy London afternoon.

Esther seemed to sense the impasse and walked over, giving subtle signals to the other characters to join her.

"It may be difficult to take the first step toward a new way of thinking or seeing the world, but after the first step, then the next, it can become quite natural," Esther suggested kindly.

"We are at your disposal, Harriet," David insisted. "We shall help you take those first steps."

Aurelia smiled at Esther, grateful for the help in getting past her momentary shock.

"I've been thinking that you might like to travel," Aurelia began. "You've traveled with the Meagleses, but this time you could choose where you go—anywhere in the world. And you could even move to a new country if you'd like. You don't need to stay in England if you don't want to."

"I could travel. Or I could move," Harriet recited, as though committing those options to memory.

"If you'd like to settle somewhere new, might the African continent take your fancy?" Pip asked. "I settled in Cairo for many years and cannot recommend it highly enough."

"I've been to Egypt with the Meagleses," Harriet said, turning a sad eye to Aurelia.

"We can take Egypt off the list, then," Aurelia said reassuringly.

"How about Australia, Harriet?" Peggotty offered. "I'm sure my brother and niece would welcome you."

"Oh, but Peggotty, your story takes place years after Harriet's. They won't be there when her new story begins."

"Lord! I didn't realize. When is her book set, then?"

"Sometime around 1826. One of the characters mentions that date." At a questioning look from Harriet, Aurelia added, "It was John Chivery. I'm not sure whether you've met him?"

"I did, once. He let me into the Marshalsea Prison to see Miss Dorrit."

"That's right! I'd forgotten that."

Aurelia picked up her copy of *Little Dorrit* from the desk and began paging through to the end of the book.

"What about Italy? France?" John Jarndyce offered.

Aurelia lowered the book, momentarily distracted by the memory of France and Vronsky's new story as a slow smile overtook her face.

"You could try France if you like, Harriet."

"I've seen enough of France at Marseilles and Calais," Harriet said with a shake of her head. "My memories of those places are not happy ones."

"And Italy? Little Dorrit—Amy—went there after her family inherited their fortune. It was a sort of—" Aurelia paused at the words 'polishing school,' not wanting to offend Harriet. "Well, they tried to get used to their wealth there, before returning to England to live a very different life than the one they'd lived at the Marshalsea."

"I don't think I should like to go back to Italy," Harriet said uncertainly. "I have traveled there several times before, with the Meagleses."

"Somewhere new, then," Esther said, nodding in understanding.

"Greece?" Aurelia offered.

"There's a war in Greece," Harriet said, sounding slightly panicked.

"There is? I'll have to remember that. Wherever you decide to go, I'd best do some research to make sure we're not dropping you into a war or a natural disaster or something." Aurelia wrote a reminder to herself in her notebook. "What about America? I think you could be a bit more independent there. You could start a business or travel the states."

"On my own?" Harriet asked in surprise.

"No, of course not," Esther said.

She had spoken just as Aurelia was about to say 'of course.' Aurelia looked at her, puzzled.

"No, certainly not," John Jarndyce agreed. "She'll need a companion, someone to accompany her."

Right, Aurelia thought, realization dawning on her. *It's 1826 for Harriet, not exactly modern times.* "A companion. Okay. Is there someone you'd like to bring with you?"

"I really only know the Meagleses. And Miss Wade, but I wouldn't like to go with her," Harriet said, shaking her head.

"No, we'll leave her out of this story," Aurelia promised. "Maybe there's a side character we can bring back," she added, picking up *Little Dorrit* and flipping through it again. "Someone who seems nice enough and might be able to travel with you. Though we can invent someone for you just as easily."

"Just... make them up?" Harriet asked.

"Simplest thing," David joined in.

He'd been pacing throughout their conversation, no doubt mulling over his own ideas for Harriet's story.

"Put a pen to paper and you can create a dozen companions. Two or three dozen if you like! This particular companion," David began slowly, picking up his pace as he invented. "Perhaps she's a solid woman, rather a martial figure, no nonsense. Someone who has served as a companion before, but perhaps she doesn't like being considered a servant, makes a fuss about not wanting to be paid while making it clear how much she expects in her pocket each year."

Aurelia gave him an indulgent smile. He was unwittingly describing Mrs. General from *Little Dorrit*, an unpleasant woman whose company Aurelia wouldn't wish on Harriet—or anyone, for that matter.

"What about your friend, Margaret?" Peggotty asked, looking to Harriet. "You said she was almost a sister to you, when you were at the Foundling Hospital."

"Yes, perhaps I could write to her and invite her to come with me?" Harriet suggested hopefully.

"I fear Margaret is too young to serve as a companion on your travels, Harriet," Esther said kindly.

"Ah, that she is," Peggotty acknowledged with a nod. "She's younger than you—I'd forgotten."

"Someone a bit older than you, with a little more experience of the world, could help guide and support you," Aurelia agreed. "We'll just have to keep thinking. I'll do a deeper dive in your book and see who I can find."

Harriet's face fell and Esther took her arm.

"If you'd like to see Margaret, I am certain that Aurelia could write a chapter or two where you visit her before departing on your travels."

"Could you?" Harriet asked, the hope back in her voice.

"Yes... Okay, sure," Aurelia said, trying to sound encouraging.

David exchanged a grimace with Aurelia, and she suspected they were both thinking the same thing: that a few chapters of Harriet sitting around and visiting with an old friend wouldn't make for very compelling reading. It reminded Aurelia of the chapters she'd written with Vronsky, where he'd visited stables and puttered around Italy before moving to France. She'd cut those chapters after Oliver had called them boring, and she was anticipating the same criticism for these yet-to-be-written Margaret chapters. Still, if that was what Harriet wanted, Aurelia would write it and do her best to make it work.

Harriet sat down next to Aurelia, looking more eager to get started than she had before.

"Oh, should we—do you want me to start the Margaret chapters tonight?" Aurelia asked.

Harriet nodded excitedly, as though she might get to see Margaret as soon as Aurelia started writing about her.

"Alright. Um..."

Aurelia pulled out a few sheets of paper and set her notebook aside. She'd been planning to start researching travel destinations for Harriet, but one look at Harriet's smiling face let her know she should save that for another time.

"Okay then," Aurelia said, picking up her pen. "Where shall we start?"

30

Aurelia spent the morning writing during her free moments in the shop, polishing what she'd already written, and moving ahead in bringing Harriet to the brink of her as-yet-undecided adventures. But she had to press pause that afternoon to head over to UCL.

She met with her old professor to go over details for the lecture series. Sophie, an undergraduate literature student who was also a regular at the shop, had joined them, excited to help in any way she could.

Afterward, she found Jack waiting for her at a café just off campus as she came rushing in.

"I'm sorry I'm late!" she said as they found a table. "I got talking and lost track of the time."

"Not to worry," he insisted. "How did it go?"

"Well, it's happening! Professor Marquez is going to do the first lecture, on Mary Shelley's *Frankenstein*, in three weeks' time. Sophie's going to make up posters and send out emails to students, and I'm going to put the word out at the shop, order copies of the book, and get things organized for having everyone in to listen. I can't believe how quickly it's coming together!"

"This is brilliant! Well done, you."

"Thank you so much for suggesting it. Everyone I've told says they think it's a great idea, so well done *you*. I don't know who's more excited about it—me or Oliver."

Aurelia and Jack had been full of a matching, boisterous energy until that moment. But the mention of Oliver's name seemed to put a pin in Jack, making his smile weaken as he slouched down in his seat and began tapping the rim of his coffee cup. She wasn't sure what had happened at first, but then she realized that he and Oliver likely hadn't spoken since that awkward dinner.

"Are you okay?" she asked, her tone soft.

Jack tried a smile and said, "Yes, I'm alright. I'm just sorry for last week. I've been meaning to apologize."

"There's no need. Really," she said more emphatically at a look from Jack.

"I didn't think he'd be so upset. And I didn't know he hadn't told you about Lottie. We don't talk about her much—at all—so maybe I shouldn't have been surprised."

"He filled me in after you left and it was fine."

Jack raised his eyebrows.

"He was a little prickly, but..." Aurelia paused, remembering Antonia's insistence that she stay out of it. "But I think he was just confused that you mentioned her since you were so young when she died."

There, that wasn't meddling, she told herself. *Not too much, anyway.*

"I wasn't a *baby*," Jack said, his eyes flashing as he repeated Oliver's words. "I remember her. I was young, but not so young that something like my sister dying didn't leave an impression." He looked down at the table, his eyes losing focus. "I remember the nurses trying to keep me away from her bed, near the end. I remember begging to be allowed to stay with her when they kept shunting me off with babysitters. And before all that, I remember her reading to me sometimes, and letting me play with her toys in her room when Oliver was busy with sports practices and games. I remember..." Jack's voice caught. "I remember being sad when I realized that she wasn't coming home again, after they'd taken her away—sad that I'd never see her again."

Aurelia reached out and gave his hand a reassuring squeeze.

"I know it was a long time ago," Jack continued, his voice stronger now. "But no one ever talks about her. It makes Mum and Dad too sad, and Oliver... well. It's this major chapter of our family history that everyone always skips past like they know it already and I still... I'm still missing some of the details."

"I imagine for them it all made more sense—they were older. But you were younger, trying to process death and what it meant without really understanding it?" He nodded and she continued. "Gosh that's a lot, Jack. I'm sorry."

"I've been wanting to talk to Oliver about it, now that we're older. But I should have picked a better time. I didn't think he'd be so... What did you call him? Prickly," he finished with a small laugh.

"I think he just wasn't prepared for it," Aurelia said. "He's not the best person for surprises."

"I've probably blown it now," Jack said, shaking his head. "If I say her name again, he'll run from the room."

"If you brought it up again, he might. I don't know... But there must be some way to help you two talk about it."

As soon as she was back at the shop, Aurelia called Antonia, anxious for her sister's advice.

"Can't I meddle, now? Oliver thinks Jack doesn't remember anything, and Jack *does*. Shouldn't I tell Oliver?"

"I think he needs to know. I'm just not sure it should come from you," Antonia mused.

"But Jack's too afraid to mention it again. And it's too sad to have this misunderstanding keeping them apart when they might be able to get past it. Maybe I could just let it slip—'Guess what? Jack *does* remember...' That could work, right? Then Oliver can decide what he wants to do about it."

"I'm glad to hear you say that, because you have to know that he might not want to do anything. They might never be best friends, Relia."

"I know," she said, her tone suggesting otherwise. "But wait until you meet him, Antonia—you'll see. He's so sweet, and you can tell he genuinely loves Oliver and looks up to him. He's excited about the lecture idea too, and he's even offered to help me organize it. I mean, I won't take him up on it since Oliver's already helping me. But wasn't it nice of him to offer?"

"It was nice of him to offer," Antonia agreed, sounding amused by Aurelia's list of Jack's charms. "He does sound sweet. Didn't you say he's like a human Biscuit?"

"He is," Aurelia laughed. "I think if he could follow Oliver around, he would. So... maybe they could be friends, at least. That would be better than being just acquaintances who happen to be related. Wouldn't it?"

Antonia went back to scolding her but didn't manage to convince Aurelia otherwise.

31

It was a struggle not to tell Oliver about what was, to her, the most interesting detail from her afternoon at UCL, but Aurelia was determined to wait rather than bombard Oliver with what she was certain would be a difficult bit of news about his own brother. At least she had other news to share. Over dinner, she filled him in on her plans for the lecture series and made him set aside the date for the inaugural event.

And just a few hours later, she was back to work on Harriet's story. Once she'd exchanged hellos with the characters, Aurelia and Harriet sat at her desk, with Aurelia determined to make progress.

"Have you had any thoughts about what you'd like to have happen next? Or where you might like to travel?"

"No," Harriet said, shaking her head. "I seem to have a good idea of where I *don't* want to go, but not where I'd *like* to go."

"Okay, then what about a traveling companion? Have you thought of anyone you'd like to go with—either from your own story or someone we could invent?"

Harriet opened her mouth as if to speak but then closed it again and shook her head before lifting a shoulder in defeat.

"Well, I've had an idea. I thought it might be best to stick with a character from your novel. Maybe it would make you feel more comfortable to have someone I could vouch for?"

"Alright."

"I was looking through it again and I found a woman who I think might be the perfect person to join you on your trip."

"Do I know her?"

"I don't think so. At least, it's not in the book."

"But you've met her?"

"Not here in the shop, but I read about her in your novel. Her name is Miss Rugg, and her father helped the Dorrits discover their inheritance—so he was a good, kind man. She was engaged once, but her fiancé broke it off. I think she might like to leave home for a bit of an adventure."

"And is she good, and kind, like her father?"

This was a more difficult question for Aurelia to answer since the novel didn't spend much time on Miss Rugg. Aurelia knew she could write more of a personality for her and make sure that she'd be a good friend to Harriet. She also thought it might be nice for Miss Rugg to have a chance to travel and enjoy herself after the disappointment of a broken engagement.

"She is. But more importantly, she will be. We'll make sure she looks after you, and I think you two could have fun together, traveling the world and meeting new people. What do you say? Shall we add her to your new story?"

Harriet took a moment before nodding and saying, "I'd be happy to have Miss Rugg as a companion, if you think that's best."

"I do! I was thinking... It's sort of a roundabout way of doing it, but that's just like Dickens—I was thinking that Mr. Meagles could ask Arthur Clennam if he had any suggestions for a companion. Then Arthur can happen to mention it to Mr. Pancks, who rents a room from Mr. Rugg. So it will eventually get back to Mr. Meagles that Miss Rugg is willing, and we can set up a scene where you two meet."

She paused to catch her breath, giving Harriet a chance to nod in agreement.

"Alright, then. I've been thinking that you and Miss Rugg should sail to America. I did a little research, and we could have you take a packet ship from Liverpool to New York. It's a long trip, about a month. But then you could stay in America for a few months, a year, a lifetime—whatever you like."

"America!" Peggotty said from the armchair across the room, popping off one of her buttons with the force of her exclamation. "That's a long way, Harriet, but not as far as Australia, at any rate."

Aurelia looked up and realized that everyone was listening in, wanting to hear what would happen to Harriet next.

"America would be quite an adventure! Boston, New York, perhaps Philadelphia—you and Miss Rugg would have plenty to entertain you there," John Jarndyce said kindly.

"That's thrillin', Harriet, to think of you seein' the wide world!" Joe added.

"Do you think so?" Harriet asked, her eyes filled with wonder and a little worry. "It seems awfully far away."

"Nonsense. There's nothing like a voyage at sea to set you off on a new adventure," David insisted, nodding approvingly. Then, with a mischievous wink, he added as an aside to Aurelia, "Might I suggest a few mercenary suitors? She'll be a wealthy woman, unmarried... You could wring a good deal of drama out of that."

Seeing Harriet blush, Aurelia realized that she hadn't thought about a love interest for her. She'd have to remember to ask if Harriet wanted one, but she'd find a way to do it without embarrassing her.

"Maybe," Aurelia told David. "But gold-digging suitors might do Harriet more harm than good, don't you think?"

"I suppose, though perhaps it might be effective in a little story I've been cooking up," David said, wandering off and taking out the pencil and pad from his pocket to jot down his idea.

Esther hadn't said anything for or against Aurelia's plans for Harriet, but Aurelia didn't notice since she was too busy enjoying her relief that Harriet seemed to be on board with her ideas. At last they could get some real momentum now that Aurelia knew what to write next, and she was eager to get going. But when she looked around her desk, ready to begin, she noticed that her notebook wasn't there. Realizing she must have left it in the flat, she excused herself and ran upstairs to get it.

Slipping into the flat and closing the door quietly behind her, Aurelia managed to get up the stairs without making a sound. She stood on the last step for a moment, letting her eyes adjust to the darkness while practically holding her breath to listen for any noise from the bedroom. Hearing none, she walked into the living room and stood, trying to think of where she might have left the notebook. Pivoting around as her eyes swept the room, she finally spotted it tucked under a throw pillow on the sofa.

"A-ha," she said softly as she walked over to grab it. Turning around again, she nearly shrieked when she saw Oliver coming out of the bedroom.

"Aurelia?" he asked groggily. "You okay?"

"Yeah! Yes," she whispered loudly, holding her hand to her chest as if its weight might help slow down her heart rate. "I'm sorry, did I wake you?"

"No. I don't know. I just woke up." He rubbed an eye for a moment, then took a few steps toward her. "What're you doing?"

"I was just getting my notebook," Aurelia said, holding it up as evidence. She hoped that in his half-asleep state, Oliver would accept her explanation and go back to bed.

"Okay." He nodded, then shook his head in confusion. "You're going to write? Now?"

"I was, yeah. Inspiration struck, so I figured I might as well take advantage."

"Okay," he said again, heading back to the bedroom before pausing and turning to her again. Taking a few steps toward the top of the stairs, he said, "The lights are on in the shop."

"I don't think they are. Are they?"

"They are. I'll go shut them off," he said, yawning as he took a step forward.

"No, that's alright!" Aurelia said, stepping between him and the stairs. "I was just... I'm going to write down there. Remember?"

"Remember what?"

"I told you, back before you moved in, that I like to write in the shop sometimes. At night."

"Oh... right. I sort of thought you were joking."

"Nope—very serious."

"Okay," he said again. "Wait... Why—" He paused, squinting at her in the dim light. "Why've you changed into clothes? You're not in your pajamas."

Aurelia looked down, stalling for time.

"I am not. You're right, I did change."

Oliver seemed to wake up a bit more at this. "Why?" he asked incredulously.

"Well... I don't want anyone passing by outside to see me in the shop, at night, in my pajamas. So I change."

Oh honestly, Aurelia thought, sighing. Why was she bothering to write a book if she couldn't come up with a decent story of her own?

"Right," Oliver said, nodding through his confusion. "Got it." He looked at her for a moment, then turned back to the stairs. "Is the radio on?"

"What?"

"I think I hear something downstairs—is that the radio?"

Startled, Aurelia looked at him and asked, "You can hear that?"

"Just barely."

Aurelia could hear Joe telling David a story about Pip as a boy. His voice sounded clear as anything to her.

"Yes, it's the radio," she said quickly. "Sometimes I listen to music while I write. Just like sometimes I go downstairs to write in the middle of the night. I have lots of odd little writing quirks,"

Aurelia said, hoping to achieve a sweeping answer to any additional questions.

"Like getting dressed to write."

"That, yes."

"And writing in the shop. At night."

"That too," she said, shrugging her shoulders.

Oliver squinted his eyes at her.

"This is all weird," he said, moving his finger between Aurelia and the stairs.

He was smiling, though, which was something. She stepped forward and gave him a quick kiss.

"I know. Add it to your list of very weird things Aurelia does."

"Like speaking in the third person," Oliver said as he turned back toward the bedroom.

"She hardly ever does that!" Aurelia called after him.

Oliver waved without turning and went into the bedroom, closing the door behind him. Aurelia dropped her head back and let out a giant exhalation. If she added up all the lies she'd just told Oliver, she wondered, how many would that be? How many had she told him altogether, in the weeks and months they'd known each other, to keep her midnight adventures off his radar?

The characters had warned her that she wouldn't be able to bring anyone into the shop to meet them, and their disappearing act each time Oliver had come into the shop had proven that. But part of her had still held out hope that there might be some way to share it with Oliver. Now, though... He could hear the characters, but 'just barely,' he'd said. If there were some way to share the shop's secret with him, she would, but how could he ever believe her when he couldn't make out the characters' voices and they vanished the second he set foot in the shop? Aurelia knew that if it were her, she'd never fully believe such a wild story—not without some kind of proof. Still, it felt rotten to lie, right to his lovely face, again and again. And the more she did it, the harder it was becoming to rationalize away.

With another sigh, Aurelia pulled herself back to the present and walked downstairs to work on the next chapter in Harriet's story.

32

The following evening, as Aurelia and Oliver were cleaning up after dinner, he reminded her about her nighttime writing session.

"So, you really go down to the shop to write? In the middle of the night?"

"I told you I do! Been doing it for a while now," Aurelia said, happy to be honest about that, at least. "I wrote a lot of my Vronsky book downstairs, at night."

"Don't you get tired?"

"I do, but you're forgetting that I can sleep in most mornings."

"That's true." Oliver paused, then added, "Have you got a good start on this new book, then?"

"Yeah, I have a few chapters now. Still rough, but I'm on my way."

"Anything you're ready to share?"

"Oh," Aurelia said, surprised. "Do you mean share with you... as my editor?"

"Either way," Oliver said with a shrug. "Me your editor, or me your boyfriend. Either one of us would be happy to read it."

Aurelia didn't know how to tell him that she didn't want him to read it yet. She knew he wasn't excited about the idea, she knew she was going to write it anyway, and she knew she'd have a hard time not taking his criticism—however well intentioned—to heart. Still, he would have to read it eventually if she was going to get it published.

"I guess I'm not quite ready. It's still early days and I haven't really got a handle on it yet. But soon?"

"Sure—whenever you're ready."

A few hours later, Aurelia sat with Harriet and shared the chapters she'd been working on.

"I think it's coming along," she told Harriet. "It's better that we used Miss Rugg instead of inventing someone. She's a fun character—person—to write."

Harriet nodded, ever quiet at Aurelia's side.

"Oh, speaking of inventing someone," Aurelia began. She looked around, realizing that the entire shop was within listening distance. She lowered her voice and continued, "David mentioned something last night and it got me wondering... Maybe we should go upstairs for a minute, so we can talk more privately?"

"With Esther?" Harriet asked hopefully.

"Sure, Esther can come too."

The three women walked up to the window seat.

Once they were settled Aurelia said, "You should think about inventing someone that you might like to meet in your story, a... suitor."

A slow blush crept over Harriet's face.

"Well, we're writing your future, aren't we?" she added with a sly smile. "You might like someone, a partner, to join you in that future."

Aurelia purposefully used 'partner' and 'suitor' instead of 'boyfriend' or 'husband.' She wasn't sure what Harriet's preferences were. There was a unique sort of connection between her and Miss Wade that Aurelia had never quite been able to put her finger on, and Aurelia didn't want to box her in.

"Have you considered whether you would like to marry, Harriet?" Esther asked.

"I... Well, yes. I've thought about it once or twice. But... Do I have to decide who I want to marry right now? Without meeting him?"

"No, you can think about it," Aurelia said, clocking Harriet's use of 'him'—though she wondered if it was just because same-sex marriage wouldn't have been an option in Harriet's time. "I know it's a big decision. And you don't have to marry at all if you don't want to. You'll have enough money to do whatever you like."

"In the meantime, Aurelia and I can help you to think about what type of man might be best suited to you."

"Yes, like someone tall, dark, and handsome, or fair and stocky," Aurelia teased, waggling her eyebrows.

Esther let out a small laugh, while Harriet's blush deepened.

"I was thinking someone kind, gentle, and sincere," Esther said, teasingly reproving.

"I know you were," Aurelia said, grinning. "But we can also make sure this saint you want for her is handsome to boot."

"This man... You'll write that he loves me, that we get married and have a life together?"

"We can write whatever you like about him."

Aurelia wasn't sure when that idea would sink in—that they could invent whatever Harriet wanted.

"But... you'll *make* him love me? He'll have no choice? I don't think I care for that." Harriet looked to Esther for support. "To make someone love me, to dictate their feelings to suit my own. It's been difficult to know that the Meagleses would never love me as a daughter or sister, but still, I wouldn't wish to force their love just to have it. Just as I wouldn't wish to force the love of a man, a husband, to suit myself."

Aurelia stared at Harriet for a moment, impressed. She was so young and immature in many ways, but her concern about manipulating the future of another character to suit her own was very insightful.

"First of all, Harriet, you are decidedly loveable and any man would be lucky to call you his," Esther began.

"That's right," Aurelia joined in. "You've had bad luck with the Meagleses, but that doesn't mean there aren't other people who would jump at the chance to get to know you and love you."

"Perhaps," Harriet said quietly.

"Look around you. Everyone here is eager to help you on your way. We are all hoping for great things in your future," Esther reminded her, nodding down toward the shop floor where the characters were gathered. "You have all of us on your side. That should be a sign to you that others will be eager to know you, as well. Not because you have bent them to your will, but because you have won their affection and care through your kindness and concern for each of them."

As Esther spoke, Aurelia thought over a collection of moments from the past few weeks. How many times had she seen Harriet taking care to help Peggotty up and down the spiral staircase, or to find her lost buttons at the end of each evening? How many times had she seen Harriet take special notice of Joe, who would often step back to let David and John Jarndyce have center stage?

"You're a kind person, Harriet, and it'll be easy to write about a man who loves you. You keep thinking. If there's someone in particular you might fancy, let me know. If not, maybe Esther and I can put our heads together and surprise you? We could leave it a complete mystery, so that you go into your new story not knowing who he might be, or you can read it first and decide if you like him."

Harriet looked to Esther.

"It sounds like there's time to think about who you want to be with, and how to meet him, right, Aurelia?" Esther said reassuringly.

"Definitely. There's no need to decide now—you have a bit more time."

Harriet, Esther, and Aurelia eventually joined the other characters back downstairs. As they chatted with everyone, Aurelia was certain she saw a little smile sneaking across Harriet's face every now and then.

33

On Saturday, Aurelia and Oliver decided on a quiet night in with takeaway and a movie. She'd had a busy week of planning for the lecture series and a full day in the shop, not to mention her busy nights writing with Harriet.

After dinner, they sat on the sofa and started their movie. She tucked herself against him and he wrapped an arm around her as they settled in. But then she spotted his finger as it began its familiar tapping against the rim of his wine glass, which reminded her of Jack and how she still hadn't told Oliver that one important detail from their conversation. Thoughts of when and how to tell Oliver began playing through her head, and soon she had no idea what was happening in the movie. She sat up and reached for the remote, pressing pause before turning back to Oliver.

"What?" he asked, dragging his eyes from the now-frozen screen. "Do you need the loo?"

"No. I need to tell you something."

Oliver looked worried and she realized her own expression must seem just as troubled.

"Everything's okay," she said quickly. "I just can't stop thinking about something that I want to tell you and now I have no idea who that person is"—she pointed to the still image on the screen of a man frozen mid-sentence—"so I figured I might as well have out with it."

Oliver raised his eyebrows, waiting for her to continue.

"You know how I met with Jack a few days ago, after I met with Professor Marquez and Sophie?"

"Uh... Yes, I remember."

"I don't think I mentioned—well, I know I didn't—that he apologized for what happened when he was over for dinner."

"Did he," Oliver said, his tone unreadable.

"He did. He felt awful for upsetting you, but there's something else he told me."

Aurelia waited to gauge Oliver's reaction. Deciding that he didn't look angry or put out, she kept going.

"He said he does remember Lottie. He told me all sorts of things he remembers about her, about that time. I don't think they're just things he's heard. He was almost five years old. That seems old enough to remember such a huge, tragic thing happening. I believed him."

After a moment, Oliver said quietly, "When I think back, I remember him being so little, practically a baby."

"You were eleven. I'm sure it seemed like he was a baby compared to you," she reassured him.

"What did he remember?"

"Um... He said Lottie used to read to him, sometimes. And that they used to play in her room when you were away for sports things."

"'Sports things'?" he repeated, a quirk to his lip in spite of the gravity of their conversation.

"Games, whatever." She smiled back, then grew serious again. "I know I'm meddling, and I'm sorry for doing it when I know I shouldn't. But when we talked after that dinner, it seemed like part of the reason you were upset was that you didn't think he remembered. So I thought you should know that he did. He does."

Oliver nodded, then looked down at his wineglass and began tapping. After a moment, he seemed to realize that Aurelia was staring at him expectantly, and he looked up at her.

"I'm not going to call him right this minute," he said, raising his eyebrows.

Hearing the hint of teasing in his tone, Aurelia held back a laugh.

"Antonia told me not to expect anything."

"Good. She's prepared you, then."

Aurelia let her better judgment take over and decided she'd best leave it there for the time being.

"Now that's done," she began. "Just how far back will you let me rewind without getting too annoyed with me?"

"Five minutes?" Oliver offered.

"Ten?" she countered pleadingly.

"You haven't been paying attention for all that time?"

Aurelia shrugged her shoulders innocently, nestling back into him as she hit rewind and waited to catch sight of a scene that looked vaguely familiar.

As they sank back into the movie, she felt his arm around her and thought he seemed alright. Even so, at times the character of his silence made her think she could almost hear the wheels spinning in his head.

They didn't mention Jack again that night, but Aurelia was certain Oliver was working through what she'd told him. She'd just have to be patient, or try to at least, to see if all that thinking would change anything between him and his brother.

34

A week went by and every night started to feel the same: Aurelia and the other characters would make suggestions for Harriet's story, but Harriet didn't seem all that interested in any of them. Aurelia was close to just writing chapters for Harriet during the day and getting her to sign off on them at night, but here, too, she was trying to be patient. In any case, with planning for the lecture series and their trip to Yorkshire that weekend, Aurelia was keeping busy enough.

By Friday morning, she and Oliver were scrambling around the flat, trying to pull together everything they'd need for their weekend away. Fezz was side-eyeing the cat carrier Aurelia had pulled out of the closet, and Biscuit was yipping at their feet, nearly tripping them in his excitement over what he clearly sensed would be an adventure.

As they walked through the shop with the final few bags and items for the car, Aurelia spotted her notebook on her desk and grabbed it, slipping it into her bag.

She had offered to postpone their trip a few times that week, thinking that Oliver might want a little more time to recover after Jack's visit and the revelation about his memories from their childhood. But Oliver kept insisting that he was fine and didn't want to break their promise to join her dad's birthday celebration.

Oliver had met her dad before, but this would be his first time at the house and his first time seeing her dad for more than a few hours at once. Fortunately, even though he'd seemed slightly nervous at the idea of spending the weekend with her father, his nervousness was quickly displaced by his happiness at how little traffic there was on the way up. And once they'd arrived, the easy drive gave him something to talk about with her dad as they unloaded bags and animals from the car. That, plus the business of introducing the dogs and getting Fezz settled, managed to break through any lingering nerves and get him feeling more relaxed.

Biscuit was relentless with her father's dogs—barking happily and trying to play with them—and his excitement and energy were infectious. They went off on a long ramble to stretch their legs and show Oliver the countryside, and by the time they got back to the house, they were ready for a good meal.

Later, they were all in the kitchen making an easy dinner of pasta with pesto when her father's phone rang. Aurelia answered, knowing it would be her sister.

"We're very busy here," Aurelia announced breezily. "No time to talk to daughters who couldn't be bothered to leave Paris for their father's birthday."

"Well, that's just mean," Antonia retorted, pretending to be offended.

"How are you? Wait, hang on—" Aurelia held the phone to her chest and turned back to her father and Oliver. "Can I leave you to it while I talk to the prodigal daughter?"

"Hi to Antonia. Oliver and I are managing just fine, go," her father said, waving her away.

Aurelia looked to Oliver for confirmation. He nodded and gave her two thumbs up, which she'd never seen him do before. He was *not* a thumbs-up kind of guy. She made a face at him and laughed, while he just shrugged before waving her away, as well.

She went into the next room, far enough to be out of earshot of the kitchen.

"Sorry. How are you?"

"'Prodigal daughter'?"

"Oh, you heard that?" Aurelia asked lightly.

"You know I did."

"Then you heard Dad says hi?"

"Hi back. Tell him I'll call him tomorrow for his birthday. How's it going there?"

"Fine. They're in the kitchen making dinner together. Biscuit hasn't made a mess on the carpet or torn apart any furniture yet, so all in all, we're off to a good start."

"And Oliver?"

"He hasn't had an accident on the carpet yet, either," Aurelia said, barely repressing a laugh at her own joke.

"Ha ha," Antonia said dryly.

"He's good. He and Dad have been chatting away, so it's going well."

"I'm calling with news, and you have to promise to tell Oliver and Dad. My local bookshop is putting in an order for more copies of your book!"

"Really? Have you bought them all?"

"I bought *some*, yes, but not all of them! I went to get a copy for a friend's mum the other day and they were sold out. I couldn't believe it—I mean, well done you, but still—*sold out*!"

"That's... amazing!" Aurelia felt surprised but also pleased. "I feel like I owe you a commission."

"Yes, I'll work that out with Oliver," Antonia deadpanned. "Alright, go back to your men. And tell them the news!"

"I will. Thanks, Tonia. Know I love you."

"You too."

Aurelia walked back into the kitchen to find her father and Oliver setting plates full of food on the table.

"A girl could get used to this."

They sat down and passed wine and bread, ready to dig into their meal. As they ate, Aurelia shared Antonia's news.

"Sold out? Congratulations, darling. That's wonderful!"

"It is," Oliver said with a big smile. "I'm not sure any of our authors have ever sold out a shop in Paris." He turned to Aurelia's father and explained, "We're a small outfit, so sales outside of the U.K. are typically pretty modest."

"Well, apparently Antonia spread the word far and wide. Though I'm still convinced she has stacks of copies sitting in a closet at her flat."

"Or?" her father asked, dragging out the word.

"Or... people are actually interested in my book."

"That's right." Now it was her father's turn to explain to Oliver, "Their mother hated when the girls refused a compliment or pretended away an accomplishment."

"She did," Aurelia agreed. "But it takes practice not to do it."

"You can practice accepting heaps of compliments when you do your book reading in Paris," Oliver said mischievously.

"What's this?" her father asked, as Oliver must have guessed he would.

"Antonia has set up a reading at that shop in Paris. She wants Aurelia to set a date, but she's dragging her heels."

"I'm not dragging my heels," Aurelia said witheringly, narrowing her eyes at Oliver. "I agreed to do it, but I just haven't picked a date yet."

"Well, don't keep your public waiting too long," her father advised. "Speaking of which, are you working on anything new?"

Aurelia looked at Oliver, who was busy twirling pasta on his fork.

"I am, actually. I only have a start, but it's coming along." Aurelia saw the question on her father's face and added, "I'm working on a sequel for Harriet from *Little Dorrit*."

"Like Count Vronsky's story," Oliver said.

"Well, it's only like his story in that it picks up where the novel left off," Aurelia explained. "Other than that, though, they're very different characters."

"That sounds intriguing. Tell me, why Harriet? And why *Little Dorrit*?" her father asked.

"Oh... I just thought it would be interesting to see what she'd do next in her life," Aurelia said.

Oliver tilted his head, giving her that kind, sympathetic look that made her feel like the worst girlfriend—person—in the world. She knew he was waiting for her to share more with her father, so she took a deep breath and continued.

"And *Little Dorrit* was one of Aunt Marigold's favorite books."

"You found some old notes of hers, right? About her favorites?" Oliver said.

"Right... I did."

"Huh," her dad let out. "I didn't realize she'd kept a reading journal."

"Um, they were just some notes," Aurelia said quickly. "Not like a diary or anything."

She couldn't remember lying to either one of her parents, even as a teenager, and it was an uncomfortable feeling. The very same feeling she'd been experiencing with the tales she'd been telling Oliver.

"Aurelia was working on something else, a different book," Oliver volunteered, "but when she found the notes, she decided to make a switch."

"And what does her editor think about this *Little Dorrit* book?" her father asked.

Oliver looked to Aurelia, pausing a moment before saying, "I want her to work on whatever book she feels inspired to write. I just wasn't sure this one was really calling to her."

"It wasn't at first, but it's fine now," she said, hoping she sounded more confident than she felt. "I'm enjoying it. Really!"

It *had* been going just fine, and even if it was 'just fine' and not 'great,' she was doing her best. She didn't like diminishing Oliver's very accurate observation that it hadn't been the book she'd been itching to write. But she didn't want him to worry when she was the one who had made the choice to write Harriet's book. She hadn't felt like she could refuse, but still—she had chosen to do it.

Oliver's expression made it clear that he didn't fully believe her, probably because her own expression was betraying her.

"It's not too late to set it aside," he said kindly. "You could pick it up again in a few months or a year."

"No, I can't," she said, realizing her sharp tone only when she saw Oliver nearly flinch in response. Her frustration was with the situation, of course, not him, and she tried for a gentler tone when she continued, "I just meant... I'm making such good progress. It would be a shame not to keep going."

And, to complete her performance, she gave a reassuring smile that she didn't feel.

35

As Aurelia and Oliver got ready for bed that night, he kept trying to catch her eye, but she felt a lingering guilt that made her want to avoid looking at him.

"Aurelia," he said at last, reprovingly.

"I know," she said, pulling a face at being caught out. "I'm sorry. I'm just... I got myself in a little bit of a mood."

"Not again," he chided, a smile showing he was teasing her.

They looked at each other for a moment, putting on stern faces, then laughed.

"I'm sorry if what I said upset you—about taking a break from your *Little Dorrit* sequel."

"No, it didn't upset me. I'm sorry if I seemed... No, it's fine."

Now she felt even more guilty for making him think he'd said the wrong thing.

"What was it you said to me when I suggested you write about someone other than Count Vronsky? 'Well, Count Vronsky's is the book I'm writing'?" he mimicked in an annoyed, snappy tone.

She managed to laugh, remembering how annoyed she'd been at that suggestion.

"Determined, decisive… stubborn. Yep, that sounds like me."

"That should have been my first clue not to badger you about your subject matter."

"You can badger me anytime you like. But I can't promise I won't cudgel you right back," she said, pausing before going on. "No, but… I'm sorry I was snappish earlier. I didn't mean to be, not when you were trying to be helpful."

"I only want to make sure you're doing what *you* want. But I've said that already, and you've said you want to write this book. So, if that's what you want to write, I promise I'm not standing in your way."

"Really?" Aurelia asked, feeling relief settling in. "But what about editing it? If you don't like the idea, I don't want to make you—"

"Nope. I'll be right beside you, making my points as you argue with me about every edit I suggest," he said, kissing her as they climbed into bed.

"Good." Aurelia settled under the covers and threw an arm over him. "I prefer having you alongside me."

After a pause, Oliver said, "On the plus side, we're back to normal again."

"What do you mean?"

"You've been very sweet. I know you've been trying to look out for me after I told you about my sister, but this is better—back to us."

"So, 'us' is me being crotchety?" Aurelia gave a look of mock outrage even as she laughed.

"Yes," he said in a very serious tone. When Aurelia nipped at his chest, he added, "No, it's you saying what you really think and me saying what I really think. That's us."

He turned out the light, which was convenient since it saved Aurelia from having to try and hide the look of shame that had washed over her face.

———◯———

The next morning, they made her father a nice breakfast for his birthday. After they'd eaten their fill, they all went on a long walk with the dogs, which helped Aurelia try to move past the previous night's conversation with Oliver. Just as they arrived back at the house, one of her father's friends arrived for a visit, so Aurelia and Oliver decided to drive into town and wander in and out of the shops. She'd grown up just outside London, but her parents had moved to Yorkshire several years ago, so it was a familiar home away from home. She liked sharing it all with Oliver, showing him her favorite farmhouse, tiny little cheese shop, and café. London felt like a place that belonged to everyone, but here—this small village in Yorkshire—felt like it belonged to her and her family.

Slightly exhausted from so much leisure time, Aurelia and Oliver went back to the house and napped for an hour. Then, deciding to walk to dinner, they joined up with her father's friends on the way and had an enjoyable stroll under the stars. Their destination was a quintessential old pub in town—low-ceilinged, with miniature tables and chairs scattered about the floor, and a wooden bar with brass fixtures set along one wall. It was Saturday night, so it was full and had live music playing, which added to the festive feel of the birthday dinner. They ate in a slightly more subdued section of the pub, then ordered a round of drinks and moved into a larger room where the band was playing classic rock covers.

Her father seemed genuinely happy; Aurelia liked seeing him surrounded by friends. And after listening to a song or two, he even coaxed their little group out onto the makeshift dance floor, where Aurelia noticed for the first time that Oliver was a truly horrible dancer. He had very little rhythm and a limited repertoire of two or three moves that he repeated again and again. She couldn't help laughing, and all the more so when he laughed along with her. Seeing him not just willing but pleased to be part of her father's impromptu dance party—even if what he was doing might not qualify as dancing—was a new and lovely reminder of how much she loved him. And seeing how much her father appreciated Oliver's efforts—even as he too laughed both at and with him—was yet another.

Aurelia made a mental note to kiss Oliver thoroughly on the way home and made good on that promise several times as the others walked on ahead.

———◯———

Oliver was chipper the next morning, though Aurelia and her father were cringing through mild hangovers. A solid breakfast soon set them right, and they went off for a final walk before packing up the car, Biscuit and Fezz included, to head back to London.

The weekend had gone well—despite her subterfuge over Oliver's concern for her career on their first night. Aurelia had loved seeing how much Oliver and her father genuinely enjoyed each other's company. But even those happy feelings from the weekend weren't enough to keep her from thinking back to David's warning that, some day, she might need to choose between Oliver her boyfriend and Oliver her editor.

36

Although Aurelia skipped visiting the characters in the shop that Sunday night—she was tired from the weekend and looked forward to a full night's rest—she woke up on Monday feeling ready to get back to Harriet's story. But first, she had to tackle her to-do list for the lecture series. It was in good shape, but she still felt a mounting nervousness as the date for the first lecture drew closer. With just a week to go, she had a case of wine in the back room (which Oliver insisted would be more than enough in spite of her doubts), extra copies of *Frankenstein* on hand, and every regular customer she could think of alerted to the event.

Oliver came home early from work that evening, just before Aurelia closed up the shop, and pointed to a new poster in the window.

"That looks very official. Did you make it?"

"No, that's all Sophie. She's been calling me every few days to see what she can do to help—it's very sweet. She's put posters up on campus, at a few local cafés, and she put that one up this morning."

"Very nice of her. Are any of your other regulars coming?"

"Mrs. Smith said she'd come, which was a surprise."

"Is she the one with the corgi?"

"That's her. And Mark's coming, of course, with Rebecca."

"With Rebecca... You're alright with that?"

"I am," Aurelia said decisively.

Mark had brought Rebecca to the shop for tea before their Yorkshire trip, and Aurelia hadn't had to pretend to like her since Rebecca was lovely. She'd liked seeing the two old school mates reunited and, it seemed very apparent, in love.

"I hope all this planning hasn't set you off course with your writing? You still haven't given me any chapters."

"Chapters, right... I can print them for you tonight."

"Only if you're ready?"

"Yeah, sure. No time like the present."

Aurelia's casual tone wasn't fooling anyone. Her heart gave a little flip, and Oliver took a step toward her as his face clouded.

"If you don't want to—if you're not ready—it's fine."

"No, it's not that," she said, moving to lace her fingers through his. "I think I'm just... I'm nervous to hear what you think. I know you weren't sure about the idea, so I feel like I've got a bigger hurdle to jump in order to impress you."

He pulled her closer and wrapped his arms around her.

"You're an excellent writer. And I'm not going into it with preconceived notions, remember? I'm on board. Promise."

She looked into his eyes and felt her body relax as she saw he meant it.

"Okay. I'll print my chapters for you tonight. But don't forget that in between reading them this week, you've also got to find time to help me rearrange things before the lecture."

"I won't forget." He smiled. "What's going where?"

They stepped apart as Aurelia began pointing around the shop.

"I was going to use the desk to display copies of the book. Then I have that table in the back room that I use for wrapping presents—we can bring that out and use it for drinks."

"Why not just use this?" Oliver asked, walking over to the Recommended Reads table. "We can clear these off and put the books here, or the wine."

He reached out to pick up the stack of copies of *Little Dorrit*.

"No!"

It came out as a shout as Aurelia rushed over to the table. They both froze at the sound of her raised voice.

"I—I'm sorry, that was much louder than I thought it would be. I just... This table always has shop recommendations."

"But isn't the shop recommending *Frankenstein* next week?"

"It is. I am, but... I'm not ready to shift these off just yet. It's a... Well, it's sort of a shop tradition. It's important."

He smiled and lifted his hands in surrender, saying, "I understand."

Kissing her on the cheek, he moved toward the spiral staircase and Aurelia realized he must have assumed that her insistence had something to do with memories of Marigold. Yet another pang of guilt at letting him believe that was outweighed by immense relief to have stopped him before he'd taken Harriet's book off the table. If he put it back after, or if Aurelia did, she wasn't sure whether Harriet would come out again.

At the top of the stairs, Oliver turned back to her.

"Does Jack know about the first lecture? That it's next week?"

"I haven't mentioned it to him. I wasn't sure if you'd want him here?"

"It was his idea. I think it'd be nice to invite him."

"Me too."

Aurelia tried to repress the smile that was threatening at the corners of her mouth.

"I'll call him now, let him know," Oliver said as he turned toward the door to the flat.

"Sounds good," she called after him.

Once Oliver was through the door, she gave a full-body wiggle of excitement, pleased that her meddling might have done some good, after all. Even her nervousness over printing and sharing the first chapters of Harriet's book couldn't dampen her mood.

Once the characters appeared that night, Aurelia started out with an apology.

"I'm sorry I missed you all last night. We were home from our trip in time but a bit tired out."

"Happy to see you back, Aurelia," Joe said cheerily. "I'll wager you were glad for a little extra sleep."

"I was, actually," she said, smiling. "But now I'm ready to dive back into Harriet's story."

After catching up with everyone, Aurelia and Harriet were back at the desk, sitting side by side.

"I don't know if you're familiar with the process of publishing a book," Aurelia began, "but usually a writer works with an editor. That's someone who looks through the manuscript and gives suggestions to help make it better."

"Oh. What sort of suggestions?"

"Well, an editor might suggest we add certain scenes, change certain characters, or rearrange some of the things that happen."

At a startled look from Harriet, Aurelia quickly continued.

"I know it might seem strange to have someone else jumping in to work on your story, someone you don't know, but I promise I'll run any changes by you first. Okay?"

Harriet nodded, though her face was still drawn.

"And the editor, he's... he's my husband, Oliver. We've worked together before, on Count Vronsky's book, and he really did make it better. I've given him the start of your book, so I'll let you know what he thinks. It'll be fine, I promise."

It will *be fine*, Aurelia promised herself too.

37

It had been a busy few days in the shop, and Aurelia was sitting at her desk enjoying a cup of tea just after closing at five o'clock. Her notebook was open and she was flipping through the pages, reviewing her ideas for Harriet. She sat back for a moment, thinking about how the writing process with Harriet had been going. Vronsky had been more opinionated—*much* more, she thought with a smile—about what she was writing for him. He wanted input at every stage, wanted to read over her shoulder and truly collaborate in developing his future. Harriet, on the other hand... Aurelia couldn't tell if she wasn't interested, didn't care, or didn't like the plans Aurelia had made for her. No, the plans she had made *with* her, Aurelia corrected herself. She'd asked Harriet again and again what she wanted, but Harriet didn't seem to have her own ideas or strong opinions about Aurelia's.

Just then, Oliver unlocked the shop door and came in, calling out a greeting as he turned and locked the door behind him. Biscuit stood up from his bed beside Aurelia, stretched, and trotted over to him.

"You're home early. I thought I was meeting you at the restaurant at seven?"

"I had one last thing to do for work, but, as it happens, it's work I can do from home."

"Right. Should I stay down here so I won't disturb you? I can keep myself busy until dinner."

"Not necessary," Oliver said, heading into the back room.

Aurelia turned, looking after him. He reemerged, carrying the extra chair Harriet had been using and placing it beside her.

"My work's with you—I've read your chapters," he said, sliding his messenger bag from his shoulder and digging inside.

"Oh," Aurelia said, slowly registering what was happening.

He lifted out a thick stack of pages and plopped them on her desk. She peered at them—just as dog-eared and marked up as the first chapters of Vronsky's book had been. Oliver was about to sit down when Aurelia held up her hand to stop him.

"Maybe we should go somewhere else," she suggested, looking around.

"What do you mean?"

"Well, the first time we did this here"—she pointed at her desk—"it didn't exactly go well, did it?"

"What do you mean?" Oliver asked again, his eyebrows supplying an added question mark.

She looked at him, her own eyebrows raised, waiting for him to put two and two together.

"Okay... The first time we sat here," he said, running his hand through his hair, thinking. "I gave you my first edits on your Vronsky book."

Aurelia raised her eyebrows even higher, waiting for the other shoe to drop.

"It went fine! You kept saying 'okay, yes, I'll work on that.'" He took in a deep breath then. "Oh... right," he said, realization dawning at last. "I don't think I've ever put together the Aurelia I knew then with the Aurelia who I know very well now." He started laughing. "You were trying not to murder me, weren't you?"

"Murder... Such a strong word," Aurelia teased. "Maim, yes. But murder?"

"Well, as I like my limbs, maybe we should opt for a change of scene." Oliver picked up her chapters, ready to relocate. "What do you reckon? Is upstairs safe? Or do we need neutral territory, like a café or the pub?"

"Hmm... Maybe we'd better find neutral territory." She stood and walked up the spiral staircase, adding over her shoulder, "Then you'll have witnesses in case I start plotting your demise."

"Cantankerous author, table for one," Oliver called after her.

Aurelia opened the door to the flat and grabbed her coat and bag from a hook.

"No, it'll be a table for two, darling," she said in a treacly voice, walking to the railing and batting her eyes at him before skipping back down the spiral staircase.

Oliver led the way to the door and she followed before doubling back to her desk. She grabbed her notebook and popped it into her bag so she'd have somewhere to scribble down Oliver's notes. She gave a forlorn Biscuit a pat and then followed Oliver out the door before locking up behind her.

They chose the pub around the corner and ordered drinks. They chatted about how their days had been while they waited at the bar, but once they had their drinks in hand and had found a table, Oliver pulled out the chapters again.

"Alright, let's have it," Aurelia said, steeling herself with a sip of her hot toddy and scalding her tongue.

Oliver didn't notice her fanning her mouth as he rearranged things on the table to make room for the manuscript.

"To start: the pace is good—you're moving things along. Brief set-up, where we are, what's happened, then you jump right into the will."

"No prolonged and boring trip to Italy this time," Aurelia said, reminding him of their first editing session together, when he'd torn apart her early chapters on Count Vronsky.

"No, you get right to it," he said, smiling. "And I love that you've managed to capture Dickens' voice but make it feel new and fresh. I wasn't sure if that was a one-off, the way you managed to do the same with Tolstoy's voice, if maybe you just knew his books and style better than anyone else's. It's such an impressive skill."

At the compliment Aurelia leaned forward, eager to hear more.

"The mysterious inheritance thing though," Oliver continued, "it might be a little too..."

"Dickensian?"

She leaned back again, sensing Oliver was moving on to his critical comments now.

"I suppose, yeah. Is Tattycoram going to find out more about who her benefactor is?"

"Harriet," she corrected.

"What?"

"Harriet, not Tattycoram. She doesn't like that nickname. It basically means tattered orphan."

"*She* doesn't like it?" Oliver asked, his mouth quirking into a smile. He was used to Aurelia talking about the characters she wrote as if she knew them, never guessing the truth since she'd explained it away as part of her creative 'process.'

"Well, the inheritance thing works," he continued. "It gets you where you need to be with Harriet, given her background."

Aurelia bristled at that. It was true, Harriet's background meant that they'd had to cook up a way of giving her money to be independent, but somehow the way Oliver said it felt like a slight. Or maybe she was being oversensitive, she told herself, and tried to tamp down her rising ire.

"I like the glimpse you give the reader of the Foundling Hospital and Harriet's history," Oliver went on, sitting forward and gaining steam as he always did when digging into someone's writing. "I guess, overall, I'm just not sure about Harriet."

Aurelia tilted her head, waiting for him to go on.

"If you want to write a *Little Dorrit* sequel, I'm on board—we've covered that ground," he said, holding up his hands in defense. "But this just doesn't read like Harriet to me."

"How so?" Aurelia asked, sitting back and crossing her arms.

"I've read *Little Dorrit*, at your insistence, and the character you're describing doesn't seem like Harriet at all. She was a quiet, tense, tightly wound girl. She ran away, but returned in the end, asking to come back under the protection of the Meagleses."

"She came back to them because Miss Wade was awful and she had no other choice. Where else could she have gone?"

"I don't know... She could have put an ad in the paper and tried to get a job as a maid for someone else."

"But some other family might have been just as bad," Aurelia said, echoing Harriet. "I wanted to give her something better to hope for in her life. She had a difficult childhood—she needs something exciting and wonderful to happen to her."

"Traveling around America in the 1820s would certainly be exciting," he said sarcastically. "And maybe even a little dangerous. I don't think it was all that easy for people to hop off to America on holiday back then. It just doesn't seem like something Harriet would do." He paused, then added, "At all."

Aurelia was trying to check her annoyance, but it was becoming more and more difficult. Harriet *was* going to do it. Oliver seemed to think he had a better grasp on Harriet than she did, despite the fact that she spoke to her almost every evening.

"Well, I think she would want to go. I think it would be easier for her to go to America to make a new life, rather than try to make her way in early nineteenth-century English society as a wealthy woman with no family."

"She has a family—the Meagleses."

"Oliver, come on!" Aurelia said, exasperated. "They were never her family. They treated her like a servant, not like a daughter or a sister. She came into their house when she was fourteen or fifteen, hoping for a family and love, and instead she got to watch their daughter, Pet, get all the attention."

"Write that, then. Write about Harriet wanting to be loved and finding a way to make the Meagleses her family."

"We—I've thought about that, but she wouldn't want to force them to love her. It's easiest to send her off somewhere new with no bad memories."

"Easier, but..." Oliver hesitated, now fully aware of her frustration, though he plowed onward. "I'm not sure it's true to Harriet. No, actually—I'm certain it's not."

"Look, I'm in her head. I *know* her. This is Harriet's story," Aurelia said, pointing to the chapters on the table.

Oliver sat back, unwilling to cede ground. "You're not writing Harriet's story, Aurelia. You're writing about a totally different character from a totally different book."

"What?" Aurelia asked, startled.

"This character you're writing is someone different. Just change the name."

"It has to be Harriet."

"What about John Chivery? Or Amy's sister? There are plenty of great characters in *Little Dorrit* to choose from—"

"I told you, it *has* to be Harriet."

Oliver closed his eyes and tipped his head back, then let out a sigh as he looked at her again.

"That's right. I'm sorry—I'd forgotten."

He reached out to take her hand, and she almost drew it back. She was ready to keep arguing and didn't understand his sudden shift to being calm and understanding.

"Forgotten what?"

"You said Marigold liked Harriet, right? Somehow I kept thinking that she liked *Little Dorrit* in general, but you did say she liked Harriet in particular."

Aurelia was practically squirming under the weight of his sympathy. She didn't feel like she deserved it, even if Marigold had been the reason she'd started writing for Harriet. It wasn't fair, but his critique, plus the reminder that she wasn't being completely honest about her connection to Harriet, made her lash out.

"Never mind Aunt Marigold. You hate my book."

"I don't hate it."

"You do. You haven't liked it from the beginning. You promised you could read it with an open mind, but obviously you can't."

"I can, and I did, but my open mind says this isn't working," Oliver said firmly, putting his hand on the pages between them. "*This* isn't about Harriet, Aurelia. When you're done being angry at me, look back at *Little Dorrit* and then read your chapters again. You're writing someone different."

Aurelia stared at his hand on the pages—*her* pages. Somehow the criticism stung ten times more coming from him. He wasn't just her editor anymore; he was her boyfriend, and she wanted him on her side. Oliver drew his hand back, waiting for her to say something.

"I've heard you out," she said as evenly as she could manage. "But I don't want to talk about it anymore. Not tonight."

"Okay," Oliver said, nodding. He put the pages back in his bag and asked, "Should we just go to the restaurant from here?"

He was trying to speak evenly, but she could hear the irritation in his voice. She felt trapped. There was no way she could package up her emotions and sit across from him at a restaurant ten minutes from now, maybe not even ten hours from now. For that matter, it didn't seem like he'd be able to manage it, either.

"I think I'm going to stay here. Why don't I meet you home later."

"You don't want to eat?"

"Not just now."

"Aurelia," he scolded.

"I know," she said, hating the whine in her voice as she acknowledged that she was being difficult. "I just need to sit here and think. On my own."

He opened his mouth to argue but then shook his head resignedly.

"I'll see you at home, then," he said on a sigh.

"See you in a bit."

He left the pub, and as the door closed behind him, Aurelia slunk down in her chair. For a moment she found herself wishing she could go home to an empty flat so they could avoid the inevitable continuation of their conversation. And that thought made her feel even worse than she already did.

38

Aurelia waited out her irritation at the pub, eventually ordering something to eat while she worked through what had just happened.

She knew Oliver had been honest not because he'd wanted to hurt her, but because it was his job to give her his opinion on her work. But knowing that didn't take the sting out of his words. Her writing felt so personal, and on top of that—like a giant cherry that he couldn't see—she had reasons for writing about Harriet that she couldn't explain to him. Their conversation had reminded her that in spite of the fact that they'd fallen in love as they'd worked on her first book, it *had* been difficult working together. He'd helped her make some major and important changes to her first book, but it hadn't been an easy process. And now that they were living together and, eventually, she'd have to go home and actually speak to him again… Well, David had been right; living and working with one another was too complicated—for her.

Aurelia had always been a little sensitive about having her work critiqued, but she'd never gotten as upset as she had tonight. Well, she'd gotten upset about some of his edits to Vronsky's book, too. So maybe it had more to do with getting criticism from Oliver, which she'd suspected was part of her problem. Because it was *her* problem; she knew that. Again, he hadn't said anything to be mean or hurtful, but he was clever and insightful—and she was in love with him and his cleverness and insightfulness—so that everything he said carried that much more weight.

And what he'd said about Harriet, about how Aurelia had written her… That couldn't be right, she told herself. She'd asked Harriet for her input at every turn. A big adventure did seem a little out of character for her, she could admit that at least, but the whole idea was to give Harriet new opportunities and new experiences—to change things up for her.

As she walked home, Aurelia imagined Oliver getting ready for bed, wondering where she was and worrying about her outsized reaction to his edits. And just like that, all her annoyance and hurt drained away, leaving Aurelia feeling guilty—for a different reason than usual this time. The mantel clock struck ten as she came into the shop. She walked upstairs, deciding she'd miss the characters that night so that she could focus on resolving things with Oliver.

———◯———

The flat was quiet when she came in, and she could hear Oliver getting into bed down the hall. She went into the bathroom to go through her evening routine, then moved into the darkened bedroom where she climbed into bed, trying not to jostle Oliver as he lay on the opposite side with his back to her.

She sighed and was almost immediately aware that Oliver was awake. She'd gotten so used to the sound of his breathing at night and knew when he was awake, just dozing into a light sleep, or deep into the kind of sleep that would allow her to sneak downstairs undetected.

With another sigh, Aurelia rolled over, facing him. He moved onto his back and a glimmer of light in his open eyes shifted as he looked at her.

"That was unpleasant," she offered quietly.

"What was?" he asked, his tone deliberately obtuse.

She found his leg with her foot and gave it a gentle shove. She saw the tension in his body relax.

"Oh, that," he said lightly. Then, quietly, "Yes, it was unpleasant."

"It's just that you're so stubborn. We'd never argue if you just gave way," she said dryly.

Aurelia hoped he could hear the smile in her voice, even if he couldn't see her face in the dark.

Oliver laughed softly. "Oh, I'm the stubborn one?"

"No. I think we both know I take that title in this relationship." Aurelia's smile dipped as she shifted to a more serious tone. "I'm sorry. I know I'm always difficult when you give me edits, but... tonight felt harder than usual."

"It did, somehow."

"I feel really strongly about this book. I don't know how to push that down or set it aside. It's just how I *feel*—I'm not sure I can change that."

"I don't want you to change. And I know I get a little enthusiastic when I'm suggesting things. But if I'm going to be your editor, I have to tell you what I think. It won't work if I'm not honest with you."

"Of course—you shouldn't have to lie or feel like you have to protect me. But this story and this character mean something to me. As I've written them."

They were both silent. There was only one solution to the problem of her not being able to take criticism from him while also needing an editor, and she was certain he knew what had to happen next.

"I love that you're passionate about books. It's one of the first things I loved about you," she said, reaching out to pull his face toward her.

He turned on his side and reached up to brush his hand through her hair, sending pleasant sparks of sensation down her neck.

"But maybe it's too hard for us if I'm passionate about *your* books," he said.

Aurelia was grateful to him for saying it and relieving her of the burden. She nodded and drew her fingers across his cheek, which was rough with the scruff he would shave just hours from now. He kissed her hand, then slid his arm around her and pulled her close.

"We'll be okay as a couple still, won't we?" she asked, unable to hide a slight wobble in her voice. "This won't be the thin end of the wedge that pushes us apart?"

"Definitely not," Oliver said, pulling her even closer. "But if we keep working together, that could become the thin end, and I don't want that."

"Neither do I," she agreed.

"I suppose, if we have to choose between working together and this…" he began, pausing to kiss her.

"I choose this," Aurelia finished for him, kissing him back.

39

Aurelia was gentle with Oliver the next day. She still felt remorseful for taking his criticism so very badly, but she also appreciated that he seemed to have processed their professional breakup so well.

They had dinner at home that night, both voting for something easy after a busy few days. As they sat at their small dining table, Oliver slid a piece of paper across to her.

"What's this?" she asked, picking it up.

"A list of potential editors. I narrowed it down and these are the ones I think might be thick-skinned enough to work with you."

She looked up quickly and saw that he was smiling, and she smiled back in relief.

"Think they'll be able to withstand a fiery temper, then?" she asked.

"My sources say yes."

Aurelia looked over the list.

"Annie, Helen, Louisa... All women?"

"Are they?" Oliver asked, his tone of false curiosity a dead giveaway.

"You're not honestly worried some other man might be tempted by that fiery temper I just mentioned?" she asked with a laugh.

"Stranger things have happened," he said, shrugging. "In all seriousness, though, they really are talented editors. Their gender is just a bonus as far as I'm concerned."

"So... Do I call them? How does this work? I've only met with a potential editor once and here we are."

"I let them know you might be calling. They're all willing to talk and see if working together might be a good fit."

"Okay, then. I'll call them tomorrow." Aurelia paused, reaching out and placing her hand in Oliver's. "Thank you."

"You're very welcome." He squeezed her hand before picking up his fork and spearing a bite of food. "And as my last act as your editor, I'm going to insist that you call Antonia and pick a date for that reading in Paris."

Aurelia had just taken a bite and nodded as she rolled her eyes at the delay while she finished chewing. "I will. Although I'm guessing she'll call me first—but I will definitely set a date."

———◯———

Aurelia's mood was a bit subdued as she waited for the characters that evening. As much as the decision not to work together had been a mutual decision—and the right one—she felt nervous about finding someone new. What if they didn't click? What if they didn't like her writing style? What if... What if they didn't like Harriet's story, either?

The characters began to materialize in front of her, and by the time they were saying hello, she was smiling again. After a few minutes of chatting with everyone, Aurelia led Harriet over to her desk.

David followed them, saying, "I understand your husband is also your editor. I'm sure it's very convenient to have an editor under the same roof. You can hand him each page as you finish writing it!"

Aurelia's mouth dropped open and she quickly closed it again.

"Oliver... he *was* my editor. We couldn't... Well, we've decided it's best if he doesn't edit my work anymore."

"He doesn't like my story?" Harriet asked.

There was a hint of something in Harriet's tone—it couldn't be hopefulness?—that Aurelia couldn't quite place.

"No, it's not that," Aurelia insisted, unsure whether she sounded particularly convincing. "It's just that it's too hard living together—being married—and working together. I'm a bit... well, sensitive when it comes to my writing. A professional breakup seemed like the best way to avoid all-out war at home."

"But you said we need an editor to make my story better and to publish it. What will we do now?"

"I'm going to reach out to a few other editors tomorrow, don't worry," she reassured her.

"Might I suggest avoiding editors and publishers altogether?" David piped up. "One may avoid a world of trouble by simply printing the thing oneself. Establishing a readership will come in time, and you can distribute Harriet's story—perhaps in serial form, a few chapters at a time—here in your shop."

Just like Dickens did, Aurelia thought with a smile.

"That's definitely an option to keep in mind," she agreed. "But it would be helpful to get a second set of eyes on my writing, so I won't give up on finding a new editor just yet."

Aurelia and Harriet sat down to begin looking over Aurelia's notes with ideas for the next few chapters, and David listened in. Harriet nodded as Aurelia talked her through each one, shrugging a shoulder whenever Aurelia asked if she should try writing it out. Aurelia looked up and caught David giving Harriet an exasperated look before turning to raise his eyebrows at Aurelia in commiseration—but fortunately Harriet had been focused on the notes and papers in front of her.

I need to start taking the reins here, Aurelia told herself. Because even after weeks of encouragement, Harriet still struggled to decide what should happen next in her story. David was full of exciting ideas, Aurelia shared as many as she could think of, and the other characters weren't shy about making suggestions too. But even with all those choices set out for her, Harriet still didn't seem to understand that anything and everything really was possible.

Maybe if I start pushing Harriet a bit more, she'll start to accept that she has more options than she realizes and we'll make more progress. Then I'd be that much closer to getting back to my own book.

Aurelia winced at the unkindness of such a mercenary impulse. She wanted to get back to the book she'd started before taking on Harriet's story, that was true. But she genuinely wanted to help Harriet find her way forward, even if—maybe even because—Harriet seemed so incapable of finding it on her own. Aurelia *would* take the reins and push Harriet along a little, but only to help her move forward and live a life Aurelia was certain would make her happy. Even if Harriet couldn't see it yet.

40

As Aurelia had predicted, Antonia called the next morning while she was finishing her breakfast.

"I'm ready to set a date for that reading at your local shop," Aurelia said by way of a greeting.

Antonia paused, taking in Aurelia's change of tune.

"You're sure? I know I've been insisting, but if you really don't want to—"

"No, I want to."

As she said it, Aurelia realized that she really meant it. She'd been energized by setting up the lecture series in the shop. It took some work to organize but wasn't the herculean task she'd imagined when she'd thought of Antonia's local bookshop putting on an event for her. She liked the idea of welcoming customers into her shop after hours, of having them all there to hear something new and to chat with one another afterward. It didn't seem like such a bother anymore.

And, of course, Oliver had asked her to do it, and she was happy to oblige.

"I really do," she added.

"I finally wore you down, then?" Antonia asked, sounding proud of her efforts.

"Mm-hmm."

Aurelia didn't mind letting her think the win was hers.

"Alright, then. I'll stop by the bookshop today to arrange it. He told me he has a few events next month, but he could fit you in."

"Oh, I was thinking later—maybe the middle of April."

"April? That's ages away," Antonia whined.

"Two months—that's hardly any time at all," Aurelia said placatingly.

"I suppose... That does give me time to spread the word, make up some flyers."

"Flyers? Really? Antonia, don't go to any trouble—"

"I'm happy to do it. I'm already imagining a photo of the book cover and your author photo arranged just so... It'll be fun."

"Hey," Aurelia said, pausing as she carried her breakfast dishes into the kitchen. "I know I've been dragging my feet, but I really appreciate you helping me get the word out about my book."

"I know. I haven't taken your reluctance for ingratitude, don't worry."

"Good. Thank you for that, and for arranging it."

"Do I have to run anything by Oliver before I set it up?"

"I don't think so. He didn't say."

"Ask him just to be sure?"

"I will. Well, I'll ask my new editor once I find one."

Antonia was silent, waiting for Aurelia to fill in the blank.

"I fired Oliver. Or he quit."

"Hmm. It was only a matter of time, wasn't it?" Antonia asked casually.

"You don't sound surprised at all," Aurelia said, surprised herself at her sister's blasé tone.

"I mean, you're very... *you*. And from what I can tell, Oliver is very... *Oliver*. Living and working together—that was destined to be a short-term arrangement."

"You didn't exactly sound the alarm when I told you he was moving in."

"That's because there are some things you just have to work out on your own," Antonia said smugly.

"We worked it out alright," Aurelia said, grimacing at the memory of their argument. "We're okay now, but it was not our finest hour. Or not mine, at any rate."

"Is it really okay, though? Or just glossed over, ignore-the-giant-fissure-in-the-floor okay?"

"I think it really is okay," Aurelia said, considering. "He and I aren't very good at pretending to think or feel anything, so I'm fairly confident there is no giant fissure in the floor."

Aurelia's confidence faltered when she remembered the fact that she couldn't tell Oliver why she was so determined to write Harriet's story. She couldn't tell Antonia either, of course. But before she could linger too long on how her secret double life was becoming one of those fissures Antonia had mentioned, her sister went on.

"Good," she said decisively. "I'm attached to him now, so I'd rather you didn't throw him over just yet or get thrown over yourself."

"I'll do my best," Aurelia said with a huff at her sister's lack of allegiance.

They talked for a few more minutes, until Aurelia caught sight of the living room clock and realized it was ten o'clock and time to open the shop. She promised Antonia that she wouldn't change her mind about the reading in Paris, then rang off and ran downstairs.

Once the blinds were up, the door was unlocked, and she was sitting at her desk with a second mug of tea, Aurelia started calling the names from Oliver's list to set up meetings with her potential new editors.

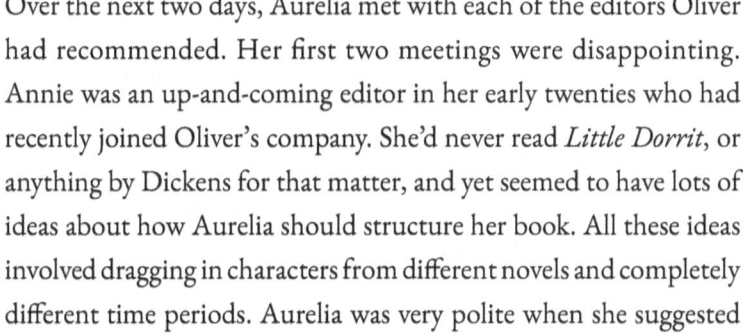

Over the next two days, Aurelia met with each of the editors Oliver had recommended. Her first two meetings were disappointing. Annie was an up-and-coming editor in her early twenties who had recently joined Oliver's company. She'd never read *Little Dorrit*, or anything by Dickens for that matter, and yet seemed to have lots of ideas about how Aurelia should structure her book. All these ideas involved dragging in characters from different novels and completely different time periods. Aurelia was very polite when she suggested they might not be a good match.

Her second meeting wasn't much better. Helen was a bit of a pushover and seemed unwilling to disagree with anything Aurelia said. Although Aurelia momentarily considered the benefit of working with an editor who would let her run wild, she knew it would be best to work with someone who felt comfortable pushing her to consider changes she might not otherwise come up with on her own. Even if she'd resist those changes with just as much stubbornness as she'd shown Oliver.

Given her lack of success with the first two candidates, Aurelia's expectations were fairly low as she walked into a café in South Kensington to meet with Louisa, the final name on Oliver's list. Shaking rain from her umbrella, Aurelia looked around and spotted a woman with short black hair, sharp cheekbones, and a wide smile.

"Aurelia?" the woman asked, raising her eyebrows.

"Yes! Hi—Louisa?" Aurelia walked over to the table and they shook hands. Louisa was tall and looked like one of those women who'd spent their teen years looking gangly and awkward before waking up one day and looking fabulous without any effort.

"Sorry to drag you out in the rain," Louisa said as Aurelia hung her umbrella from the back of her chair before taking a seat.

"Oh, it's no bother. Hard to avoid it in London." Aurelia smiled. "Do you—do I detect an accent?"

"You do. I'm Canadian. I moved here with my girlfriend about five years ago. She's from Bristol, but I managed to get her to agree to move to London as a compromise."

"There's nothing wrong with Bristol… but well done," Aurelia said conspiratorially. "If you're giving up home, might as well pick somewhere that's new for both of you. And you could do worse than London."

"It's no Toronto," Louisa said facetiously, "but it'll do."

A waiter came by and they ordered tea and two different kinds of cake to share.

"Well, this is off to a good start," Aurelia said.

"Oliver might have suggested I'd need to feed you if I wanted to make a good impression."

"Did he?" Aurelia laughed. "Did he also tell you I'm a monster to work with and to run while you can?"

"Yes, though he didn't use the word 'monster.' What was the word he used? 'Tyrant.'"

They both laughed and Aurelia relaxed into her seat.

"At least you're stepping in with your eyes wide open," she said.

"Why don't you tell me about this book you're working on?"

Aurelia launched into a description and then, as they worked their way through cake and tea, she found herself explaining why the story meant so much to her and why it had to be about Harriet. But, of course, she didn't say that she'd been meeting with Harriet at night and chatting with her about her story. Nearly two hours passed before they agreed to give working together a go. Aurelia handed Louisa a copy of her draft, and they made plans to meet again soon to discuss her initial feedback.

As she walked back to the shop, Aurelia grew excited at the prospect of working with Louisa. While she felt slightly nervous about hearing her thoughts on the chapters, it wasn't as overpowering as what she'd experienced when she'd shared them with Oliver. There was a new freedom in being able to take Harriet's story in whatever direction she chose, and Aurelia spent the rest of the afternoon at the shop researching the places and attractions that would have lured visitors to America in the 1820s.

41

After weeks of planning, it was finally time for the shop's very first lecture. Oliver came home early from work to help Aurelia set up. She'd had chairs delivered and they set them up on the shop floor, moving the armchair to make room. As they were rearranging things, Oliver pointed to the Recommended Reads table, but at a look of panic from Aurelia, he left it where it was and started arranging the wine and cups on the table they'd brought out from the back room.

Sophie was the first to arrive, eager to help though there wasn't anything left to do. A gathering of about thirty people eventually trickled in, including familiar faces: Mark and Rebecca; Kali and her husband, Tom; and Jack. David and James had let her know ahead of time that they couldn't make it but promised to try for the next one if all went well. The shop was tightly packed, but it made it all the more cozy and welcoming.

Professor Marquez was very engaging and had the whole shop rapt with attention, though Aurelia couldn't help but look around and marvel at having pulled the whole thing off. Eventually, Oliver took her hand, smiling with a distinct twinkle in his eye as he continued staring ahead at Professor Marquez, as though to let her know that he understood her distraction.

Aurelia had been so absorbed in getting ready for the lecture itself that she was pleasantly surprised by the gathering that remained afterward to catch up, drink wine, and discuss what they'd just heard. It reminded her of her nights in the shop with the characters and made her wish there was some way to join the two crowds together.

Jack and Oliver were deep in conversation, though Aurelia was happy to hear some laughter coming from their corner of the shop, too. She kept Kali's husband Tom company while Kali spoke with Sarah, who had met with her a few weeks earlier and was now trying to recruit her to work exclusively for the National Gallery giving tours to families with small children. And as she chatted with Tom, Aurelia watched Mark nodding slowly at something Mrs. Smith was saying. She wasn't sure she'd ever seen them talking and felt a thrill to think that the lecture had brought so many of her friends together. That settled it for her, and she made sure to arrange a follow-up event with Professor Marquez before the night was over.

———◯———

Aurelia debated whether to join the characters that night, but as she lay awake just before midnight, restless with the excitement of the evening, she decided she might as well make the most of her inability to sleep.

But once she'd gotten downstairs and said hello to everyone, progress on Harriet's story was slightly delayed because they all wanted to know how the lecture had gone.

"What a shame we just missed it," Joe said. "Only a few hours difference and we could have had a listen in, as well."

"Not exactly, I'm afraid," Aurelia said with a smile. "If those people had been in the shop at midnight, you wouldn't have been able to appear."

"It is a shame," John Jarndyce said with a sigh. "I quite liked *Frankenstein*, though it is a touch darker than my tastes generally run."

"I wish I could have had you all there, or here, to hear it. Come to that, I wish you could meet my friends—so many of them were here tonight."

"And your husband?" Esther asked. "Was he in attendance?"

Aurelia mentally repressed a threatening blush.

"Yes, Oliver was here too. I hate that I can't introduce all of you. I know he'd love the chance to meet you."

Her smile dimmed a little at that. Oliver really would love to meet fictional characters, to see what Aurelia was so lucky to experience nearly every night. But she didn't have time to linger on those thoughts as the characters continued to ask her questions about the event and her friends.

Eventually, Aurelia and Harriet were sitting at the desk, and Aurelia was ready to get back to writing.

"Perhaps… Perhaps we should wait to continue?" Harriet asked. "If Oliver is no longer your editor, surely you need time to find a new one?"

"Oh—but I've just found us a new editor!"

"You have?"

"Yes, and she's wonderful."

"She is?"

"Mm-hmm. Her name's Louisa and she's reading your chapters now. But she likes the overall idea for your book, so we're off to the races again."

"Races?"

"I just mean we're ready to keep writing. I've got so many ideas for you, Harriet!" Aurelia said encouragingly, making good on her plan to take charge and push Harriet's story forward. "We've finally got you and Miss Rugg in America, now it's time to set you off on some real adventures."

"Adventures?"

"Yes! I'm thinking since you'll land in New York we'll keep you there for a few months at least. You can visit museums, galleries, and the theater. And you can go shopping and out for walks along Broadway and the Battery."

Harriet raised her eyebrows at these unfamiliar names.

"They're all very fashionable things to do in New York during your time."

"I'm not particularly fashionable. I won't fit in there, will I?"

"Of course you will! You'll have your inheritance, and Miss Rugg will be by your side to help you." Aurelia pulled out several sheets of blank paper and her pen, then started writing.

Esther walked over to the desk and put her hand on Harriet's shoulder.

"How is the story coming along?" she asked.

"It's been a little slow-going, but we're about to pick up speed," Aurelia replied. "We've got Harriet and Miss Rugg to New York, and I think we'll keep them there for a while. I was just telling Harriet about all the things they can do there—the theater and galleries. We'll keep them occupied."

"Have you ever been to the theater, Harriet?" Esther asked.

"No, never."

"Oh, you'll love it!" Aurelia insisted. "It's like seeing the world through someone else's eyes for a few hours."

Aurelia continued writing and missed the glance that Harriet and Esther exchanged.

42

Aurelia rode the high of the first lecture's success throughout the following day. It was quiet in the shop after yesterday's excitement, but she was encouraged when someone came in to ask about the poster that was still in the window, and whether there would be any other events in the future.

She was able to confirm that there would be, since Professor Marquez had already called to let her know that one of his Ph.D. students wanted to present a portion of her dissertation on a seventeenth-century author, Aphra Behn. At first, Aurelia thought it might be a little esoteric for her customers, but then she remembered seeing Mrs. Smith nod in interest at some of the more complicated points Professor Marquez had discussed the night before. Maybe it would be right up their alley after all.

Over the next week, during nights and days in the shop, Aurelia continued writing about Harriet's adventures in America. She was drawn to the idea that Harriet, at just nineteen, would have the world open to her to explore. Not to mention, Harriet's invented inheritance and the fact that she was unmarried gave her a freedom that few women of Harriet's time would have been able to enjoy.

Once Aurelia had wrapped up writing about Harriet's stay in New York City, she began researching where Harriet might travel next.

"There was a regular route for tourists up the Hudson River by steamboat," she told Harriet one evening. "You can stop in Albany and other towns along the way until you reach Saratoga Springs."

"Another boat ride?" Harriet asked, frowning.

"Yes, but you can get on and off this one, so it won't be as bad as your trip across the Atlantic. And once you arrive in Saratoga Springs you can stay for a bit."

"What will we do there?"

"It's a spa town, so there will be other visitors to meet and lovely walks around the countryside. We can have you take a trip to Niagara Falls from there. Have you heard of the Falls?"

"Yes," Harriet on a soft sigh.

"Great—then you know they're supposed to be amazing!"

Aurelia tried for her most encouraging tone, taking Harriet's response as a sign that she was still struggling to believe that writing about these adventures meant that she'd actually get to experience them.

"The Falls aren't far from Saratoga, and it seems a shame to have you so close without going to see them," Aurelia continued.

"Alright," Harriet said, sighing again.

"I've heard of this Saratoga Springs," John Jarndyce interjected. He'd been tuning in and out of their conversation as he chatted with David and Joe. "It's something like Bath, only smaller."

"That's right," Aurelia agreed. "It was a popular spot for people who wanted to escape the city and sort of get back to nature. Though it wasn't exactly wild country—just more rural than New York City."

"As for Niagara Falls, I have read that one may climb into caverns behind the water. The noise is said to be terrific—nearly deafening," David added.

"Deafening?" Harriet said softly. "Caverns? I shouldn't like to go into any caverns, I don't think."

"But it sounds so exciting!" Aurelia said, once again trying her best to be encouraging.

"I've seen waterfalls before, in Switzerland," Harriet said. "I suppose I don't need to see another one?"

"Nonsense!" Aurelia chastised. "The Falls are practically one of the wonders of the world. They're much bigger than anything you would have seen in Switzerland."

With that, Aurelia began writing. Harriet watched her pen move across the page for a few minutes, then stood and walked over to join Esther and Pip. Aurelia registered movement as Harriet walked away, then lost herself again in the adventures she was spinning.

43

It had been just over a week since Aurelia and Louisa first sat down to discuss Harriet's story, and now they were set to meet that afternoon at the same café to discuss the chapters Aurelia had shared. Aurelia was a little nervous as the hours ticked by and their meeting drew closer, but still nothing near as anxious as she'd been to hear Oliver's notes.

Louisa had arrived first again and had a teapot, two mugs, and two slices of cake waiting for her.

"I figured you wouldn't mind?" Louisa asked, gesturing to the cake and tea as Aurelia took a seat.

"No, this is excellent, thanks. I can tuck in without having to wait."

They caught up for a few minutes while starting in on their cake, and then Louisa reached into a bag at her side and pulled out Aurelia's chapters. They were slightly tidier than the typical stack of pages that Oliver used to return to her—no dog-ears or sticky notes poking up from the top. But Aurelia did notice that Louisa had several lined pages clipped to the front with notes scrawled in neat, careful handwriting.

"So, you've read it?" Aurelia asked, her nervousness returning.

"I have. But first I read *Little Dorrit* since I'd never read it before. It was great—a little softer than *Bleak House*, in a way? I see why you were inspired by it."

Aurelia nodded, waiting.

"The last time we met, you were telling me why you wanted to write about Harriet, why she meant so much to you as a character." Louisa paused. "But when I read through *Little Dorrit* and then your chapters, there was a bit of a disconnect for me."

"A disconnect?" Aurelia repeated.

She had to admit she'd been hoping for high praise despite her nerves. Now she felt emptied out, her stomach no longer working itself into knots but instead devoid of any feeling.

"Yeah. She's this fiery, passionate creature in *Little Dorrit*. But I'm just not getting that in these chapters."

"Well, there's just not a lot for her to get worked up about at the beginning," Aurelia said, though she knew instantly that Louisa was right. Even in the most recent chapters she'd been writing, Harriet was moving along without much of the spark she'd had in *Little Dorrit*. But, she told herself, that was just a reflection of how she'd been in the shop—quiet, agreeable, without a lot to say about what Aurelia was writing.

"I guess that's true," Louisa said, scrunching up her face as she thought about it. "But overall, there's just something missing here. I wondered—and I know you said you really wanted to write about Harriet—but I wondered if maybe you could focus on Miss Rugg instead?"

"Miss Rugg?" Aurelia repeated, trying to follow Louisa despite still being stuck back at her first comment—*a bit of a disconnect.*

"You seem to have really connected with Miss Rugg in these chapters. I liked getting to see more of who she is and loved that she was up for setting off on this trip, jumping at the chance to put her broken engagement behind her."

"But Harriet's getting a new start, too," Aurelia said mechanically.

"She is, yeah. But it's different somehow. Miss Rugg seems game for it, but Harriet... I don't know. She used to get dragged along on all those trips with the Meagleses, and I got the sense she didn't really like traveling."

"She didn't like traveling as their maid, being stuck serving Pet and having to eat her meals separately from the family. But I don't think she hated traveling full stop," Aurelia said, hating the defensiveness that had crept into her voice.

"Maybe," Louisa said, unconvinced. "What if you reversed things? Have Miss Rugg inherit the money and invite Harriet to join her? Or have Miss Rugg find someone else to go with her?"

"But what about Harriet?"

"I'm just not that drawn to her as a main character. At least not as she is here," Louisa said, putting her hand on the pages in front of her. Aurelia instantly recalled Oliver reaching out a hand in just that way and what it had signaled.

"Have you talked to Oliver about the chapters?" Aurelia asked, trying to keep her voice steady.

"No—did you want me to?"

"No. No, I didn't. It's just that you have some similar feedback. He doesn't like Harriet, either. Or at least not as I've written her."

Louisa nodded sympathetically, seeming to appreciate that her feedback, combined with Oliver's, was difficult for Aurelia to hear.

"I think you're a great writer," Louisa said encouragingly. "I'd like to see some of the changes I've mentioned in the next draft. But I'm not worried that you're not capable, so that's a relief as an editor. I know you've got it in you to write a really good story, and so do you since you've done it before."

"Count Vronsky's story," Aurelia said flatly.

"That's a fantastic book, Aurelia," Louisa said. "Dig back into these chapters and remind yourself that you've got the skills to work out these kinks and get another great story on paper."

Aurelia nodded, her eyes on the dregs of their tea things littered across the table. Louisa was silent and Aurelia realized she was waiting for her to respond.

"I do want to focus on Harriet. But I'll try to find a way to give her more of a... a spark, as you said."

"Okay. You do that and let me know when you're ready for me to take a look at your revisions."

"I will," Aurelia said, attempting a smile.

Walking back to the shop, Aurelia tried to keep the tears she felt building from letting loose. It was harder to ignore when two different people had given her the same feedback—*this doesn't sound like Harriet*—but Aurelia didn't know what to do about it. Harriet had agreed to everything she'd written. She wasn't sure how to draw

Harriet out more, given how much she'd struggled to come up with her own ideas or accept that *any* idea was possible.

Unlocking the shop door and settling back down at her desk—after greeting Fezz in the armchair and Biscuit stretched out below it—Aurelia began to think through how she might rework things to bring out more of the passionate nature that Harriet had shown in *Little Dorrit*.

44

Saturday found Aurelia at her desk, still trying to work out how to fix whatever she'd bungled with Harriet's story. She hadn't told Oliver about Louisa's feedback yet—she was too embarrassed. Not to admit that he'd been right, but to admit that she didn't have quite as much of a grasp on Harriet's character as she'd been insisting. And she was equally embarrassed to think what Dickens' most Dickensian character would think about how she'd handled one of his characters, so she hadn't told David either.

After a few hours at her desk with only a handful of customers having come in and out to distract her, Aurelia heard Oliver padding down the spiral staircase, Biscuit at his heels. She looked up to see he had his coat in hand.

"Where are you off to, then?"

"Jack's invited me over to watch football."

"Football? I'm not sure I've ever seen you watch a game. Any game, really," she said, repressing a laugh.

"Not exactly top of my list, but he asked and I didn't want to say no."

Aurelia stood and walked over to give him a kiss.

"I think that's very sweet. Are you going to bring anything?"

"I was going to bring Biscuit," Oliver said, holding up the lead in his hand as proof.

"That's not what I meant," she laughed. "I think you're supposed to bring beer or little bites or something. Isn't that what people do when they're going to watch a game?"

"I think that's just what people do when they're watching American football... I'm not sure." He began turning around as he said, "Maybe I shouldn't bother."

"No! Don't be silly. Just stop in at a shop on your way and buy some crisps or something. You told him you'd go, so you can't back out now. And Biscuit looks like he's up for a day out."

They looked down at the dog, who was looking from one to the other, tail wagging merrily.

"You're a good big brother," she continued, walking him to the door. "I'll expect a full report on the game—the match?—when you get back."

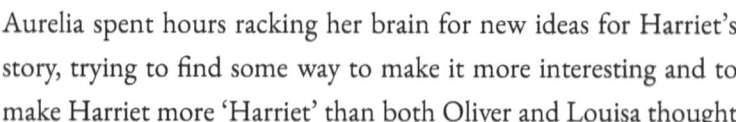

Aurelia spent hours racking her brain for new ideas for Harriet's story, trying to find some way to make it more interesting and to make Harriet more 'Harriet' than both Oliver and Louisa thought

Aurelia had written her. She took a break when Oliver returned and followed him upstairs for dinner and a debriefing on how his day with Jack had been. Although relieved for the distraction Oliver had brought home with him, once they'd finished eating she explained that she needed a few more hours to write in the shop and insisted he shouldn't wait up for her.

Back at her desk, Aurelia hoped inspiration would strike as she flipped through what she'd written so far. But everything felt wrong now. She was starting to see what Louisa and Oliver had been talking about but was at a total loss as to how to fix it. She couldn't exactly take them up on their advice and tell Harriet she wanted to write about a more interesting character. She'd been trying her best; even if it wasn't a story her creative mind had been eager to write, she'd really tried to do right by Harriet. And Marigold, by extension. Aurelia felt panicky at the possibility that she'd failed them both instead of helping.

She looked at the mantel clock: midnight was drawing closer and she was running out of time. Anxious to come up with a fix, she began jotting down ideas that grew further and further away from anything she would have ordinarily suggested for Harriet. But she was desperate to find some way to salvage Harriet's story, no matter how outlandish.

As the characters appeared and Aurelia greeted each of them, she became uneasy. Once she and Harriet sat down at her desk, Aurelia decided to present her new ideas to Harriet as a thrilling change, rather than something she felt forced to do in order to make her a more compelling character on the pages of her new story.

"I've been plotting, Harriet," Aurelia began. "We've got you traveling to some well-known tourist spots in America. But there's not much drama there. Everyone is well-behaved, nice, and—well, a little boring."

Harriet stared at Aurelia, seeming to sense she had more to say.

"I thought maybe we could shake things up a bit. Maybe instead of sending you to Saratoga Springs and Niagara Falls, or having you go to the theater in the city, maybe we should send you straight out west, to the frontier."

"The frontier," Harriet repeated.

"Yes! Out where things were still unsettled, uncharted. You could be part of the early settlers who helped create new towns and cities." Aurelia tried to sound upbeat and eager, but Harriet looked entirely unconvinced. "You could really make a new life there, make it whatever you like!"

"I don't... I don't know," Harriet said, sounding annoyed rather than uncertain.

"I think this could be a great adventure for you. Much more exciting than just staying in hotels and seeing the sights."

"*Much* more exciting!" David burst out, walking over to them while rubbing his hands together like a gleeful villain.

"I don't—" Harriet began again but ended with a sigh as she shook her head.

Aurelia started digging through the scattered notes on her desk as she continued, "I've been working out some ideas about what you could see and do. Let me show you."

"Excellent! This is just what I've been hoping for," David said happily. "A story needs action, intrigue, and a little danger to keep readers on their toes."

"Danger?" Harriet and Aurelia said together.

"Just the threat of it, of course. Enough to make the reader worry only to ease their minds once you come out alright in the end."

Aurelia considered this before nodding and turning back to her notes.

"A little danger then," she agreed. "Or the threat of it, anyway."

"No," Harriet said quietly.

Too quietly, since Aurelia didn't hear her as she continued lifting pages and tossing them aside, trying to find the ideas she thought were most likely to pique Harriet's interest.

"No," Harriet said, this time a little louder.

"What's that?"

"No," Harriet said resolutely, standing as she spoke. "No, no, no, no, no!"

She was shouting now and had Aurelia's full attention at last.

"'No' *what*?" Aurelia asked, looking as perplexed as she felt.

"No to traveling west. No to New York, no to the blasted Hudson River. No to America! And *no* to adventure!"

Harriet's cheeks were flushed and there was no doubt now that she was angry. Very angry. David took a step back, holding up his hands as if to ward her off.

"Alright, okay," Aurelia said, trying to get her bearings. "You don't want to go west. I sort of had it plotted out, you going out there, but, okay... I can try to make something else work."

"No, Aurelia! No more plotting or planning. I don't want any of it!" Harriet had begun pacing the shop floor, from the desk to the front door and back again. "This was supposed to be *my* story, but you've filled it with long travels and boat rides and strangers. It's nothing like me! It's nothing that I want!"

Aurelia's mouth hung open and she blinked as she took in Harriet's words. The other characters exchanged glances but otherwise remained silent as they watched the scene that was unfolding.

"But... I asked... You said okay to America, okay to New York—"

"You wanted me to go away, and I didn't want to go to Egypt again, or France or Italy, and I was running out of options. Better America than the moon!"

"Why didn't you tell me? I've been writing and writing, thinking it was what you wanted!"

"It's nothing like what I want! I traveled with the Meagleses because I had no choice, because it was my job to go with them. I never got to choose where or when, I just had to follow along. I thought letting you write me a new story might help you, that it was something Marigold would have wanted for you, to help you in your grief," Harriet added, softening only slightly. "But as much as I loved Marigold, I don't think she would have wanted this for *me*."

Aurelia's eyes widened. Was it possible that neither one of them had been fully invested in writing her new story? That they'd both done it only because they thought it was what Marigold would have wanted?

"I... I'm sorry, Harriet. I offered to write your story because I really did want to help you. And yes, I thought Marigold would have wanted me to help you too." Aurelia paused as Harriet began her pacing again. "When you couldn't decide where to start, I thought I was helping by giving you a few pushes. And then every time I pushed, you went along with it, so I thought... I thought it was what you wanted," she finished weakly as she remembered all the times she'd taken Harriet's quiet acquiescence as uncertainty—instead of dislike.

"I only agreed to travel because you seemed to want me to. You wanted to send me off on adventures and now I'm stuck in America with Miss Rugg—who I'm certain is nice enough, but I've never met her before and now we're trapped and traveling for months on end, with no return in sight. You have me surrounded by acquaintances and strangers. I'm meeting people on the boat and in New York, but no one is a *friend*."

Harriet's pacing had grown faster as she grew more and more agitated, her hands working into fists at her sides.

"Oh, Harriet…"

Aurelia knew Harriet was right—she hadn't thought of it that way as she'd written new characters for Harriet to meet, but it was true. She hadn't written her into any close friendships. Turning to David, whose own book was peppered with good friends, she saw real sympathy in his eyes as he regarded Harriet.

"I'll write more friends for you! That's no problem. Of course you should have friends. That was… Oh, it was a terrible oversight, but I can fix it."

"No! No more writing. No more fixing anything," Harriet said with a fiery look.

"But…" Aurelia's mind raced to come up with options, even though she'd spent weeks doing just that when Harriet clearly hadn't liked any of them. "But I *can* fix it—we can. If you want to get on a boat back to England, I can write that. I'll do it right now!"

Aurelia, anxious to appease her, moved to her desk to start writing immediately, sensing that Harriet's anger was reaching a fever pitch that threatened an explosion.

"I never wanted to leave England. I don't want you to write me returning, I want you to rip up those pages so that I never left in the first place!" Harriet was passing the small table at the front of the shop yet again, but this time she stopped her pacing and stared down at it. Her breathing was fast and her chest was heaving as she took great gulps of air. "Better yet, I'll go back myself!"

Harriet reached out a hand to try and knock the stack of copies of *Little Dorrit* from the table, but her hand passed right through them, dissolving into a sweep of white studded with scattered words before resolving back into her hand once again. Harriet tried again and again but she couldn't budge the books. She stomped her foot, threw back her head, and released a shout at the ceiling.

Esther rushed over to her, reaching out an arm to try and calm her.

"It's no use, Esther!" Harriet exclaimed, tears falling down her cheeks now as she moved away. "I want to go back. I'd rather be miserable in my old life than pretend I have any hope of a future." She brushed the tears from her cheeks and turned to face Aurelia. "Send me back, Aurelia! I want to go back. Now!"

"I... Please, Harriet—I've never taken a book off the table like that." Aurelia walked toward her and then stopped, unsure whether being near her would calm or inflame her. "If I take it off tonight, I'm not sure that we'd be able to get you back again. Some other characters from your book might appear instead."

"You wouldn't want to leave us, would you, Harriet?" Peggotty asked, worrying her hands together. "Take time to think it over, dear."

"Yes, perhaps in a few hours you'll feel differently. Give it time," Esther said gently.

"I don't need time," Harriet sobbed. "I don't want to count to five and twenty, I want to go home. *Right now!*"

Aurelia struggled to keep up with what was happening. Quiet Harriet, who'd sat beside her all these weeks and barely spoken above a soft murmur, was now shouting and angry—*at her*. She looked around the shop, trying to piece together what Harriet was saying and how to salvage the disaster she'd created.

"Alright, what about this?" Aurelia asked, slowly taking a few steps toward her. "What if I open the door? If I step outside, everyone, you included, will go back into your books. Then tomorrow night, if you still don't want to be here, I'll take your book off the table."

Harriet looked at Aurelia, her breath ragged with her crying.

"I promise, if that's what you want, I'll do it." Aurelia's heart was breaking to see her so upset. "But please—give us a chance to talk again tomorrow night?"

Harriet closed her eyes for a long moment and nodded. Aurelia looked around at the others.

"I'll open the door then." She tried for a calm, reassuring tone, though she felt anything but calm. "Once I step outside, you'll be pulled back into your books. Alright?"

They nodded, everyone looking shellshocked by Harriet's passionate outburst. As Aurelia reached up to unlock the door, she registered that her hands were shaking. She looked back at all of them, wishing she could think of something heartening to say, but nothing came to her. She opened the door, stepped outside, and pulled it closed as she peeked back into the shop. The characters immediately melted into mist, drawn back into their books and lives, leaving the shop behind.

Aurelia waited until the last swirl of parchment-colored vapor had disappeared, then walked back into the shop, closed and locked the door, and burst into tears.

45

Harriet's angry outburst not only startled Aurelia but gave her yet another solid bit of proof that what Oliver and Louisa had been saying was true: Aurelia had written pages and pages of a story that was much too far off course. By assuming she understood the root of Harriet's lukewarm agreement to her plans, Aurelia had come close to alienating the poor girl completely, rather than helping her find a better ending to her story. And hadn't Aurelia just been teasing Oliver about not recognizing that her silence during their first editing session wasn't a sign that she'd accepted his criticism? It wasn't until he knew her better that he understood she'd been both processing his feedback and preparing to pummel him for it. Now Aurelia understood that Harriet's silence had carried its own hidden meaning, one she very much wished she'd tried to interpret sooner.

Even though Aurelia had told herself that it might be hard for Harriet to come up with new ideas when Harriet had been so conditioned not to expect much from life, maybe—very probably—she hadn't been as patient and understanding as she could have been. Harriet had grown up in service, always having to keep her opinions and thoughts to herself, to 'behave.' Speaking up for herself obviously didn't come to her easily, at least not until she'd been pushed to the brink as she so clearly was now.

Aurelia had to face the fact that the problem might have started when she'd begun thinking of Harriet as a project, a task to check off her list so that she could get back to writing her own novel. That wasn't what she'd intended when she took on Harriet's new story, and it hadn't been a conscious goal once she'd started writing—not really. But still, Aurelia's reluctance had been there, even if she'd wanted to help Harriet and do something in honor of Marigold. The inescapable truth was that her reluctance might have ruined any chance Harriet had for a happier ending, and that truth set Aurelia's stomach churning with regret.

When she opened her slightly puffy eyes the next morning, Aurelia was happy to remember that it was a Sunday. The shop would be closed and she would have time to think through how to convince Harriet—and herself—that she could rework a new ending for her. She and Oliver had slept in, finally waking when Biscuit insisted it was time to get out of bed. After a leisurely breakfast, they decided to take the dog for a long walk along the river, giving them an opportunity to take advantage of the sunshine that was beginning to break through a bank of morning clouds.

It was one of those early March days that hinted spring wasn't just coming but had settled in for a good while. As they walked toward the river, Aurelia grew quiet, thinking back over last night's events, Oliver's and Louisa's comments, and questioning how she could have strayed so far from a character she thought she knew so well.

"Hey," Oliver said quietly, putting a hand to her back as they walked. "Are you alright?"

"Me?" Aurelia asked, reorienting herself to the moment. Oliver smiled and raised his eyebrows as he waited for her to answer. "Yeah, I'm fine. Just a lot to think about."

"Like what?"

"Oh, it's nothing. We don't have to talk about it."

"Are you sure?"

"No," Aurelia said, dragging out the word. "I mean, I guess we shouldn't, right?"

Oliver laughed. "What, is it top secret? Do we need to speak in code?"

"No, it's just—I'm thinking about my book. Harriet's story. I'm sort of struggling, but I didn't know if you would want to talk about it—if we should talk about it."

They continued walking, Oliver silent at her side. After a moment, he put a hand out to stop her, then turned her to face him.

"I don't think we should have anything that's off limits," he said, shaking his head. "Do you?"

Aurelia smiled. "I don't," she said, shaking her head in return.

"If you want to talk about your book, I want you to talk about it. I'll try to take off my editor hat and just listen, okay?"

"Okay," Aurelia agreed. "And I won't get tetchy if you criticize it." Oliver raised an eyebrow. "I will try very hard not to get tetchy if you criticize it," she quickly amended.

They both grinned at each other. She put her arm around him as they continued walking, and he did the same. Her heart swelled and she was distracted for a moment by new and welcome thoughts of how much she loved this man walking beside her. She had yelled at him, fired him, and here he was, still standing by her side, not holding a grudge.

"So, why are you struggling? What's going on?"

"It's not working... I've got it all wrong somehow." She paused and Oliver waited for her to continue. "You were right. Louisa said the same thing, but I've only just seen it myself. What I was writing wasn't true to Harriet, to what she wants—or what she would want," Aurelia corrected herself. "I'm not sure what happened, but... I think a part of me liked the idea of a woman of that period having a total blank slate, total independence to go anywhere, be anything she wanted. But I see now that even if that's the kind of future that would interest one character, that character definitely isn't Harriet."

They had gotten to the river and gravitated toward a bench. Biscuit flopped to the ground to rest as they sat down.

"What was it that made you see it?" Oliver asked.

Aurelia hesitated, wondering how close to the truth she could get. In that moment's hesitation, she realized that she'd just promised him there wouldn't be any 'off limits' topics between them, and here she was, continuing to hide a very big one.

"Aurelia?" he prodded.

"I'm just thinking," she said quietly.

Was this it, then? Was this the moment to tell him everything—no more secrets and sneaking about? She and Oliver were growing closer and closer. They were living together, for goodness' sake. If not now, when? Aurelia sensed that it would only get harder from here if she didn't tell him everything now, or at least soon. But... she wasn't ready for this conversation. She wasn't ready for whatever his reaction might be to hearing that she could see and talk to fictional characters in the shop at night. As much as she loved and trusted him, it always came back to her knowledge that if Oliver told her the same thing, she'd worry that he was having visions or was unwell. And in spite of the fact that she knew he loved and trusted her in return, his reaction wouldn't be—couldn't be—as simple as saying 'I believe you.'

Still, as necessary as they were, the secrets and lies were starting to hurt.

Taking in a deep breath, she once again reached for something close to the truth without hitting on it directly.

"Um... Well, you know how I've said I feel like I know my characters, like I hear them talking to me?" She looked to Oliver and he nodded. "Last night Harriet didn't just talk to me—she shouted. I guess I hadn't really been listening for her voice, but I suddenly heard it, loud and clear."

Oliver smiled.

"I won't judge you if you say 'I told you so,'" Aurelia said. "I absolutely have it coming."

"No, I won't say it," he said, picking up her hand and twining his fingers with hers. "Sometimes it's easier to see things from the outside." He shrugged his shoulders. "Especially when I come to it with no preconceived notions or plans. A writer has to spend time thinking out what should happen, when, and how... It can be hard to step back from that."

"Well, now I've stepped back, but I don't know how to rework it," Aurelia said with a humorless laugh. "I was so locked in on this one way forward. I thought it would give her all these opportunities, but now, if she doesn't want opportunities, what sort of story am I supposed to write?"

They were both quiet for a while, looking out toward the river.

"Try reading through *Little Dorrit* again," Oliver suggested. "Skim through some of Dickens' other novels too. You have that selection on the table in the shop—maybe looking at his storylines for other characters will give you some ideas for Harriet?"

Aurelia frowned as she considered this. She'd looked through *Little Dorrit* but that had been a few weeks ago. Maybe it wouldn't hurt to review it again. And while she wasn't sure how the other novels might help, at least Oliver's suggestion was better than floundering with no plan at all.

"I'll do that," she said, nodding decisively. "I'll give it a try this afternoon."

She'd have to. Harriet had only promised to give Aurelia one more night before giving up on the whole project.

When they got back to the flat, Oliver changed to meet David and James while Aurelia gathered up her copies of *Little Dorrit*, *Great Expectations*, *Bleak House*, and *David Copperfield*. She'd been planning to join everyone for drinks, but she needed to make some headway on resolving her Harriet dilemma before seeing the characters again that night.

After waving Oliver off, she pulled out a new notebook and pen, then brought the lot of it down to the window seat in the shop. As she paged through *Little Dorrit*, she was reminded of how young Harriet was—still a child, really, despite the fact that she was nineteen. Although she'd been unhappy with the Meagleses, she didn't just run away; instead, she'd gone to Miss Wade for protection. When that didn't work, she went back to the Meagleses rather than strike out on her own. Aurelia now understood that Harriet wasn't in search of adventure so much as company. But how to find the right kind of company to make her happy?

After paging through the books for hours, Aurelia hadn't come up with any brilliant ideas, and the minutes to midnight were ticking past. What she needed now—apart from a brilliant idea—was time. And so, rather than join the characters at midnight, Aurelia decided she needed another day to think through what she would say to Harriet to convince her that she was willing to really listen to her this time. That would also give her time to find a new idea that would interest Harriet more than everything she'd offered up to now.

Last night's emergency maneuver gave Aurelia an idea: she waited until just before midnight, then stepped outside the shop and waited on the pavement, bringing Biscuit with her to avoid any barking that might wake Oliver. With her ear to the door, Aurelia listened for the clock at the back of the shop to chime midnight. After waiting a few extra minutes for good measure, she went back inside. No one had appeared. It was empty save for Fezz, who was curled up in the armchair and oblivious to Aurelia's and the dog's footsteps padding up the spiral staircase to bed.

46

Pouring rain had replaced the previous day's sunshine. Aurelia didn't mind the change in weather, though, since she knew it would keep customers away and give her a chance to continue coming up with options for Harriet's story.

Sitting at her desk in the quiet shop, Aurelia moved on from *Little Dorrit* to skim through the other books from the table. Pip and David had lived abroad and also had unique experiences at home in England. Esther had stayed in England throughout her novel, though she met an intriguing cast of characters and had unique experiences of her own. Each of them had described their lives in honest detail, sharing their happiest moments but also moments that caused them shame and embarrassment. Their stories and the characters they described were unmistakably Dickensian—he never seemed to spare anyone with his pen—but Esther, David, and Pip still managed to tell their stories with a distinct voice and perspective.

Aurelia had been looking out the window, her eyes staring through the rain to the square beyond, when her brain caught onto something in that train of thought. She looked around the shop, almost as if trying to find the idea so she could pin it down. Standing, she walked quickly to the shelves that housed all the shop's copies of Dickens' books and began pulling down one of each title. Her heart started racing as her thoughts took shape.

Carrying the books back to her desk in a tall, heavy stack, she set them down and began paging through them, one by one. *Hard Times*: third person narrator. *Our Mutual Friend*: third person narrator. *Little Dorrit*: third person narrator. On and on, and all the same: omniscient, unidentified third person narrators. All but three, that is, and they were on the table: *Great Expectations*, *Bleak House*, and *David Copperfield*, all of which were narrated in the first person by Pip, Esther, and David.

Aurelia squinted across the shop to stare at the table. Was that why she and Harriet had struggled to find common ground on her story all along? Was Harriet supposed to write the story herself? Maybe that's why Harriet hadn't been able to tell Aurelia what she wanted—she needed to put things into her own words, her own voice.

"That's it," Aurelia said aloud, startling both Fezz and Biscuit. She smiled, certain she'd figured out what had to happen next. Her face fell, however, when she realized she couldn't just hand Harriet a pen and paper—she wouldn't be able to hold them. Having Harriet narrate aloud to Aurelia wasn't ideal, either, since it would put Aurelia in the middle again.

The rain had begun to let up, and Mark arrived for a visit. Aurelia didn't mind the distraction now, knowing she had at least come up with what seemed like the best possible pitch to keep Harriet from leaving the shop for good.

47

Just before midnight that night, Aurelia stood in front of the table in the shop, spinning the pretend wedding ring around her finger and hoping Harriet would let her explain her plan before demanding that Aurelia make good on her promise to take *Little Dorrit* off the table.

The characters barely finished materializing before Aurelia blurted out, "Harriet, I'm sorry!"

Everyone turned at the sound of her voice, then looked to see what Harriet would do or say. There was tension in the air as all eyes focused on Harriet, but she stood silently watching Aurelia, who took it as a sign to keep going.

"I was a bully. When you didn't say what you wanted, I went ahead and did what *I* decided you'd want. I didn't mean to upset or control you—I really just... I got caught up in my own ideas." Aurelia paused. She couldn't be sure, but it looked as though Harriet's face was softening. "Please forgive me?"

Harriet worked her hands for a moment, then let them drop. "I forgive you, Aurelia."

"Oh, thank you! Thank you, Harriet." They smiled at each other, and Aurelia took a step closer. "I don't suppose you'd be willing to hear yet another idea of mine? Not an idea for what should happen in your story," Aurelia added quickly, "but an idea about how to write it—*who* should write it."

"Alright." Harriet nodded. "I'm willing." Her confidence seemed to have grown now that she and Aurelia were on equal footing again. There were no quiet or resigned responses from her tonight.

"I've realized something," Aurelia began. "We have three people in this shop—David, Esther, and Pip—who all wrote their own stories. They describe what happened to them from the present, looking back on their pasts. What if you write your own story—you, not me—describing your future the way that *you* want to live it?"

Harriet thought it over, then said, "But I've never written a book before."

"That's alright. Don't worry about what it should or shouldn't be. You can just write whatever you like, however you'd like to write it."

Although Aurelia meant what she said, she had a sudden realization about this new plan. Would Harriet write something that would be publishable? What if it turned out to be a handful of pages? Or a thousand? And if Harriet wasn't a strong writer, then whatever she wrote might be good enough to set her on a new path, but perhaps not good enough for Louisa to agree to publish it. *Well,* she told herself, *too late now.* She'd have to figure it out once the story was written.

"I can help," David was saying. "I've written a book or two myself, as you know."

"I would be happy to help you, as well," Esther joined in. "You will find it quite manageable once you become accustomed to the process."

"There is one thing we need to work out..." Aurelia started before hesitating. "I'm not sure how you'll actually put any words on paper since you can't hold a pen here. I was thinking you could bring your own, but you'd have to remember to bring it back with you each night—otherwise it'll disappear from the shop like Peggotty's buttons."

Peggotty and the others laughed. Her lost buttons, which flew from her dress like projectiles whenever she laughed or made a sudden movement, would disappear each dawn along with the characters, floating up from the various hidden corners of the shop to rejoin Peggotty back in her book.

"Unfortunately, I do not believe Harriet could bring her writing home. I have often jotted down notes and ideas while in the shop," David said, pulling out his notebook. "But when I return here each night, the pages are empty save what I had written prior to leaving my novel."

"Oh," Aurelia said on a dejected sigh.

"I do wish it weren't so," David said, shaking his head. "There are many ideas I should like to bring back with me for my next story. Sadly, they seem to disappear from my memory as well as my notebook each time I return home."

"If I can't leave paper here, and can't bring it back with me, I won't be able to write my story at all, then," Harriet said, sounding disappointed.

Disappointment seemed like a positive sign—it meant she really did want to try it—though Aurelia still didn't know what to do.

"There is one possibility," Pip said slowly. "Joe and I used to sit together with a slate and pencil on the marshes." Pip paused, looking to Joe and raising his eyebrows questioningly.

"Aye, Pip!" Joe said excitedly, seeming to catch on. "That's it!"

"What is?" Harriet asked.

"I would write on the slate to show Joe what I had learned." Everyone was silent, waiting for Pip to connect the dots. He pointed to Harriet and continued. "Since we always know we're about to leave our stories and appear in the shop a moment or two before it happens, that would give you enough time to gather up a paper and pencil from your novel. You could use that to write in the shop, and Aurelia could look over your shoulder and write out your words with her own pen and paper. The words will be yours, but Aurelia will be able to keep them here after you return to your novel each day."

"That could work, Pip!" Aurelia turned to Harriet. "I could just copy down whatever you write—word for word, no changes—and keep it here until it's finished."

Harriet nodded, her eyebrows furrowed as she thought it through: writing her own story, having Aurelia copy it, being in charge of her own fate.

"On second thought," Aurelia added suddenly, "Pip said I could look over your shoulder as you write, but maybe it would be more comfortable for you if we let you write for a bit, and then I can copy what you've written just before dawn. That might help you feel a little freer to write what you like."

They all waited in anticipation as Harriet began pacing the shop, considering the plan. Soon, she stopped and looked around at everyone.

"I'll do it," she said, smiling. "I'll write my own story, just like Esther. And you, David—and Pip." Her smile grew as everyone gathered around to congratulate her.

Smiling along with the others, Aurelia released a long exhalation. As much as she was relieved to have won Harriet's forgiveness, she was also happy to know that she hadn't stopped her from getting a chance to live a better future. Now it would be up to Harriet to decide what that future would hold.

48

Aurelia's happy mood lasted until a few days later, when Oliver's mother called and invited them to dinner. It was an invitation she'd been both dreading and anticipating with some curiosity.

Although his parents were divorced and each had remarried, they still seemed to operate as a unit. His mother, for example, had extended the invitation to Aurelia as something '*we'd* love,' as in, 'We'd love to have you two for dinner.' Oliver had explained that 'we' was an overinclusive term that could mean his mother and father; his mother and stepfather; or his mother, stepfather, father, and stepmother.

Never having met all four in one go, Aurelia was relieved to hear that Jack would be joining them too since she thought his presence might diffuse the parents' attention. The three of them had decided to drive to the family dinner in one car. Making plans together definitely seemed like a good sign for the brothers—they'd even met for coffee earlier in the week.

Oliver was somewhat quiet on the drive, though that might have been because Jack was busy filling Aurelia in on what lay in store for her that evening.

"Mum isn't much of a cook, but Geoff will have put on something good. What do you think, Oliver? Two puddings?"

"Either two puddings or three sides," Oliver said.

"Last time I brought a girl home it was two puddings. Has he ever done three sides?"

"Um, once or twice," Oliver said, looking embarrassed.

From that, Aurelia guessed he'd brought a girlfriend or two home in his day, and she put her hand on his arm to reassure him she wasn't jealous. He seemed to relax and took his eyes from the road for a moment to give her a smile.

"Loads of food, got it," she confirmed. "So, it's Johanna and Geoff. Then your dad's Michael and he's married to Ellie."

Hearing Jack and Oliver refer to them as 'Mum' and 'Dad' hadn't quite locked their actual names in Aurelia's memory, and she was nervous she'd slip up and call someone the wrong thing.

"You've got it," Jack said.

"I'm guessing this won't be as chaotic as my family gatherings?" she asked Oliver.

"Well, no kids running around. But six—now seven—adults trying to coordinate drinks and food—"

"And seating arrangements," Jack interjected.

"—can get a bit…"

"I think the word he's looking for is, actually, chaotic," Jack laughed.

As they pulled into the driveway, Aurelia thought she spotted a few faces peering out of windows before the front door opened and all four parental units spilled outside. They waved and nudged each other, making Aurelia smile at their shared conspiracy even though she knew it was about her.

Stepping out of the car, she waved back and then headed for Oliver's mum, the only one of the four she'd met before. Handing her flowers and a bottle of wine, Aurelia was pleased when his mother's face opened into a broad smile. On the two occasions they'd met, his mother had been a touch reserved, making Aurelia wonder what had happened between then and now to make her so effusive.

"No traffic?" Johanna asked.

"No, it was easy going," Oliver said, giving her a hug.

Jack hugged her next and her smile grew.

"You came together," she observed, more of a statement than a question.

"We were coming from the same direction," Oliver explained. "Made sense to go in one car."

What a few weeks ago might have been a dismissive tone, Aurelia noticed, was softer now. Their mother seemed to notice it, as well.

"It does," she said, eyes traveling over all of them. "It does."

Aurelia watched as Oliver and Jack greeted their assorted parents, then stepped forward as Oliver reached out a hand to lead her over for introductions. Everyone insisted on hugging her, and she was happy to oblige.

"Come in, come in," Geoff called out, putting his hand on Aurelia's shoulder as he led her inside.

Geoff was warm and loud, seeming to draw Johanna out from what might otherwise have been a quieter shell. Michael and Ellie were a bit more stoic, though Aurelia wasn't sure if that was just because they weren't the ones hosting this time around.

The house was clean with a hint of clutter here and there. Johanna and Geoff had lived in the house for years and Aurelia was looking forward to seeing the room Oliver had lived in from the time he was a teenager. Johanna offered to give her a tour, but Geoff wanted them to eat first since dinner was ready. As it turned out, he'd made not just three sides, but also two puddings, leading Oliver and Jack to exchange raised eyebrows and a burst of laughter each. Johanna looked between them, smiling through her confusion.

"Apparently this much food is a sign that I'm a popular girlfriend," Aurelia told her in an undertone. "They gave me the inside scoop on the way here."

"Did they?" Johanna asked, disbelieving.

"They were practically taking bets on whether I'd rate high enough for one pudding or two." Johanna opened her mouth to protest, so Aurelia reassured her, "No, it was all in good fun."

"Is Aurelia telling you how I gave her a brilliant idea for her shop?" Jack asked from the other end of the table.

"What's this?" Michael asked. "A brilliant idea from this one?"

"Yes, try to contain your surprise," Jack deadpanned, still grinning. "Just ask her."

"It's true—all credit to Jack. He suggested I host a lecture series at the shop and invite professors and grad students to come in and talk about different books. We had the first one a few weeks ago and it went off really well."

"That's great," Michael said, no longer teasing.

"I think the customers really liked it. We're having the next one in a few weeks' time."

"We should go in for it," Ellie suggested. "All of us."

"We should!" Geoff agreed. "It would give us a chance to see the shop, and where you're living now."

"The shop's not that big," Oliver began to protest.

"Nonsense," Aurelia said, smiling at his effort to spare her. Then, turning back to his parents, she added, "Remind me and I'll give you the date and time before we leave."

"Oh—I met that friend of yours, Kali, at the lecture. Did she tell you?" Jack asked.

"No, but I saw you talking to her."

"She runs museum tours for little ones, explaining the artwork to kids," Jack told the others. "She's going to come by the theater so I can give the kids a tour behind the scenes. We thought they might like seeing the curtain go up and down, and watching us move the sets on and off stage."

"I bet they'll love that!" Johanna exclaimed.

"Backstage might be a little dangerous for children," Oliver said, his eyebrows drawing together.

"No, we'll clear things up before they arrive, make sure there aren't any *Phantom of the Opera*-type mishaps."

"I suppose... You're right," Oliver allowed after a moment. "That could be great fun for them."

Aurelia reached out and took hold of his hand under the table.

49

After dinner, Oliver gave Aurelia a tour of the house, ending in his childhood bedroom. As expected, there were books in every corner. It was more of a guest room now, so the bits and pieces of his youth weren't as obvious as they might have been, but she could still imagine him sitting at the desk doing his homework, or sprawled out on the floor reading.

He led her over to a bookcase and took down a framed photograph of three young children. Leaning into him, she looked down at their faces.

"That's you," she said quietly, pointing. "Jack... and Lottie?"

"Mm-hmm. I was probably nine or ten years old there. That was our old backyard."

They looked caught in a moment, as though they'd paused only to indulge the photographer before running off to continue their game or adventure. Aurelia felt a smile pull at her mouth as she looked at Oliver's young face, which appeared both happy and serious as he sat in the middle, his arms slung around Jack and Lottie. He had four living parents to Aurelia's one, but she had the sister he'd lost. Life was funny, that way—giving and taking and making you adjust, constantly adjust.

"You all look very sweet. Well, Jack has a little frown in his eyes, doesn't he?"

Oliver let out a breath of a laugh and said, "He wanted the family cat in the photo, but she wouldn't oblige."

"Sounds like Fezz—everything on his own terms."

"That's most cats, isn't it? Not like Biscuit."

"No one's as obliging as Biscuit," she countered.

"You didn't bring him. You should have," a voice called from behind them.

They turned to see Oliver's mother standing in the doorway.

"You know how Biscuit gets," he said. "I thought it'd be too…"

"Chaotic?" Aurelia offered.

"We don't mind chaos here," Johanna teased. "Though the kitchen is a bit of a disaster."

"We'll come down and help," Aurelia said, moving toward the door.

"No, Oliver can go down," Johanna said, stepping into the room and sweeping her arm as though showing him the way. "Go on."

He hesitated, looking back at Aurelia.

"I'll be down in a minute," she said, sensing that Johanna wanted her to stay behind.

He nodded and headed for the doorway, where his mother pulled a tea towel from her shoulder and handed it to him as he passed.

The two women looked at each other for a moment, each smiling.

Johanna walked toward her, pointing at the framed photograph that Aurelia still held in her hands, and said, "They were beautiful children." Her face took on a faraway look as she stared down at their faces.

"They were," Aurelia agreed. She paused, then added, "Oliver is a really wonderful human, Johanna—and Jack too. I wish I could have met Lottie. I'm so sorry…"

She had felt she ought to say something about Lottie, to acknowledge her in some way, only to realize that she wasn't sure how.

Johanna put her hand on Aurelia's arm.

"Thank you. I wish you could have, too. I'd have liked to see them all here tonight, grown up and sitting together." Johanna looked up at Aurelia, then. "Seeing Oliver and Jack, though—seeing them together… Well, I've seen them together, of course, but not like they are tonight. There's something different between them. And Jack went to your shop, for the lecture… And he said he's been seeing Oliver…" Johanna trailed off, her voice threatening tears.

Aurelia put the photograph back on the shelf and put her arms around Johanna, who froze for a second before gripping her back in a stranglehold of a hug. Tears began pricking at Aurelia's eyes—not from pain, though Johanna's grip was good and strong—but from a release she hadn't known she'd needed. She'd been hugging friends, family, and Oliver for months now, but this was something else. A hug from a mother was just different, and she hadn't realized how much she'd missed it until this very moment.

"I'm sorry about your mum, Aurelia," Johanna said through tears. "I'm sorry about your mum, and Lottie, but I'm so glad you're here. Oliver needed you, I think. No—I *know* he did."

Aurelia's tears spilled onto her cheeks then, and she was embarrassed as she caught her breath in a small sob, but Johanna just patted her shoulder as she kept hugging her.

What startled Aurelia most was that she wasn't shocked at the sudden pain of hearing Johanna refer to her own mother. Instead, it was that she'd almost been wanting her to say it, ever since she'd arrived. Being at Oliver's house, surrounded by his collection of too many parents, had made her feel the absence of her own mother in a way that, for the first time, didn't feel quite so hopeless.

Jack walked into the room and both women turned to him, tears on their faces and arms around each other. He stepped backward, as if to leave, before pausing.

"Everything okay here?"

"Yes. Go away—we're having a moment," Johanna said, patting Aurelia's shoulder again as she spoke. There was a smile in her voice that eased Aurelia's sadness and made her smile too.

"Right," he said, holding his hands up and backing slowly out of the room.

Johanna turned back to Aurelia and her smile widened.

"Next time you're here, I'll have Geoff make you three puddings," she declared with a nod. Then, with a watery laugh, she reached out and gave Aurelia another hug.

50

Before heading back into the city, Aurelia had given Oliver's parents the date for the next lecture and they'd promised to come. Oliver had even suggested that she invite her dad so they could all meet, which set everyone off in excited twittering about how they could all go out to dinner afterward and get to know each other. It was another big step—introducing the parents—but Aurelia and Oliver were both taking it in stride.

Aurelia was aiming for the same sanguine approach to her evenings with the characters. Nearly a week had gone by since Harriet had decided to write her own story, and though she was no closer to getting started on it, Aurelia was determined not to push her. Instead, she wanted to let Harriet come to it in her own time. David, on the other hand, felt no restraint and offered his ideas in a near-constant stream. The other characters often intervened, drawing Harriet away for a chat to give her a break from David's incessant drive to create.

Although she knew Harriet didn't want a grand adventure, Aurelia still thought she might be tempted by a smaller one, like starting her own business, running her own school, or buying a large estate to manage. Each of those would have been a major undertaking for a woman in Harriet's time, but Aurelia knew Harriet could tackle a challenge and conquer it. Harriet, however, politely vetoed each idea, and—this time—Aurelia was quick to take Harriet's no for an answer.

The other David in Aurelia's life—the one that existed outside the shop during daylight hours—had invited her to dinner that Saturday, specifying that they'd be leaving James and Oliver to fend for themselves. As always when David suggested they meet over a meal, Aurelia had been careful to confirm they'd be going to a restaurant instead of David and James's flat. David had a blog where he parlayed his job as a history teacher into sharing the results of his experiments with historic recipes. He loved testing them out on James and Aurelia, and even his students, but the results could be hit or miss.

When she reminded him of this as they sat down to dinner, he rolled his eyes at her.

"I've only served you something inedible once," he insisted.

"Twice."

"That's not bad, actually," David speculated. "Considering how often I'm in the kitchen."

"You're a very good cook when you're not subjecting me to your medieval cooking research." Seeing his mouth opening in protest, Aurelia added, "Some of those have been pretty good. Just weird-looking. Or with some odd name or mystery ingredient. But good!"

"Which is the perfect introduction to my main topic for this evening," he said importantly, taking a dramatic pause. "James wants to publish a cookbook with the recipes I've covered in my blog."

"Oh, I love that!"

"Really?"

"Definitely. You've done the work already, haven't you? Experimenting and then writing up your posts. It's all there, ready to go."

"James thinks I could do some 'light' editing to the posts and then write up an introduction for each time period. What do you think?"

"I told you—I think it's brilliant."

"No, what do you think about James and me working on it *together*?"

"I see," Aurelia said slowly, her face breaking into a wry smile. "You're asking because I failed miserably at the editor/writer/relationship thing with Oliver?"

"Exactly."

She gave him a hard stare, but her mouth betrayed her as it quirked into a smile.

"I'm not sure I like being your expert on failed working relationships, but I suppose I might as well share my hard-earned wisdom with my best friend."

"That's the spirit."

"Let's see… The posts are good, but you'll need to edit them to make them work as a book, which means James is going to tell you to cut things and move things around. Now, take a moment," Aurelia advised. "Does the thought of that make you angry, or panicked, or ready to run from the room?"

"No," David said, shaking his head decisively. "I'm not precious about my posts. He can tear them up if he wants to."

"Then I say go for it," Aurelia laughed. "I'm much too precious, apparently."

"That's it?"

"Well, I guess you'll have to be prepared to talk about it over dinner, at the weekend, on holiday… It'll be hard to escape the project until it's finished."

"Now, *that* could get annoying. But maybe we'll set some boundaries, like 'no book talk after dark'?"

"That's a very wise idea," Aurelia agreed.

They shifted to talking about work and how he was already counting the days until the next school holiday, when he remembered her lecture series.

"James and I are on for the next one. When is it?"

"Two weeks away." She paused. "Oliver's parents are coming, and my dad."

"Are they?" David's eyebrows shot up. "Things are getting serious, hey?"

"We moved in together! Things have been serious for a while now," she said with a laugh.

"How're we feeling?" he asked, his tone more subdued.

"Fine. Great, actually. It just feels very normal—like, of course our parents should meet."

"Not nervous at all?"

"Not really. I don't seem to get nervous with Oliver. Okay, I was a little worried about him moving in..." Aurelia had to remind herself that she couldn't explain why she'd been nervous about having Oliver move into the same place where she chatted with fictional characters each night. "But... once he moved in, everything just felt like it was all working out the way it should, you know? Like he was always supposed to move in and we were always supposed to be together." She looked at David. "So. Thank you again for that."

He smiled at her and sighed contentedly, no sign of humor or teasing in his voice as he said, "You are so very welcome."

51

After another few days, and in spite of the characters' efforts, Harriet still couldn't get started on her new story. Just as before, the possibilities seemed to overwhelm her, which required lots of breaks from brainstorming to reassure her that they would, eventually, find a thread she'd want to follow.

Aurelia woke late on Sunday morning to the smell of bacon frying and the sound of one of her aunt's old records playing. She stretched full across the bed, smiling like a cat in sunshine. Fezz, seeming to sense that she was awake, jumped up and began rubbing his face against hers, purring happily.

"I take it Biscuit is occupied with the bacon?" she asked the cat as she scratched his cheeks.

"Do I hear the dulcet tones of Sleeping Beauty?" Oliver called from the kitchen.

"You do. Do I smell the artery-clogging scent of a Sunday fry-up?" she called back.

"Definitely not, this is all fat-free."

Aurelia laughed, pulling herself out of bed and throwing on a jumper and a pair of leggings she had tossed on the floor the day before. She emerged from the bedroom and stood at the bathroom door. Oliver was standing over the stove, with Biscuit sitting at attention at his feet.

"How much time do I have?"

"Hmm... Enough time to splash some water on your face, but not enough time to shower."

"Got it," she said, and stepped into the bathroom.

Walking into the kitchen a few minutes later, Aurelia joined Oliver at the counter and put her arms around him, her chin resting on his shoulder as he transferred food from the frying pan to their plates.

"You've been holding out. Now that I know what you're capable of, I'll expect a full breakfast every Sunday."

"Oh no, next Sunday I expect breakfast in bed from you."

"Yet reality so rarely meets our expectations," Aurelia said wistfully. The record skipped and she held up her hand. "Wait for it..." The record picked up again a few seconds later. "That song always skips." She started to step away to help bring breakfast to the table when Oliver took hold of her hand.

"What's this?"

Aurelia didn't understand what he was asking at first, then she felt his fingers move over the metal band and she realized—she'd forgotten to take the pretend wedding ring off her finger. It was no wonder as she'd practically been asleep on her feet when she'd climbed into bed after saying goodbye to the characters.

"That... That is a ring."

Her mind was still sluggish from sleep, and she willed it to wake up and help her dig herself out of the mess the ring had put her into.

"Should I meet the man who seems to have proposed to my girlfriend?" Oliver raised a teasing eyebrow. He let go of her hand but didn't move from the kitchen. He was waiting for a response and Aurelia was still trying to invent one.

"I should get around to introducing you, shouldn't I?"

Aurelia let out a short laugh that was entirely unlike her own. She knew she would have to give him more of an explanation. She didn't usually wear rings and suddenly she was wearing something that looked very much like an engagement ring.

"I found it in my jewelry box the other day and thought, 'I never wear rings, why not.'"

The obvious question was, why that finger? It seemed silly to think someone could never wear a ring on that hand without appearing to be engaged or married, but there it was.

"It only fit that finger," she added lamely.

Oliver looked amused by her fluster. He kissed her cheek and carried their plates to the little table by the front windows. Aurelia watched him for a moment, reassuring herself that he'd seemed to accept her explanation, then poured coffee into the mugs he'd set out and followed him. Sitting down, she took a grateful sip of coffee. She was about to change the subject, say something light about tucking into breakfast, when she noticed he was preparing to speak.

He looked thoughtful and Aurelia's brow furrowed as she tried to guess what he might be working up to say.

"Speaking of rings... What are your thoughts about marriage?" Oliver asked.

Aurelia made an effort not to change her expression, which wasn't hard as she couldn't make up her mind which emotion to express. She was confused and curious all at once.

"Are you opposed to the fundamental idea of it," Oliver continued, "or are you in favor?"

She sensed that Oliver was trying to strike a certain tone—serious but not too invested in her answer just in case it came out the opposite of his. He picked up a piece of bacon and took a bite as he waited for her to respond. She smiled at him, her heart swelling a little more with love for him.

"I'm in favor," she said lightly. Then, joking aside, she added, "It's worked out quite well for most of the people in my life."

"Mine too," Oliver said, relaxing a bit. "I mean, at least the second time around for my parents." He pushed his food around the plate with his fork, then continued, "I've always thought it was strange that proposals are meant to be this big surprise. 'Will she say yes?'"

"Right," Aurelia agreed. "A couple should have some idea whether they want to spend their lives together. It seems so odd to think the first time it would come up would be in the midst of some grand, elaborate proposal."

Oliver nodded, staring down at his plate before looking at Aurelia again.

"So... Neither one of us is opposed to the idea of marriage in general."

"Correct." Aurelia took a bite of toast, thinking the topic was over.

"And, in terms of whether you'd want to spend the rest of *our* lives together... Any thoughts on that idea?"

Well, then: topic still very much on the table, Aurelia thought.

She put down her toast and kept her eyes on her plate for a moment, feeling the significance of whatever answer was about to escape her. Raising her eyes to look him full in the face, she blinked as she took in his familiar features. She felt a sudden calm and there was no hesitation when she spoke next.

"I'm very happy with you, Oliver. The idea of spending our lives together has crossed my mind a few times... More than a few times," Aurelia acknowledged with a smile. Now was certainly an occasion for honesty. "And I'm not opposed to the idea of that, either."

He reached over and took her hand. "I'm very happy with you, Aurelia," he said, running his thumb over the back of her hand. "And I'm definitely not opposed to spending our lives together." They smiled at each other, both breaking into grins. Oliver stood and reached across the table to kiss her.

"So, we're both alright with marriage, we're both alright with spending our lives together. What do you reckon?" Aurelia asked.

They kissed again and Oliver sat back in his seat, picking up his fork again. "I reckon we've just had a grand, elaborate proposal."

"We're engaged, then," Aurelia declared, taking it in.

"We are indeed," Oliver agreed. Aurelia reached for her fork and he nodded toward her hand. "We'll have to find you a new ring for that finger."

Leaning back, Aurelia held out her hand to stare at the ring. "You know, I'm not sure I should let this one go. I think this might be a *magic ring*," she said teasingly, turning her hand for Oliver's inspection.

"Magic, is it?"

"Well, it did just make an engagement appear out of thin air."

They ate their breakfast, cleaned up, and got ready for a long walk in Richmond Park with Biscuit. Aurelia kept thinking over how it had happened. Such a small conversation over a small thing—a ring—had transformed them from dating to engaged. It felt like everything and nothing had changed, all at the same time. Mostly, she felt a new sense of comfort in knowing that the person she loved most felt the same way about her. She had known he loved her, of course, but now she knew that he, too, wanted to make it permanent.

Downstairs in the shop, Biscuit started pulling at Oliver, wanting to get outside to start their walk.

"You go ahead," Aurelia said from the spiral staircase, where she was sitting on the bottom step as she pulled on her shoes. "I'll find you in the square."

"Alright—see you in a minute."

Oliver gave her a soppy grin as he stepped through the door, and Aurelia smiled just as soppily back, shoes forgotten while she watched him cross the street toward the square. With a happy sigh, she stood and slipped on her coat as she passed the Recommended Reads table. Looking down at the books, her mind started running over the ideas they'd been working on for Harriet's story, wondering what everyone might come up with when she saw them that night.

At that thought, her smile fell and she froze.

She'd be seeing the characters tonight. The fictional characters she saw most nights at midnight. The people she hadn't yet mentioned to Oliver. Oliver, who had been her boyfriend, and was now her fiancé. Oliver, who would one day be her husband.

They'd just promised each other a lifetime and he was still in the dark about what, exactly, Aurelia's life entailed. She had the sudden, desperate wish to talk to Elinor—a character from *Sense and Sensibility* who had become a friend last year, someone whose advice was always so reasonable and reliable. Aurelia's eye caught on the copies of *Bleak House* that were stacked on the table, and she realized she knew someone whose advice was likely to be just as helpful as Elinor's.

"Aurelia!" Oliver called out as he opened the door, setting the bell ringing and pulling Aurelia out of her thoughts. "Are you with us?"

"Yes! Sorry, here I come."

52

Aurelia rushed through saying hello to the characters that night, confirmed that Harriet didn't have any new ideas about her story, and then practically herded Esther upstairs to the window seat. She was nearly breathless by the time they sat down, and Esther was looking at her as though she might have become slightly unhinged. Which... fair.

"I'm sorry." Aurelia thought it best to begin there. "I've been wanting to talk to you all day and having to wait hours and hours until midnight has been miserable."

"Is something the matter? Have you taken ill?"

"No, I'm fine! Just a little rattled. Something happened today, something really good, but I realized I needed to talk to someone about all of it and you were one of the first people I thought of."

"I would be happy to hear your good news and am very pleased you thought to share it with me."

Esther smiled encouragingly, and Aurelia suspected she was still coming across as a bit off. She took a deep breath and blew it out slowly to center herself.

"Before I can share my good news, I have to confess a few things. And apologize. And then when I'm done with all of that, I need your advice."

"That sounds like quite the agenda," Esther said with a smile.

"It is. Do you mind?"

"No. In truth, you have me quite intrigued."

"Okay. Confessions first. Oliver and I aren't married."

Esther drew her head back.

"I thought...?"

"No. I said we were married because we're living together. And in my time, couples live together all the time when they're not married—it's not scandalous, I promise."

Esther's eyebrows drew together, clearly trying to decide for herself where this information fell on the scandal scale.

"Our parents know and they're fine with it." Aurelia felt like a child trying to convince a babysitter to let her do something that was absolutely not allowed. "It really isn't a big deal in my century. But I didn't want to shock everyone, especially when we'd all just met, and so... I lied." Aurelia knew there was no gilding that one. "And I'm sorry for that."

Now it was Esther's turn to blow out a breath.

"It's a lot, I know. If you need a minute, I can walk around and let you think."

"No, there is no need to leave." Esther held out her hand as if to stop Aurelia. "But just to ensure I understand you... You and Oliver are *not* newlyweds."

Aurelia shook her head.

"You live together, out of wedlock."

Aurelia nodded.

"And that is not cause for scandal in your time."

Aurelia shook her head again.

"Your parents know of your living arrangements."

Aurelia nodded.

"And they have no objections."

Aurelia shook her head and added, "Our friends know, too—everyone does. Oh, except for all of you. And again, I'm sorry. I really thought it was best. But I apologize for doing it." She paused before asking, "Are you very upset?"

"I am not upset. I am happy to know the truth, although it does take some getting used to. Such things would lead to a woman's ruin in my time—it is difficult not to worry for you. But, I suppose, you did not want to trouble us with worrying?"

"Exactly, not when people nowadays don't think twice about it. Some of the characters I've met in the shop have worried about me staying out late or having dinner with a male friend alone—"

Esther's eyebrows shot up.

"Which is all totally normal too," Aurelia quickly went on. "Sometimes, I feel like the differences between our times are easier to get past by making up a white lie to skip over them. But I do hate lying. Even though... Well, I seem to do a lot of it these days. And that's where I need your advice."

"Alright." It was Esther's turn to nod.

"Oliver and I got engaged this morning. Oh—that's the good news I wanted to share!"

Esther laughed. "Congratulations! That does ease my mind about your... confession, as you called it."

"Maybe I should have led with that," Aurelia said with a smile. "We're engaged and I'm so happy and I was practically floating around earlier until I started thinking... He still doesn't know about the shop, about all of you. No one does, not even my sister."

"Truly? But I recall you saying you are very close with your sister."

"I am—we are. It's just that there's no way for me to prove to anyone that all of you exist. You saw what happened when Oliver came into the shop. Or maybe it happened too fast for you to see it... You all disappear whenever anyone other than me is here. What would you think if Ada or John Jarndyce told you they could talk to characters from books but that you'd just have to take their word for it?"

"Yes... Yes, that I do understand," Esther said soberly.

"And there's also a part of me that still worries... That still thinks maybe this isn't real, maybe it *is* all in my imagination after all."

Aurelia hadn't planned to share that particular fear, but now that the floodgates were open, it had slipped out.

"Not that you're not real, or not—"

"There is no need to explain," Esther promised. "If I had not met you, then I would have questioned whether I'd imagined your aunt Lucy, just as you must question whether you've imagined all of us. The strangeness of what happens in your shop does make it difficult to accept, let alone share."

"But don't I have to tell him now? Now that we've promised to love each other and stay together forever? How can I let him say 'I do' if he doesn't know about this?" Aurelia asked, waving her hands toward the other characters who were gathered downstairs.

Esther bowed her head, deep in thought. Aurelia resisted the urge to keep talking, hoping that if she gave Esther a minute, she might come up with a genius solution.

After a long pause, Esther spoke.

"You wanted my advice?"

"Yes, please."

"Then my advice is to wait for your moment. I suspect there will come a time when it will be clear to you that you are ready to share your secret, and that Oliver is ready to hear it. That time may be tomorrow, or it may be a year from now. But I do not think putting pressure on yourself—to tell him now that you are engaged, or by a certain date—will make the telling or the hearing of it any easier. Wait for your moment and tell him then."

Aurelia nodded slowly, thinking that through.

"So don't rush it."

"No, I would not advise that. Desperation to ease one's conscience often leads to poor execution and even less desirable results."

"Wait for the right moment, then."

"I think it would be best."

That means don't run upstairs and wake him up to rant about talking to characters, Aurelia instructed herself. *Or blurt it out in the middle of dinner just to get it off your chest.* If only she could let Antonia in on her secret, she knew that was just the sort of advice her sister would give her.

"I don't suppose you have advice about how to find the right moment?"

Esther laughed. "I think the right moment will find you, not the other way round."

"Worth a try," Aurelia said, laughing and shrugging her shoulders. "Oh—one more question. Do you think I should tell the others, about how Oliver and I aren't really married?"

Esther narrowed her eyes thoughtfully then said, "I do not think it is necessary. If you would like to, then of course you may do as you wish. But some secrets are not worth telling, and I think your white lie, as you called it, did not cause us any harm."

Harm. Just a few weeks ago, Aurelia had told herself that her lies to Oliver weren't meant to hurt him. And they weren't. But whenever the moment arrived to tell him the truth, she knew she'd have to face the hurt he'd inevitably feel—even if he could understand why she'd done it—at being left in the dark for so long.

Aurelia realized that Esther was looking at her, likely waiting to see if she had any other confessions ready to burst out. She put on a smile and thanked Esther, relieving her from her advice-giving duties for the evening. They went downstairs and Esther led her over to Joe and Peggotty, who were standing near the front windows having a chat.

Aurelia felt a little better, though now she was preoccupied with wondering when 'the moment' was going to arrive. She knew Esther was right; the worst possible scenario would be to let the truth about the characters slip out just because she felt like it, not because Oliver was ready to listen or she'd found the best way to explain it. She had to trust that they'd get through it, that he'd do his best to believe her when she found the right time to tell him the unbelievable.

She'd been distracted by those thoughts ever since she and Esther had come back downstairs and tried to tune back into the last few minutes of conversation with the characters before dawn. David was inventing wildly, as usual, coming up with bigger and bigger ideas to try and tempt Harriet into picking one for her story.

"No, no. Nothing so big and grand for our Harriet, Davy," Peggotty insisted. "She's a wee little thing. Think of something smaller and more manageable for her, won't you?"

Maybe it was her distraction, or maybe it was everything that had happened that day, but Peggotty's words caught at her mind. *Smaller... More manageable...* A small idea for Harriet.

A small change.

Aurelia had been thinking about small changes that very morning, after she and Oliver had proposed to one another. She'd thought about how a small thing could make a big ripple. Like putting on a ring. Or learning one new fact about your brother. What a difference small changes could make in a person's life.

So, what sort of a small change might make a difference in Harriet's?

53

Aurelia talked it over with Oliver and decided she would wait until she was in Paris—just a few weeks away now—to tell Antonia about the engagement in person. It was big news to share over the phone and she wanted to be able to hug her sister, temporarily lose her hearing at the sound of Antonia's squeal of delight, and gush about that lovely proposal while sitting right next to each other instead of too many miles away. Aurelia wasn't very good at keeping things from her sister, but Antonia would be busy with the kids and planning for the bookshop event, giving them plenty to talk about on the phone between now and then. Oliver and Aurelia would tell his parents and her dad when they all met for the next lecture, and they decided to tell Jack when they had him round for dinner the following week. In the meantime, Aurelia enjoyed having a secret *with* Oliver for a change, one that was theirs to keep and, soon, share.

The day after their impromptu engagement, Aurelia read back through the books on the table, this time to think about what a small change in Harriet's life might look like. Here she'd been imagining big, revolutionary changes for Harriet—like inheriting a small fortune, taking on an occupation, or traveling the world. But now she realized that they didn't need to blow up her life to create something new. Instead, they could tweak one aspect of her life, make one change that could then reverberate and set off a series of changes throughout her future. That still left the small problem of which small change would have the most impact, or—more precisely—the most *meaningful* impact, on her life.

As Aurelia skimmed through the books again, she thought of how Esther had written about her life by concentrating on the people around her, particularly those she loved, like John Jarndyce, her guardian; Ada, the young woman Esther had been hired to look after; Caddy Jellyby, who had become an unexpected friend; and her love interest, Allan Woodcourt. Esther had been raised in a loveless home by a woman who only later in her life was revealed to have been her aunt. Maybe it was because of that cold upbringing that Dickens had rewarded Esther with a collection of characters that became her adopted family. And David Copperfield had been raised by a loving mother, but after her untimely death, he was sent to work and fend for himself in London at a young age. Like Esther, David had created his own circle of friends and loved ones, including the Micawbers, who had taken him in as a lodger; Peggotty, of course; his friend Traddles; and, eventually, his aunt, Betsey.

Aurelia put down her copy of *David Copperfield* and picked up *Great Expectations*. Pip and Joe were brothers by marriage, though Pip was nearly twenty years younger. Pip's parents had died when he was too young to remember them, so he'd been raised by his sister and Joe. Pip had created a tightknit group of friends for himself—Joe, who had been like a father to him; Herbert Pocket, who, like Pip, had been caught up in Miss Havisham's web; and Wemmick, who became a trusted adviser.

All of these characters had built their own families from assorted friends and distant relations. And, as Aurelia thought about it, she realized that many of Dickens' characters had done the same: Amy in *Little Dorrit*, Oliver in *Oliver Twist*, and Jenny Wren in *Our Mutual Friend*. Where relatives or society had failed them, Dickens' characters often took matters into their own hands—if not consciously—to find the affection and support that a ready-made family should have given them.

Wouldn't that be a small change? Aurelia asked herself as she looked out the window to the square beyond. If Harriet could make just one or two friends, she could build those friendships into relationships that would last for a lifetime. They could give her a different kind of opportunity than the ones Aurelia had been imagining, like enjoying cozy dinners by a fireside, having someone to run to when she had a problem, and sharing laughter over a distant memory. Wasn't that what Harriet had been missing as an orphan and now, as a young maid in a household that didn't care all that much about her?

―――◯―――

In the shop that night, Aurelia decided not to mention the idea to Harriet directly but to draw out the other characters' stories and help Harriet see that she too could make her own family. They all chatted for a bit, with Aurelia biding her time until she spotted her chance—when Esther and John Jarndyce began telling Harriet a story about Ada. Aurelia joined their circle and waited for them to finish.

"You seem to love Ada as a sister, Esther," Aurelia observed.

"I do," she said, smiling. "I never had a true sister, but she and I share a bond that must be similar."

There's my opening, Aurelia thought before asking, "Wouldn't you say Caddy is like a sister, too?"

"Oh, certainly!" Esther said.

"And John," Aurelia said, gesturing to him, "he's something like a father to you, isn't he?"

"He certainly is. I never knew my father, but I have no doubt that John has filled the role admirably."

As she spoke, Esther looked at Aurelia, her eyebrows twitching slightly in a subtle question. Aurelia nodded, hoping Esther had caught on to her plan.

Nodding back, Esther added, "Even though I did not benefit from the love and support of my relatives, I seem to have found both from the friends who came into my life." She placed a hand on John Jarndyce's arm. "I consider myself very fortunate for that."

"Nonsense," John said. "We are the fortunate ones for knowing you."

"Peggotty," Esther said, gathering Peggotty's arm in hers as she joined their circle. "You would consider David to be a son, would you not?"

"I would, indeed." Peggotty's chest swelled with pride, sending several buttons flying. "I knew him since he were a babe and now he's a father and a famous author—but still my Davy."

Hearing his name, David walked over, expanding their circle still further so that Pip and Joe decided to join, as well.

"What's this?" David asked.

"We were speaking of families," Esther said. "Those we find and those we make for ourselves." Aurelia was pleased to sit back and let Esther lead the charge. After nearly ruining her friendship with Harriet by tugging her along from idea to idea, she thought it was probably best to let someone else do the tugging.

"Interesting," David said, making a face as he mused on the topic. "I did indeed forge a collection of people who are dear to me from among a scattering of friends. Aunt Betsey *is* a relation, of course, but we had to find our way to each other."

"Pip's done the same, haven't you?" Joe said, nudging Pip. "I'm his brother-in-law, right enough, but he found others he made into a kind of kin."

"That's true. No parents, but I did just fine with you and our friends."

"All of us, then, have sewn together our own patchwork family," Esther said, nodding around at the group before landing her gaze on Harriet.

She seemed to catch on—maybe they *had* been laying it on a bit thick.

"You think I should create my own family? As part of my story?" she asked.

"Hmm," Aurelia said, hoping she sounded as though she'd only just made the connection herself. "There's something to that.

Maybe, instead of trying to think of what you want your entire life to be, you could think about the handful of people you'd like to have with you?"

"I recommend starting with an uncle," Pip said.

"Or an aunt," David offered.

"Aye," agreed Joe. "An uncle for you, Pip, but an aunt for a young lady."

"Yes, an aunt. You know how much I loved Aunt Marigold," Aurelia reminded her.

"Perhaps," David said, shifting into his authorial voice, "you might have an aunt contact Coram House, rather than a rich stranger. She might have learned of your existence through... a letter, perhaps, that she had promised not to open until the very month and year your story begins."

"That's good, David," Aurelia said, her own ideas sparking now. "Harriet's mother might have written a letter about Harriet, and made her sister promise not to open it until after she died."

"Learning of your existence," David went on, picking up the story, "the aunt contacts Coram House immediately, feeling saddened to think that obeying her sister's wishes meant that Harriet was on her own for so many years. The aunt will be childless," David said, almost as an aside, "and happy to devote her life to a niece."

"Won't it be odd, though?" Harriet asked. "If I write about someone loving me? Won't I be forcing them to care for me?"

"Wouldn't finding a relative who wants to know you, after years of thinking you were on your own, be a welcome surprise?" Aurelia countered.

"Yes... Yes, it would."

"Wouldn't an aunt feel just the same—overjoyed to discover a niece to love?" Esther added.

Harriet nodded with a slow smile.

"And I've been thinking," Aurelia said. "Writing your entire life story is a big project. You could get started on a path without plotting out the rest of your life. Just write about finding your aunt and maybe having her invite you to move in with her."

"Well, perhaps she'll need to write a little more than that," David argued. "She'll need a colorful collection of neighbors living around her aunt's—what? Cottage, certainly? Yes—living around her aunt's cottage."

"Sure," Aurelia readily agreed. "More people to meet and add to your family circle."

"I like this for you, Harriet," Esther said eagerly. "Set yourself on a path, as Aurelia suggests, and you will be certain to find your way from there. Perhaps you might invite your friend from the Foundling Hospital, Margaret, to join you once you are settled with your aunt?"

Harriet's face lit up and a smile tugged at the corner of her mouth. Aurelia nearly slapped her own forehead—how could she have forgotten Margaret, the girl Harriet had described as being like a sister to her? *This is it*, Aurelia told herself, *this is going to work.*

"Do you think... Do you think I could?" Harriet asked.

"Not just could, but should," Aurelia said with a decisive nod.

Harriet looked around the shop, taking in everyone gathered around her. "You'll help me write it, then?" she asked, catching each character's eye.

A chorus of promises brought out the brightest smile Aurelia had seen on Harriet's face, which was glowing with possibility.

54

The last time she'd spoken with Louisa, Aurelia had promised to reach out to her once she'd decided how to move forward with her novel. That had been nearly two weeks ago, and Aurelia felt it was time to sit down with her and explain everything that had happened. Well, explain a version of what had happened—minus the part about Harriet exploding at her and deciding to write her story on her own.

They met at the same café, and this time Aurelia was the first to arrive. Keeping with tradition, she ordered tea and two slices of cake that arrived just as Louisa sat down to join her.

"I assumed?" Aurelia asked, waving at the table.

"Absolutely! We are so very in sync."

"Maybe even more so now than before," Aurelia began as Louisa took a bite of cake. "I've been rethinking your notes."

"Yeah?"

"You were right about the story and Harriet. It just took me a while to see where I was going wrong."

"It can be hard to step back from your own work," Louisa said with a smile. "And sometimes when you do, you still want to go your own way, which is fair."

Aurelia smiled to hear Louisa say nearly the same thing Oliver had, as if it were an editorial mantra.

"No, I definitely don't want to keep pushing the story where it was headed. To be honest, I don't want to keep writing it full stop."

Louisa put her fork down and wrinkled her forehead in concern.

"Full stop? Are you sure? I think there's something there you can rework."

"I don't know... I was so invested in Harriet, but I know it wasn't the right story for her. I'm just not sure where to take it without her."

"What about Miss Rugg? What if you make her your protagonist and have someone else go with her on the trip to America? That wouldn't take too much reworking."

Aurelia took a sip of her tea and thought over Louisa's suggestion. She had made Harriet miserable by writing a new chapter in her life that she didn't want. What if Miss Rugg would feel the same?

"I don't think Miss Rugg is right for me, either," Aurelia decided, shaking her head. "Or maybe it's that I'm not right for her," she added with a laugh.

"It seemed like you were having fun helping her and Harriet widen their horizons."

"I was, but something just wasn't working. Especially with Harriet, but with Miss Rugg too, I think. Neither one of them had much say in their lives, did they? Directing what happened to them started to feel like I was just one more person dictating their futures without their say-so."

"First Dickens, then you?" Louisa laughed.

"Yes, though he's not exactly easy on his characters."

"Him? You were about to send Harriet over Niagara Falls in a barrel!"

"I never! Well, I mean… if I'd thought she'd have been willing, maybe."

They both laughed and Aurelia appreciated being able to talk about her failed plot with a little less defensiveness than she had before.

"Whether it's Harriet, Miss Rugg, or someone else, you seem to like writing about women who break free. Maybe that's something you can salvage?"

"Hmm… I hadn't thought of it that way. Before I started working on Harriet's story, I was working on something else—a book about a man who starts a new job at a small auction house and discovers an art forgery scam. I liked the idea of him stepping into this new world and realizing it was darker than he'd imagined, and that he might mistakenly think he was clever enough to play it to his advantage. I was thinking the character would be a man, but maybe…"

She trailed off, already starting to imagine the character as a woman, how that would change the story, how it might give her new angles to explore.

"Maybe you should let me know once you're ready for me to read about this young woman and those forgeries," Louisa finished for her.

"I will," Aurelia said with a smile.

She and Louisa chatted over the rest of their tea and cake, and Aurelia realized that a weight she hadn't been aware of had been lifted. Giving Harriet the power to use her own voice meant that Aurelia was free to use hers. She could write her own books now and wouldn't have to write anyone else's characters but her own. If she wanted to write another sequel, it would be her choice. But if she found a character who needed a better ending and didn't feel inspired to write one for them, now she knew how to help that character help themselves.

55

As Aurelia and Oliver made their way to a restaurant to meet David and James for dinner that evening, she finally filled him in on her decision to stop writing Harriet's story.

"You're *not* going to write about Harriet?" Oliver asked, stopping in the middle of the pavement and causing a woman who'd been walking behind them to nearly trip over him. After apologizing to her and drawing Aurelia aside, Oliver said, "I thought you were absolutely set on writing her story?"

"I was." Aurelia saw Oliver's eyebrows shoot upward as she continued. "I know I said over and over again that I wanted to write about her—I know." Aurelia tried to think of the best way to explain it to him through her usual half-truths. "I realized that her story was better left to the imagination. The things I wanted her to do and be weren't really *her*."

"Weren't they?" Oliver asked, trying not to smile.

"I suggest you keep biting your tongue on that 'I told you so.'" Aurelia laughed. "I gave you your chance a few weeks ago and you passed."

"Oh, I know better than to let that slip," he said with a grin.

They kept walking and Aurelia went on. "I told Louisa about my art book, and she said maybe I should make the main character a strong, independent female type since that's how I was trying to write Harriet."

"Well, you know plenty of those to draw on for source material."

"I do, but I thought you didn't like the idea of me writing about another character from a novel?"

"No, I mean the real, actual women in your life, not from a novel. There's your mum, your Aunt Marigold, you, your sister, Kali. From what you've told me—and what I've seen—you've been surrounded by 'strong, independent female types' your whole life."

"That's very true," Aurelia said, smiling to hear that Oliver had taken note of each of the very important women in her life. And she mentally added to his list the female characters she'd met in the shop over the past year: Elinor, Marmee, Rachel, Esther, and many others.

They were nearly at the restaurant, a little place just off busy King's Road in Chelsea, when they passed a jeweler's that had closed for the day. Oliver nudged Aurelia over to the shop windows and took her hand in his, running his thumb over her makeshift engagement ring.

"Speaking of inspiration, does anything here inspire you?"

Aurelia skimmed her eyes over the rings on display, each sparkling in the light from streetlamps and passing cars. Her smile at Oliver's invitation to window shop faded as she thought about trading her mother's ring for something new.

"What? What's wrong?" Oliver asked, concern etched across his face.

"Oh—nothing's wrong," Aurelia said, putting her hand on his chest to reassure him. She tilted her head to one side as she looked at the ring on her finger, which she'd taken to wearing all the time now that Oliver had seen her wearing it. "I've been thinking... You remember I told you this was a magic ring?"

"I do," he responded with a soft chuckle.

"I don't know if I mentioned this, but it was my mother's ring. She gave it to me ages ago, and I don't really wear rings, so I'd sort of lost track of it. But now I guess I've gotten used to it. And it led to our engagement in a way, didn't it?"

"Well, in part, anyway. A very delicious breakfast was also involved."

"How could I forget? Yes, shared credit with your bacon." They both laughed and Aurelia leaned in to kiss him. Pulling back, she held up her hand and turned it to face him. "Would it be weird if we made this my engagement ring? Would you hate that?"

"Of course not, if that's what you want." Oliver took her face in his hands and kissed her in return. "I like that it's special to you, and that it means something to both of us." They started walking toward the restaurant again, each with an arm around the other. "Though it does feel anticlimactic not to do *something* to mark the occasion."

"Maybe there's something we could do to mark it together? A nice dinner? A trip somewhere?" Aurelia asked.

"A trip... What about Paris? You're headed there anyway for your reading—what if I go with you?"

"Oh, that would be fantastic!" she exclaimed, nudging against him. "Can you get off work and join me?"

"I think so. We'll have to find someone to watch Biscuit and Fezz."

"Maybe David and James could watch them? We can ask tonight."

"What about Jack?" Oliver suggested. "I bet he'd be willing."

Aurelia noted that his tone was normal, no sighs or eyerolls at the mention of his brother's name or at the idea of asking him to be responsible for something. Add to that, Oliver had been the one to suggest it, not her.

"I bet he would," she agreed.

Pausing at the door to the restaurant, they looked at each other.

"Paris, then?" Oliver asked.

"Paris it is."

56

Just two weeks later, Harriet had written her story. Freed from the pressure of having to plot out her entire life, and confident knowing that she was creating a raft of friends that would be by her side through her life's ups and downs, Harriet had written out the next year of her life, deciding to leave the rest to fate.

As they'd planned, Harriet wrote for a few hours each night, then let Aurelia transcribe what she'd written, page by page, using the shop's typewriter. Most of the characters, like Count Vronsky before them, had never seen a typewriter before, but they soon got used to the sound of Aurelia clacking away. And although sometimes she would suggest minor changes as she typed, the bulk of the story was Harriet's.

Well, Harriet and David's. He had Dickens' ability to conjure up fun and unique characters, and Harriet liked peopling her new neighborhood with everyone David imagined for her. It was clear, though, that she was most excited about seeing her friend Margaret again and knowing that her aunt would take in not one but two foundlings. Aurelia had thought about reminding Harriet to write a love interest or two for herself but saw that David had taken care of that. At least a handful of the male characters he'd described to Harriet seemed likely to turn her head without risking a broken heart. And after seeing Harriet's secretive smiles as she wrote about these characters, Aurelia thought it was probably best to leave Harriet's love life to fate, too.

The morning after Harriet announced that she was satisfied and didn't want to write another word of her story, Aurelia stood at her desk, looking down at the thin stack of pages in front of her. It was a short story at best, nothing close to long enough for a novel. Not only that; there was a beginning but no middle or end. Dropping into her chair, she let out a long sigh. This was the right story for Harriet, but now the trick would be getting it published. Aurelia had to admit that she didn't want to publish it under her own name. It wasn't her style of writing, and it would feel strange taking credit for something that wasn't hers. The book she'd written with Vronsky had, of course, included his ideas, but Aurelia had been the writer—she'd shaped the structure, organized the action, and written the scenes that set out his new life.

If she couldn't get Harriet's story published as a novel, Aurelia would have to find some other way to get it printed. Her understanding was that the only way to bring a character out of a story was to set their book on the small table in the shop. *Book*—as in a bound set of pages. Shopping Harriet's story around to a few literary journals by using a pen name might be an option, but again, the story had no real ending, so it would be a long shot finding a journal that would want to print a hodgepodge of events and characters. Aurelia couldn't even be sure whether the shop's table would register a journal as a source of characters, and if it did, it might release two characters from another short story and not Harriet's.

Flipping her thumb through Harriet's pages as she thought through her options, Aurelia looked up when the shop door opened, setting the bell ringing. She stood and helped what became a steady flow of customers over the next few hours. Once the store was quiet again, just after lunchtime, she locked the door and ran upstairs to grab a quick bite to eat. Aurelia stood at the kitchen counter, eating a yogurt and looking across the living room toward the sofa where Fezz was sleeping, stretched out at full length across two cushions.

She smiled at the sight of him, then spotted a book on her coffee table. Aurelia froze with her spoon midway to her mouth as she processed what it was—a photo album her sister had put together a few years ago. She abandoned her yogurt on the counter and strode into the living room. Dropping to the floor, she pulled the photo album toward her and flipped through the pages. It was a fully bound album—just like a real book—with the photos printed directly onto the pages. Antonia had ordered it, simple as that.

Aurelia ran back down to the shop and started pulling open her desk drawers, searching for a business card she'd tucked away a while back. She had a few customers that sometimes liked to have their older books rebound, and she remembered one customer said he liked to bind all his books by color according to each author. While she had no problem with mismatched paperback and hard cover books on the shelves of her flat, she was suddenly thankful for the eccentric customers that had put her in the way of a local bindery.

"Ha!" Aurelia exclaimed, finally excavating the business card from under a stack of random papers. Within a few minutes she had called the company, confirmed they would be happy to print and bind a one-off copy, and made an appointment for the following afternoon.

Although she couldn't be one hundred percent certain that a custom-bound book would work on the table, she decided it was worth a shot.

Before heading down to the shop at midnight, Aurelia gathered some of the best books from Aunt Marigold's personal collection. There were a few leatherbound ones with gilded edges and a few hardcopies bound in cloth or cardboard with beautiful endpapers. When the characters appeared, Aurelia shepherded Harriet over to her desk where she had the books stacked and waiting.

"Now that you've finished your story," Aurelia began, "we need to find a way to get it published. But since it's only a part of your story, a new beginning really, I don't think we can get a publishing company to print it."

"But it needs to be printed, doesn't it? If we want to put it on the table?" Harriet began anxiously working her hands.

"Yes, but don't worry! I think I've figured out how to print it ourselves. I'm going to visit a bindery tomorrow. I'll bring the typed copy of your story, they'll bind it for you, and then we can see if it works on the table."

"And do you think it will work?"

"Honestly, I can't *promise* it will, but I really think it might. And if not, we'll find another way." Aurelia hoped she sounded more confident than she felt. "Here, I've set a few books out to give you some ideas of how we could have your story bound. There are different types of covers—cloth, leather, and paper—different endpapers, different ways to have them cut the edges of the pages..."

Aurelia opened the books and pointed out each option. The other characters gathered around and began making suggestions, helping Harriet choose the materials that would make her new story a reality.

57

Arriving at the bindery the next day, Aurelia had a copy of Harriet's story as well as her marching orders from Harriet about how she wanted her story to be bound. A man in his early twenties greeted her in a small display room, his shaggy hair and stylishly casual clothes suggesting he might be an artist in his spare time.

"Aurelia?"

"Yes. Hi."

"I'm Sean, we spoke on the phone." He began pulling out stacks of sample books and laying them on the counter.

"Actually," Aurelia said, holding out a hand to stop him from bringing out every sample in the place, "I've narrowed down what I want."

"Wonderful! What're you thinking?"

"We—I—want a pale grey cloth binding." Some of the characters had pushed Harriet toward a leather binding, but she kept running her hand over the cloth cover of one book in particular, and they'd realized that a softly colored cloth cover was clearly more her style.

Sean pushed aside some of the sample books and opened one, flipping through the pages and landing on a section of cloth swatches in grey.

"Wow!" Aurelia breathed out, running her hand over the options, just as Harriet had done the night before. "Who knew there were so many shades of grey?"

"Do you know what kind of endpapers you'd like?" Sean asked. "That might make it easier to pick which grey option is best."

"Oh, good idea. We want—I want—marbled endpapers in purple." Aurelia had shown Harriet a few books with marbled endpapers and she'd been drawn to those. None were in purple, but Esther suggested the color and Harriet's smile in response meant they'd found the right match.

Sean pushed aside more sample books as he searched for the one he wanted.

"Here we go," he said as he began flipping to a section with purple options.

"Wow," Aurelia said again. "There are dozens!"

"Take your time, flip through and see what takes your fancy."

He started putting away some of the other sample books as Aurelia turned the pages of the two in front of her, trying to match up the purple and grey options that seemed most like Harriet. After a time, she found a soft grey linen that went well with marbled endpapers in a mix of light and deep purples that seemed to evoke Harriet's kindness mixed with her passionate energy.

Sean began marking her choices down on an order slip.

"So, what is it you're binding? Family history? Pet project?"

"I... I guess it's a pet project of sorts," Aurelia stammered. "It's a short story."

"Is it yours?" he asked.

"No... It's a friend's."

"That's nice. Making it up as a gift?"

"Yeah, I guess. Yes," she said with more confidence. She couldn't think of how else to explain it, so she decided to stick with that.

Sean paused at a section of the order form and looked up at Aurelia.

"What would you like on the cover? Your friend's name? A title?"

The characters had gone through a long debate about this. Harriet had suggested just printing her name on the cover, but Aurelia thought it needed a title to make sure the shop's table would recognize it as a book. Everyone suggested various possibilities, some serious and some silly, but Peggotty had been the one to choose the winning title. She reminded everyone of something Aurelia had said earlier in the evening—'a new beginning'—and that had stuck.

"I'd like the words 'A New Beginning' printed for the title, with 'by Harriet Coram' below that."

After writing out the words, Sean had Aurelia confirm that everything looked the way she wanted it. They chose a gold foil for the letters and a simple but elegant font.

"With our schedule, right now we're looking at... about three weeks to put this together for you."

"Three weeks?" Aurelia asked in surprise, realizing that would mean they'd have to wait until after her trip to Paris to test out the book.

"Yeah, I'm sorry. We've got a big order ahead of yours."

Aurelia must have looked as crestfallen as she felt, and Sean took pity on her.

"Well… it's just the one copy. I can sneak it ahead of the queue for you."

"Really? But won't I be putting someone else out?"

"No, it's no trouble. We should be able to get it to you early next week. How's that?"

Aurelia's mind raced: early next week—she was leaving for Paris at the end of next week, so that would give them just enough time to test it out before she left.

"That's perfect. Thank you!"

She paid the deposit, thanked Sean again, and stepped outside. As she walked back toward the shop, she couldn't help smiling in excitement at everything that lay ahead. Seeing the book come together made her feel certain that it would work—that the shop's table would recognize it as an actual book and that Harriet would have her new ending. No—her new beginning.

58

Aurelia marveled at how many events and to-dos were on her list for the coming week. There was another lecture that evening and dinner with the parents, testing out Harriet's story, then traveling to Paris with Oliver for her book event. She was eagerly anticipating so many things that it was hard for her to focus on any one of them for very long.

Sophie had come through again with some clever posters advertising the lecture, and Oliver had coordinated the chair rentals and made a reservation nearby for a late dinner with his collection of parents and her dad. At the lecture that night, there were a few new people in the shop—word seemed to be spreading—along with Aurelia's friends, family, and customers. She and Oliver had introduced their parents and then sat them together, laughing as the five of them immediately began talking animatedly over news of the engagement. When Jack arrived just minutes before the lecture began, he joked that for the next one, they'd have to send people up to the mezzanine for standing room only.

There was a pleasant buzz in the air after the lecture, and Aurelia enjoyed circling the shop, catching up or checking in as everyone gathered around with glasses of wine. She introduced herself to the newcomers and invited them to come back again for tea and a chat during business hours. She even sold a few books, which Oliver volunteered to ring up for her, including a copy of *Little Dorrit*.

Once the shop emptied out, Aurelia and Oliver led the parents to a nearby restaurant for dinner. All of them chatted happily about the lecture, the shop, and the engagement. Johanna had even started talking about plans for the wedding with Aurelia's dad. Miraculously, the parents wanted to stay out a bit longer, lingering over dessert and coffee, while Oliver and Aurelia were ready to pack it in after a long day. They left the parents and headed home to Biscuit and Fezz.

———◯———

It had been a perfect day by most measures, but something had been tugging at Aurelia's mind. All the excitement and anticipation over the lecture and getting the parents together had distracted her from pinning it down, so it wasn't until she was alone in the bathroom getting ready for bed that she understood what it was. This wasn't the first time it had occurred to her, but tonight—gathering the parents together, sharing news of their engagement—the thought now struck her with force: she'd be planning her wedding and getting married without her mother. Aurelia felt the pain of it as if she'd been struck across the face and she leaned against the bathroom counter, trying to simultaneously process that thought and the sudden grief it'd brought on.

Brushing tears from her eyes, it took her a moment to realize that Oliver had appeared in the doorway. He walked toward her and she crumpled into him, tears instantly dotting his shirt.

"It's alright," he said quietly.

"I'm sorry," she said, her voice muffled by tears and the fact that her face was burrowed into him.

"It's alright," he said again. "I meant to check in with you earlier, but things got so busy with setting up for the lecture."

"I just… dinner tonight, without Mum… It's been on my mind, but then somehow I'd forgotten until just now."

"I know," he said, running a hand over her back.

"Once again, me and my waterworks," she said, pulling away while attempting and failing to strike a casual tone as she remembered Oliver just recently had to pick her up after Mark's news about moving on from Marigold.

"Hey," he said, putting a hand to her chin to draw her eyes to his. "The waterworks are absolutely fair. Take as much time as you need."

She put her arms around him again, at first wanting to shed a few more tears over his kindness. Instead, she felt as though someone had pushed a button to slow everything down. Her breathing came easier and she was able to feel the comfort of his arms around her, the heat of his skin pressing through his shirt against her cheek, and the slow rise and fall of his chest, which seemed to set her own lungs on pace. Aurelia took another deep breath and kissed his cheek as she stepped back from him.

"Okay," she said with a nod. "I'm alright."

Oliver nodded back and watched as she splashed water on her face and then toweled it dry.

"You know that saying, 'not losing a son but gaining a daughter,' or vice-versa?" she asked after a moment.

"I do."

"I've been thinking about that a lot lately. How I'm gaining a brother and two sets of parents with you. And you're gaining a sister with her family, and a dad. I wish I could have shared Mum and Aunt Marigold too, but..." She paused to take a deep breath since tears were threatening again. "But I really do feel lucky—to have Johanna and Geoff and Ellie and Michael and Jack."

"And me?"

"Oh, you're a given. I feel luckiest about having you, of course," she said, managing a smile.

"I feel just the same—about you, about your dad, about Antonia, Max, and the kids. I know it's not what we'd choose—losing Lottie, your mum, and Marigold—but we've done alright somehow."

He pulled her closer, gently squeezing her arm.

"I haven't thanked you, for Jack—"

"No, Oliver—" she began to protest.

"No, thanks *are* due," he insisted. "I thought I knew—I thought I understood... But I didn't. And it's helped, talking to him. It was so long ago, but hearing his memories of Lottie and talking to him about her—it's helped."

Aurelia bit her quivering lip and nodded before saying, "I'm so glad. It makes me so happy that you're spending time together."

"Me too."

"So..." Aurelia began, sensing they were both ready to shift the mood. "I should meddle all the time?"

"Yes, perfect lesson to take away," he said, smiling as he teased her back.

"Right. Good."

Biscuit appeared in the doorway, and they looked down at his hopeful face.

"I'll take him out," Oliver offered. "We'll just be a minute."

"No, I'll come with."

She followed him to the bottom of the stairs, where they put on coats and shoes.

"Can you believe our parents wanted to stay out? Do you think they're still chatting over coffee?" Oliver asked.

"Oh, they're probably deep into wedding planning by now," Aurelia said, adding a shiver of horror at the thought.

"I'm imagining the worst," Oliver said with a groan. "My mum has probably forced your dad to give her his number so she can pester him with ideas."

"Are you kidding? He'd love it. Just wait until he hears Jack does set design—they'll be on three-way calls plotting something horrific."

"We want something small, right?" Oliver asked tentatively as they walked into the shop and down the spiral staircase.

"Definitely. No set pieces, nothing over the top."

He sighed audibly in relief.

The shop floor was still filled with the rented chairs, empty now, as well as a table full of discarded cups and half-empty wine bottles.

"I'll help you when we get back," Oliver promised as he watched her eye the wreckage.

"Let's wait until morning," Aurelia said as she stifled a yawn.

They walked past the Recommended Reads table, where she looked over the titles yet again. After her conversation with Oliver, and after having her friends and family in the shop earlier, she couldn't help but think of Harriet, Esther, and the others, and the family circles each of them had created for themselves. She knew that she, too, had her own circle, made up of people who were related to her by blood, circumstance, history, and even a certain kind of magic.

At the door to the shop, Oliver took her hand and they walked out into the warm spring night together.

59

Having told the characters that the book would be ready in a week, their excitement and nervousness grew as the nights passed. Then, once Aurelia told them she'd gotten the call to pick it up the following day, it seemed the time had come to make a plan for testing it out with Harriet.

"Explain it again, could ye?" Joe asked Aurelia.

"Sure. Once we take Harriet's old book off the table, there's no guarantee that she'll appear from it again if we try putting it back. And, once we put her new book on the table, there's also no guarantee that she'll appear from that. When I did this with Count Vronsky's new book, he didn't appear at all." The faces around her fell in disappointment. "But," she added in a cheerful tone, "two other characters came and let us know that he was doing well. So, it wasn't quite the same as getting to see and talk to him again, but at least we knew he was happy."

"That's some consolation, then," John Jarndyce said.

"I wish I could make promises about what will happen," Aurelia said apologetically, "but the shop is still something of a mystery, even to me."

"Then we shall see one such mystery unfold before our very eyes!" David enthused. "I look forward to observing it."

"What do you think, Harriet?" Esther asked gently. "Would you still like to try it?"

All eyes turned to Harriet.

"I would," she said determinedly. "In fact, I'd like you to try it tomorrow night, Aurelia."

Everyone exchanged glances.

"Tomorrow night? But wouldn't you like to see the book, how it's been bound?"

"I can already picture it in my imagination," Harriet said confidently. "And if I come back to visit, I'll see it in person then."

"In that case, tonight could be your last night in the shop."

"I understand. But tonight could also be the last night that I return to my old story with nothing to look forward to in my life. It could be the last night of being lonely, the last night of not having a family, and the last night of not having friends."

There was silence in the shop as everyone took in Harriet's words and understood more fully the life she was leaving behind. Her determination reminded Aurelia of Vronsky's last night in the shop and his eagerness to move on to the new life they'd planned for him.

"Then tonight is a night for celebration," Pip said sagely. "We shall miss you if we fail to see you again, Harriet, but we will send you off with best wishes for a brighter tomorrow."

"Well said, old chap," Joe said, patting Pip's shoulder.

"Here, here!" chimed in David.

The characters rallied around Harriet and tried to keep their spirits up despite the uncertainty that lay ahead.

Just before dawn, Esther drew Aurelia aside.

"Try as I might to displace it, worry is my overwhelming emotion. Do you truly think Harriet will be alright?"

"I do," Aurelia said with a firm nod. "It worked before, so I'm convinced it has to work again."

"If she does appear from her new story, will she know us?"

"That's a good question, actually. I don't know, but I think she might. Others have told me that even though they don't remember the shop when they're back in their novel, once they return here, their memories of it come with them. But I didn't get to meet Vronsky again," Aurelia said, not managing to hide her disappointment at the thought. "So I don't know if he would've remembered me and the shop if he'd appeared from his new story."

Peggotty had arrived at their side and asked in a whisper, "Will she be the same Harriet we know?"

"I don't know," Aurelia said, shaking her head. "I'm sorry."

"I hope she will be. But perhaps, a more contented version of our Harriet," Esther said with a soft smile.

With dawn breaking across the shop, there were tearful goodbyes as the characters waved to Harriet before being swept back into their books on the table. Aurelia held on to Esther's hope as she walked to the table and cleared away its copies of *Little Dorrit*.

60

At lunchtime the following day, Aurelia went to the bindery to pick up Harriet's book. It was wrapped in thick brown paper and tied with twine, and Sean unwrapped it to show her how it had turned out. It was beautiful, a slim little volume that belied the great possibilities inside. Aurelia thanked Sean and carried it home, held snug across her chest as she imagined what might happen that evening.

———◯———

It was five minutes to midnight and Aurelia was pacing the shop floor. She'd waited for Oliver to come home from work and head upstairs before unwrapping and setting out Harriet's new book on the table, as she didn't want to have to invent answers to the questions he might have if he spotted it. Now, pacing past the table, she had to resist the urge to run her hand along the top of the book and its lovely gilded lettering. She didn't want to do anything that might interrupt the arrival of its characters.

As the clock began to strike midnight, Aurelia was in familiar territory. Just as she had many months ago after setting out Count Vronsky's new book, she counted the mists that appeared from the table, trying to figure out whether any of them were coming from Harriet's book. At first she couldn't be certain but then—there they were! Two mists, rising up, falling over the edge of the table, and forming two distinct shapes. Both women, one older, and one—

"Harriet!" multiple voices called out at once, including Aurelia's.

It *was* Harriet: smiling and clasping the hand of the woman next to her. And yet, Aurelia immediately saw that there was something different about her, a new confidence and lightness, as if she'd cast off the sadness she'd carried with her for so long.

"It worked!" Harriet said brightly.

"Is it really you? Our Harriet?" Esther asked, though her smile suggested she knew the answer.

"It is!" Harriet stepped forward and embraced Esther. They pulled away and Esther held Harriet's face in her hands, scanning it as if to be sure it really was her. Harriet laughed and kissed Esther's cheek, then stepped back and linked arms with the woman who had appeared with her. "I'd like to introduce you all to my aunt Polly."

Polly looked a bit stunned as she took in the characters who greeted her, as well as the bookshop.

"Should we let Polly know where we are, Harriet, and how we know you?" Aurelia prompted.

"Yes, that's right! I'm sorry, Aunt, I forgot you have not visited here."

"Where is *here*, dear?" Polly asked in a lowered voice as she leaned into Harriet.

"This is Aurelia's bookshop, and this is Aurelia."

"Welcome!" Aurelia said, stepping forward. "I know it's a bit unusual, but I hope you'll enjoy your time here."

"It is unusual, Aunt, but wonderful! I've been here before, and met everyone, and now I can introduce you to them."

Harriet was bubbling over with energy and excitement, making Aurelia smile. She was amazed at the changes brought about by just one year in a loving home.

The characters stepped forward as Harriet introduced them to Polly, and then listened as she explained everything that had happened—her old book, her new book, how the characters and Aurelia had helped her. Harriet also pointed out the different areas of the shop and took her aunt on a tour. As they walked along the mezzanine, David joined Aurelia in looking up and marveling at them.

"It is rather wonderful, is it not?" he asked.

"It is," she agreed.

"I am undecided as to whether I should like to meet my characters in person. Some of them, perhaps, but others... It is just as well they remain on the page and in my imagination."

"It's a risky venture," Aurelia said with a laugh. "But Harriet didn't create any mean characters in her new story, so at least we didn't have to worry about meeting any villains."

"Even so," he mused, "my characters speak and think only the words I give them. It is strange indeed to consider they might have a life of their own, apart from the one I devise for them. Yet there stands Polly, thinking and saying things that Harriet did not write."

"And there's Harriet, thinking and saying things that Dickens didn't write."

Aurelia didn't add that David himself was thinking and saying things that Dickens didn't write.

"I suppose," he said, sounding unconvinced. "Though I like to think my characters are *mine*, that I'm the one who created them."

"Well, of course you did. But you've also created something that gives your readers room to stretch their own imaginations. In a way, once people start reading a story it becomes something new and different for each of them."

"True," David said thoughtfully. "Each reader can imagine a whole new set of thoughts, a new backstory, and a new future for a character, just the same as any writer."

"But the seed is ours," Aurelia reminded him.

"Also true," he said with a smile, looking over at Harriet and Polly once more.

Later, when dawn approached, the characters agreed they'd like more time with each other. Aurelia promised to keep their books out for as long as they wanted. And as they disappeared with the first light of day peeking through the shop's blinds, she was looking forward to seeing them all again soon.

61

With just two days until they'd be leaving for Paris, Aurelia knew she'd need to catch up on her sleep or risk dozing off in the middle of her event. She spent one more night with the characters, then let them know she'd need to miss their last night together before her trip. They made her promise to bring back stories of her time in Paris to share with them on her return. In the meantime, Aurelia had kept Harriet's book tucked at the back of the table, and—fortunately—Oliver hadn't noticed it at all.

―――○―――

Although she'd planned to get to bed early the night before they left for Paris, Aurelia got swept up in trying to pack for a combination work trip, engagement trip, and visit with her sister. Their bedroom had seemed like a disaster when Oliver first moved in, but now, with the wreckage of her packing attempts scattered around the room, 'disaster' really was a fitting description. Oliver was working late to wrap things up at his office before their trip, so Aurelia had invited Kali over to help her figure out what to wear for the reading. She'd also filled Kali in on their engagement, which had nearly derailed the evening since Kali wanted every detail and Aurelia kept having to get her back on task.

"So this is the one?" Aurelia asked, holding up a dress for Kali's inspection.

"Definitely. Very Parisian chic, but not so cool that you'll put people off and make them think they can't ask you questions afterward."

"Okay," Aurelia said with a nod. "This one it is." She laid the dress across the bed and sighed. "I think we deserve a refill after that hard work."

"Yes, please," Kali agreed as she followed Aurelia back into the kitchen.

They refilled their wine glasses, then walked into the living room and sprawled out across the sofa.

Kali was about to take a sip when Aurelia held out a hand to stop her.

"Wait! We need another cheers."

They clinked glasses even as Kali rolled her eyes saying, "The first one was enough."

"It wasn't, because you kept insisting we were toasting my engagement when I wanted to toast your amazing, exciting, brand-new job."

"It is pretty exciting," Kali said with a grin. "I wasn't really looking to work full time just yet, but Sarah's offer made it too hard to say no."

"I love that they were complaining about your private tours being too popular before they realized that meant they should snatch you up for themselves."

"There is a nice sort of justice there." Kali cackled. "*I* love that we both have things to celebrate—including an engagement and a book tour!"

Kali raised her glass again and they clinked glasses once more, but this time Aurelia was the one rolling her eyes.

"A tour with only one stop? I'm not sure that qualifies."

"Of course it does," Kali insisted. "Today Paris, tomorrow the world!"

"Well, tomorrow Paris, anyway. Oh!"

Aurelia hopped up from the sofa, pulled a book off a nearby shelf, and ran it into her bedroom. She came back and settled on the sofa again.

"What was that?"

"I just remembered I should bring my own copy of my book for the reading. I wanted to throw it into my suitcase before I forgot."

"Are you nervous?"

"Not really... A little? I'm sure I'll get more nervous as the minutes tick closer."

"Are you going to let Oliver sit in the audience?" Kali asked. "Or will that make you more nervous?"

"I'm worried it might, so I told him to hide in the back so I won't see him."

"What about your new editor—what's her name—is she going?"

"Louisa. And no, she's not coming along. But she did say she'd like to see the first chapters of my book when I get back. That reminds me—"

Aurelia hopped up from the sofa again, this time going to a different bookshelf and pulling out a notebook. She brought it to her bedroom, then came back again and dropped onto the sofa.

"And that?"

"It's a notebook so I can write some ideas for my new book while I'm away."

"This is the one about a Dickens character?"

"No, actually. Well, it was, but I'm going back to the art idea I'd been working on—the one you were helping me with. Which means now I'll be ready to reach out to that reformed forger you mentioned."

"Perfect—I have his contact info, so I'll forward it to you."

"Talking to him will be a huge help. I've been going back through my notes and I have so many questions and so much research to do. Plus I need to rework my outline and early chapters since I'm going to switch it up and make the main character a woman. Louisa suggested I write about a strong female, then Oliver reminded me that there have been a lot of those in my life, so I'm taking bits and pieces of all of them—all of you."

"Aw... That's very sweet! It looks like you've got two editors for the price of one, then."

"I have, haven't I?" Aurelia agreed, and they both clinked their glasses again.

Kali soon left to give Aurelia time to finish the rest of her packing. When Oliver returned home he managed to pack in an annoyingly short amount of time, but at least they were able to get to sleep at a reasonable hour. Well, Aurelia got into bed at a reasonable hour but didn't actually fall asleep. Her mind was working over everything that lay ahead—taking an early train to Paris in the morning, her book event, getting back to writing her next book, the fact that the experiment with Harriet had worked—really worked! It was all exciting, but a bit nerve-racking too. Then, of course, she couldn't help but hear the soft voices of the characters in the shop below as they chatted through the night. Eventually, Aurelia's mind switched off and she fell into a deep and restful sleep.

62

Walking along the Seine, Aurelia tried to take everything in. There was the sound of water lapping against the banks and boats bumping alongside the quays; the murmur of French being spoken by passersby; the smells (some good, some bad); and the overall joy that seemed to emanate from her at the mere fact of being in *Paris*. Antonia got to enjoy it every day—get used to it, even—but Aurelia found herself trying to cherish and record every moment in her memory.

She'd gotten through her reading the night before and even earned some applause from the small crowd that had gathered in the bookshop. The attendees were mostly expats (along with Oliver and her family, of course), with a few Parisians thrown into the mix. They all seemed to be drawn to the fact that Count Vronsky chose to settle in Paris when he had his pick of the world. Aurelia wondered if part of their attachment to the story also stemmed from Vronsky's early melancholy, even if it had eventually shifted to happiness with his life in Paris. Was there ever a French story that was entirely happy? Vronsky's seemed to fit the bill of mixing the bitter and sweet of life in a way that appealed to her small group of Parisian fans.

And now here she was, walking past the Seine just as Count Vronsky did every day in his new story. He'd told her once that he liked knowing he might never capture its beauty with his paintbrush, but that it was worth trying nonetheless. Sitting on a slab of stone near the water's edge, Aurelia smiled at the thought of him. They had given him a new ending which was, really, a new beginning. Harriet, too, had her new beginning now. Not quite the story Aurelia had imagined for her, but a story that was just right for Harriet and one she knew would have made Aunt Marigold happy.

Staring across the water toward the opposite bank, Aurelia dug out her notebook and a pen and began jotting down a few thoughts for her own book. Just like Vronsky's paintings of the Seine, she couldn't be sure whether her writing would perfectly describe the emotions, scenes, and characters that populated her imagination in a way that would resonate with readers. Still, she loved working toward the possibility that it might.

63

An hour later and Aurelia was walking up to a table at an outdoor café that was filled with familiar faces—Antonia and her husband, Max; Antonia's children, Julia, Owen, and Hugo; and, grinning up at her, Oliver. Antonia broke into applause as Aurelia approached, and the others joined in. At first Aurelia felt a flush rising up her neck, but then she decided to embrace it, and she gave them all a dramatic curtsy.

Moving toward an empty seat between Oliver and Julia, she leaned down to give him a brief kiss. She tried to communicate with her eyes that she wished they had time for a longer and more private hello, and Oliver, seeming to either intuit her message or to want to share his own, put his arm around her as she sat down, drawing her close.

The children had been mid-argument apparently, and immediately took it up again once Aurelia was settled.

"It's not fair, though, Mum, is it?" Owen was asking Antonia.

"Life's not fair, Owen," Julia said knowingly.

"That's the most annoying thing to say!" Owen spat.

"Well, it's true."

"What's this?" Aurelia asked, having missed what was fair and what wasn't.

"Julia has invited herself to stay with you and Oliver," Max began.

"And I said no problem," Oliver continued.

"And I added a proviso that she'd need to wait a year, once she's fourteen," Antonia joined in.

"That sounds sensible," Aurelia said, looking around to gauge everyone's reaction.

"But it's not fair!" Owen said, dropping back into his chair with a huff.

"I have to wait a year, Owen," Julia said magnanimously. "You're younger, so you have to wait longer. That's just the way it is."

Who is this wise young woman? Aurelia wondered. Well, wise, but also enjoying every minute of her age advantage.

"I assumed you wouldn't mind?" Oliver asked Aurelia in an undertone.

"Of course not! But will you mind? Having a teenager in our midst will be a challenge."

"I think we can manage," Oliver said, adding more loudly so the group could hear, "Julia can help you out in the shop during the day."

"That's true. I can get you vacuuming and dusting, just like Aunt Marigold used to have me do when I was your age."

Julia let out a small groan.

"Absolutely. Put her to work, Aurelia," Antonia said with a mischievous smile.

"Mum!"

"Doesn't sound so exciting after all, does it, Owen?" Max asked, elbowing his middle child.

"I want to vacuum at Aunt Aurelia's!" Hugo announced peevishly.

"You can vacuum the next time you visit with your mum, Hugo. And then, when you're fourteen, you can come and stay with me, too."

"Just 'me'?" Oliver asked.

Aurelia looked at him in confusion for a moment before catching onto his meaning.

"Us!" she added, correcting herself. "You can come and stay with your uncle Oliver and me."

Suddenly, Julia's chair lurched backward a few inches and she immediately shot Owen a warning look. He'd apparently kicked her chair under the table.

"Don't!" she said, dragging the word out in an annoyed whine. Despite her attempted maturity, she couldn't seem to hold it in.

"That's enough of that, please," Antonia said in a stern voice that carried with it a tinge of Julia's annoyance. She eyed each child in turn, then shifted her attention back to Aurelia and nodded at her hand. "Let's see it again."

Aurelia dutifully displayed her left hand with her engagement ring.

"I still don't recognize it. But it was one of Mum's?"

"Mm-hmm."

"Couldn't have found one for our engagement, Antonia?" Max teased.

"Never. I'm far less practical than my sister," Antonia said, hugging her own engagement ring protectively against her chest.

"We looked at other rings," Oliver began, a little defensively.

"But I wanted this one," Aurelia finished for him. Smiling, they held each other's gaze for a moment even as chaos erupted when Hugo tipped over his glass of juice. Aurelia pulled her napkin from her lap and tossed it into the fray, then felt Julia tapping at her arm. Turning to her niece, Aurelia saw Julia leaning in toward her and did the same.

"Next summer, Aunt Aurelia, you promise?" Julia whispered.

"Absolutely," Aurelia whispered back. She tugged at Julia's braid and added, "I'll have to start working on a reading list for you, get you up to speed on the shop's best books."

With another groan, Julia threw her head back melodramatically, but Aurelia could see she was secretly pleased to have something only the two of them would share.

Aurelia smiled across the table at the joyful noise her family was making, and then slowly drifted away with her own thoughts.

One day, the shop would be Julia's. She was Aurelia's only niece, and the bookshop was always passed down from aunt to niece. But, of course, Julia could decide on a different career if she wanted. Aurelia had learned all too well from Harriet that she'd have to let Julia choose her own path—even if she might want to nudge her in a certain direction. In the meantime, Aurelia hoped Julia would come to love the shop as much as she did, and a summer immersed in it was a good place to start. Aurelia could share all the things she loved most about it, all its quirks and secrets.

Well, all but one. Aurelia would find the right moment to share that secret with Julia, just like she'd find the right moment to share it with Oliver. She bit her lip, wondering once again when that moment would arrive and hoping she'd recognize it when it did.

Oliver gave her arm a gentle squeeze and asked, "Where've you gone?"

"I'm here! Just thinking about next summer, the future…"

"And? How is it looking?"

She settled beside him, tucking her head against his shoulder as her eyes ran across the table to her family, then out to the bustling street beyond the café before she looked up at him.

With a smile she answered, "I think it's looking very, very good."

Recommended Reads

Bleak House (1853)

- Esther Summerson: A kind woman who refuses to let her difficult childhood turn her bitter.

- John Jarndyce: Equally kind, though life has shaken his faith in humanity.

The Jarndyce family's long-running battle over an inheritance centers the action in this novel, bringing together Dickens' usual collection of unique and charming characters. Although the title sounds dreary, Dickens contrasts hardship and ease, kindness and selfishness, displaying both the good and bad sides of human nature.

David Copperfield (1850)

- David Copperfield: a man who perseveres through adversity and works hard to achieve success in both his work and personal lives.

- Peggotty: Devoted to David after practically raising him, she is goodness and joy personified.

Many aspects of this 'novel' are autobiographical, including David/Dickens having to work as a child and later striving to become a successful author. From the iconic opening line to the heartwarming end, Dickens lets the side characters take center stage, leaving the reader just as in awe as David when each new person steps into his life.

Great Expectations (1861)

- <u>Philip Pirrip (Pip)</u>: from a tiny boy to an adult, we watch Pip shift from wishing for more to having a deeper appreciation for what he already has.

- <u>Joe Gargery</u>: A male version of Peggotty, devoted to Pip even as he struggles to understand what's best for him.

Many readers associate all Dickens novels with being forced to read this one in school. There are interesting characters (as always), but if you're looking to read your first Dickens novel, I'd follow Aurelia's advice and start with *David Copperfield* or *Little Dorrit* instead.

Little Dorrit (1857)

- <u>Harriet Coram</u>: raised in an orphanage, Harriet learns to break free after a lifetime of being scolded for expressing her thoughts and emotions.

One of my favorite Dickens novels. This one also incorporates some autobiographical elements, and highlights wealth disparities and the challenges (emotional, ethical, and physical) that come with both poverty and wealth. Don't miss the beautiful BBC adaptation starring Claire Foy and Matthew Macfadyen.

Dickens doesn't spare his characters; even the kindest ones have flaws and make mistakes, just like his villains. As someone who experienced childhood poverty and saw London at its best and worst, Dickens was particularly interested in social class and the effects of the economic disparities he saw and experienced. As a result, he often depicted his wealthy characters as cruel and insensitive, and his impoverished characters as occupying the moral high ground. He wrote characters that will always stick with me, like the Micawbers from *David Copperfield* and Flora Casby from *Little Dorrit*. But he also wrote characters that have troubled generations of readers—like the highly problematic, anti-Semitic depiction of Fagin in *Oliver Twist*. Dickens eventually recognized what he'd done and tried to make amends, but it is an important reminder that we should always read critically—whether the book is a 'classic' or not.

Acknowledgements

One year ago, I decided to finally put this series out into the world. And over the past year, I've been saying that if I knew then what I know now—that it is a LOT of work to be an indie author—well... I would have done it anyway. And I'm so glad I did! I've learned so much, am still learning, and appreciate everyone who has helped me get *The Midnight Book Club* into print and on bookshelves, and now *Booked at Midnight*, and soon... book three in the series.

I'll start my thanks once again with the folks who, out of the kindness of their hearts (and because of my desperate pleas), read drafts both early and near-final to share their feedback: Braden, Caroline, Deb, Jaime, and Liz. Thank you for your always-thoughtful insights.

Thank you to my family for your excitement over every step: a bookshop stocking my book, a good review, an upcoming event. There's a reason Antonia is so supportive of Aurelia's first book—it's because she had very good real-life models.

Jen Prokop, your editing skills are unparalleled; I'm in awe of how you see threads that need to be pulled together that I didn't notice, or see new and better ways to push the story forward.

Thank you again to Lena Yang for the fantastic cover, and for putting up with dozens of emails about tuxedo cats.

Thanks are due to Kristen O'Connell for her marketing guidance, and to Eleanor Smith for revisiting Aurelia's world to proofread and polish my many writing idiosyncrasies.

Cassidy at Grump & Sunshine Bookshop, thank you for being my Maine home base and for continuing to answer my one million questions.

I also need to thank Professor Rosemarie Bodenheimer at Boston College for offering a semester-long graduate course on Charles Dickens. Your enthusiasm for his novels sparked mine and I cannot thank you enough.

To the readers who have embraced this series: I'd hoped that you would connect with Aurelia, her shop, and her journey, but your kind and warmhearted enthusiasm for her and this series has far surpassed those hopes. Thank you!

And, always, thank you booksellers and librarians for being you.

About the Author

Emily lives in Maine, her recently adopted homeland, with her three cats. She owns too many books, likes tea and coffee (don't ask her to choose), and is still knitting more projects than she can count. When she isn't writing, reading, or knitting, she's talking to the wildlife in her backyard. They haven't answered back—yet.

You can learn more about Emily by visiting her website or scanning the QR code below. And if you want to read more about Aurelia, Oliver, Biscuit, and Fezz, her website is also where you'll soon find a sneak peek at Book Three in the Midnights On the Square series.

www.ewandersen.com

If you have time and are so inclined, writing a review or rating this book on Goodreads, StoryGraph, Amazon, or your local indie bookshop's website would be so very helpful.

Thank you for reading!

www.ingramcontent.com/pod-product-compliance
Lightning Source LLC
LaVergne TN
LVHW091701070526
838199LV00050B/2245